We're Off
to See
the Killer

We're Off to See the Killer

William Murray

A *Perfect Crime* Book
DOUBLEDAY
NEW YORK LONDON TORONTO SYDNEY AUCKLAND

A PERFECT CRIME BOOK

PUBLISHED BY DOUBLEDAY
a division of
Bantam Doubleday Dell Publishing Group, Inc.
1540 Broadway, New York, New York 10036

DOUBLEDAY is a trademark of Doubleday, a division
of Bantam Doubleday Dell Publishing Group, Inc.

Book design by Tasha Hall

Library of Congress Cataloging-in-Publication Data

Murray, William, 1926–
   We're off to see the killer / William Murray. —
1st ed.
       p.   cm.
       "A Perfect crime book."
       I. Title.
PS3563.U8W45   1993
813'.54—dc20   93-3564
                                                    CIP

ISBN 0-385-47035-5
Copyright © 1993 by William Murray
All Rights Reserved
Printed in the United States of America
October 1993

2   4   6   8   10   9   7   5   3   1

First Edition

This one is for my friend
Michael Skinner, master magician.

"Life is a gamble at terrible odds. If it was a bet, you wouldn't take it."

—Tom Stoppard

We're Off
to See
the Killer

1 / Hankypoo

"HEY, WHAT'S YOUR PROBLEM?" the thin man asked. "It's a fifty-fifty proposition. I thought you were a player."

"Fifty-fifty? How do you figure?"

"There's fifty-two cards in each deck, right?"

"Right."

"So the chance of matching two cards exactly is one in fifty-two."

"So?"

"So I get fifty-two chances to do that, right? That's a fifty-fifty proposition, any way you figure it."

"I guess."

"So are you game?"

"Yeah, go ahead."

"Here, I'll let you shuffle the cards and then you can turn them over, too," the thin man said. "That way you can't say I was fixing the decks or pulling anything on you. Okay?"

"You want to cut 'em?"

"No, no, I won't touch 'em."

"All right."

"I'm just trying to give you an even chance, that's all."

"You're into me pretty good."

"Yeah, I know. That's why I'm doing this," the thin man said. "I don't want you to go away mad. I want you to have a chance to get your money back, okay?"

"Yeah, okay."

"A hundred dollars a pass?"

"Make it two hundred."

"You sure?"

"Yeah, I'm sure."

The thin man handed the two packs of cards to his friend, who was short and stocky, with a bald spot in the back surrounded by dark, bristly hair cut very short. I couldn't see his face, because he was sitting nearest to me, two stools away on my left, and his back was turned toward me so he could face his companion, who, apart from being very thin, looked more like a store clerk than a hustler. He was about forty, with a pale complexion and a small, receding chin under a long nose and with a prim, tight little mouth. His eyes, a pale blue, seemed larger than normal, probably because he wore very thick, rimless glasses. A light-brown toupee sat on his oblong skull like a small prayer rug and he was dressed in a shiny blue suit that hung lopsidedly on his wiry frame, as if it might have been loaned to him or acquired in a thrift shop. Only his hands gave him away; they were quick-fingered, manicured, obviously his only valuable asset.

"So go ahead," the thin man said. "We got an hour, maybe more."

"Sure, sure," his friend answered, picking up one of the decks and beginning laboriously to shuffle it.

I was only mildly interested in this scene, and then simply because I had an hour or so to kill myself until May Potter arrived. I was planning to take her to dinner downtown, maybe introduce her to my friend Vince Michaels, who was working at the Three Kings, take in a show, then whisk her back to my motel room early enough so we could become elaborately reacquainted. My own working day was over and I'd had enough of my fellow artists for a while, after having had to mingle with them intensely for two days now. I didn't want to talk or see or perform any more magic for at least the next twelve hours. Not unless it was Vince Michaels; I'd have gone anywhere at any time to watch Vince Michaels work. But for the moment I was happy to be sitting at this bar in the Xanadu alone, just nursing a light Scotch along and allowing myself to relax, waiting for May's flight to get in from L.A. at about eight. I looked at my watch; it was ten of seven, a relatively quiet weeknight in Las Vegas, with no major conventions in town. Our gathering of a hundred or so closeup artists huddled together in two rooms at the Ramada, you could hardly call a convention, not by Vegas's standards.

"Okay, are you ready?" the thin man asked, as his mark continued to shuffle.

"Yeah, I'm ready." He placed the two decks face down on the bar between them. "You sure you don't want to cut them?"

"No, what for? If I win, you'll say I cheated."

"I never said you cheated, Benny."

"I trust you, Ted. Go ahead, turn 'em up now. Two at a time, right? Like I told you."

Ted began turning over the top cards of both decks simultaneously and placing them face-up in two separate piles. I took a sip of my Scotch and waited, not too interested but mildly curious. I hadn't seen or heard of anyone pulling off the Matching Card Proposition for a long time—years, in fact—and I had a pretty good idea it might work very well on Ted. I hadn't even seen his face yet, but I can spot a mark when I meet one, even from behind. It was his pal Benny I was worried about. A man can get himself hurt pulling old card tricks on suckers in this sophisticated age, especially in Vegas.

Ted worked his way through the packs the first time without turning up two identical cards and laughed. "Well, all right," he said.

Benny smiled, reached into his pants pocket, produced a fat roll of hundreds and dropped two bills on the counter. "See?" he said. "What did I tell you?"

Ted scooped up the money. "Again?"

Benny shrugged. "Sure, why not? It's fifty-fifty, like I told you."

Ted started to shuffle the cards again and I went to a pay phone to call the airport, found out that May's plane out of Burbank was coming in twenty minutes late, stopped off in the men's room to pee, then returned to my post at the bar. I still had about forty minutes to kill and I liked this particular spot, a nook off the main casino lounge called the Oasis. The area was softly lighted, with an old-fashioned horseshoe-shaped wooden bar surrounded by small round tables and framed by fake but luscious-looking tropical vegetation. The cocktail waitresses wore flowery sarongs slit up the side to their hipbones, but the bartender was a tired-looking Polynesian dressed in white beachcomber pants and a loose, short-sleeved Hawaiian shirt. He poured generous drinks and minded his own business. Best of all, the bar itself was one of the few left in town free of electronic poker machines and thus conducive either to meditation or conversation, two pastimes not taken seriously in Las Vegas, a town hostile to introspection and intellectual communication.

I settled into my seat again just as Ted turned over two queens of clubs. "Shit," he said.

"Like I told you, it's a fifty-fifty proposition," Benny said, taking back his two hundred. Ted grunted, but didn't answer. Benny blinked the big blue eyes at him and tried to look distressed. "Hey, I'm sorry," he said. "I know I'm into you pretty good, Ted, and I don't feel right about it. How much time we got?"

Ted held up a hairy wrist displaying a large gold watch. "Maybe forty minutes," he said. "I have to pick up Mr. Baldwin at eight-thirty."

"That's enough time for you to get even, if you're feeling lucky," Benny said. "Want to press a little?"

"Four hundred," Ted answered. "We'll run the cards eight times."

"Suit yourself, Ted."

"You're one lucky sonofabitch," Ted said, "but it can't last forever. First, I gotta go." He swung himself off the stool with surprising agility for a man of his bulk and I caught my first look at his face. It was round and swarthy, with small black eyes set close together over a stubby nose and fleshy lips. He wore dark-gray slacks, a blue cashmere sports jacket and looked out of costume in them, not because he was in his late forties but because he should have been in uniform; he looked like a cop.

After he'd gone, Benny began drumming the fingers of his left hand lightly on the surface of the bar. The two packs of playing cards lay face up on the counter, the two queens still showing. Benny caught me looking at him and smiled. "It's a way to kill time," he said, as if apologizing to me.

"It's a good way," I answered, "if you can keep him doing it long enough."

"I beat him out of about two grand this afternoon playing poker down at Binion's," he said. "I feel bad about it."

"Of course you do," I said. "I would too. Why don't you take turns?"

"What?"

"Running the cards," I explained. "First him, then you."

Benny smiled. "Oh, he doesn't trust me," he explained. "He thinks I'd fix the game."

"Why would he think that?"

"We only got acquainted this afternoon. He doesn't know me. This way he's the only one who touches the cards, see? I guess he figures it's his turn to get lucky."

"I gather he wasn't much of a poker player."

"Not much," Benny admitted, "but then that's a game of skill, not luck."

"I guess you must like him a lot to want to give him a chance to get his money back," I said, smiling.

"Well, he seems like a nice-enough guy," Benny said, "and I've got time to kill, too." He held out his hand. "Benny Wilder."

I shook it. "Lou Anderson."

"What do you do, Lou?"

"Interpersonal relations," I said. "I'm here with a convention."

"Is that so? Doing much playing?"

"Not much. You can't beat the casinos. Mostly, I'm just taking in some shows."

"Well, they got some good ones. Let me buy you a drink."

"No, that's okay, Benny," I said. "Two's my limit here. I have to pick up a lady at the airport."

"Where are you staying?"

"Right here, at the Xanadu."

"Me too," Benny said, his eyes looking beyond me toward the returning mark. "Maybe I can buy you a drink later."

"Sure, why not?"

I sat in place for another twenty-five minutes and watched Benny and Ted split two more runs through the decks, then, as Ted began still another deal, I signaled for the bartender and dropped a twenty in front of me. Just as I was pocketing my change and getting ready to leave, I heard Ted grunt in disbelief. "Goddamn!" he exclaimed angrily. "I don't believe this shit!"

I glanced at the cards and saw the two eights of hearts nestling next to each other, only about a fourth of the way into the two packs. "You are the luckiest sonofabitch—"

"Hey, Ted, we can stop right now. I—"

"No way," Ted said, scooping up the cards again and beginning to shuffle. "No way at all. We got five to go."

On my way out, I caught Benny's eye. He smiled and nodded, but the light-blue eyes remained coldly concentrated on the action before him. Ted was shuffling the cards faster, totally and angrily hooked into Benny's proposition. There's one born every minute, an impresario named Barnum once observed. As I headed out through the lobby, I was wondering idly how much Benny would take him for before they parted company.

Charlie Pickard looked older than his sixty-four years. He was overweight, smoked two packs of cigarettes a day, drank too much bad coffee and booze, and exercised as little as possible. As a trainer of racehorses, he also had to get up too early in the morning, never later than four-thirty, and he put in seven full working days a week. I always figured he had the constitution of a yak and had once joked with him about it. "Hell, Shifty, if I ever find out there's an easier way to make a living," he had answered, "I'm sure gonna be pissed off I didn't know about it." And as for the coffee and cigarettes and alcohol, I knew better than to try and talk him out of those. He was going to live his life exactly the way he wanted to live it and that was that. He was single, had never had any children, and lived alone. "I ain't leavin' a thing behind, Shifty," he had confided late one night. "I'm takin' whatever I got left with me."

It was Eddie, his number-one groom, who was the first to notice that Charlie wasn't his usual self that morning. Eddie emerged from doing up one of the newly arrived two-year-olds in the second stall down the shedrow from the tack room to find the trainer sitting at his desk, staring blankly out the doorway. It was about nine-thirty, with most of the work done, but Charlie still had two horses out on the track, one with Polo and the other under some new exercise boy from Panama, and Eddie knew Charlie would have been out there with them. He put his brushes down, looked at Charlie, then took a couple of hesitant steps toward him. "Boss?" he called out. "You okay?"

Charlie didn't answer. Eddie stood there, not knowing what

to do, his pale, wrinkled face concentrated on the problem. To his horror, Charlie suddenly seemed to tilt to one side. The trainer's mouth opened as if to say something, but no sound came out, then he fell off the chair, landing on his side, his mouth still open. Eddie began to run toward him just as Luiz, the new groom, came around the end of the barn dragging a rake along behind him. "Luiz, go get help!" Eddie called out, as he reached the trainer. "Something's happened!"

The young Mexican was new and spoke very little English, but he was quick and smart and he knew a disaster when he saw one. He dropped the rake and ran across the way to Mel Ducato's shedrow, where he had an uncle who spoke the language and knew all about how to deal with gringos.

When the ambulance came to take Charlie away, about twenty minutes later, the trainer was still conscious, but he couldn't speak and seemed to be unable to move his left arm. As they loaded him onto the stretcher, his ever-present brown cap fell off, revealing a white forehead and bald dome. He must have looked naked without it.

May Potter was one of the first off the plane, which landed forty minutes late. As usual, she was wearing jeans, boots, and a man's plaid shirt, with very little makeup on and her stringy brown hair pulled back into a ponytail. She looked as if she might have come straight from work, but I was happy to see her. I had been out of town so much since the New Year, working a series of cruises back and forth down the South American coastline, that we had hardly spent any time together, only a couple of overnights snatched during my periods on shore while May was also working for Charlie. Since he'd acquired three new owners, and with the sudden influx of the new stock coming in from Clarendon, some of her working days had been eighteen hours long. Charlie had been slow, as usual, about hiring extra help and the burden had fallen mostly on her, since Charlie had begun to trust her more and more with the animals and had allowed her to manage most of the routine chores that needed to be done around a horse barn every single day of the week. May was a worker, all right, and she never said no to any job offered her. Between her schedule and mine, it hadn't been easy to carry on a romance.

When she saw me, though, those big green eyes lit up and

she ran up to give me a hug, dropping her small canvas tote bag to the ground. "Hey, you're lookin' good, Shifty," she said. "Let's go party!"

"Is that all you brought?" I asked, indicating the bag.

"Hell no," she said, grinning. "I spent all day buyin' myself two new outfits for you. We're goin' to a couple of shows, ain't we?"

"You bet. Whatever you want. How long can you stay?"

"Through the weekend," she said. "I told Charlie I needed the time and things is easier now since that new Mexican kid come on. We got four days, Shifty."

"That's terrific. I may go back with you, unless I stay on here for a week to fill in for Vince at the Three Kings," I said. "He may have a quick gig in Japan, he told me. It came up yesterday through the convention and I said I could step in, if he needed me."

"That's your magician friend."

"Yeah, you'll love him."

"He can't be better than you."

"He is," I said. "He's the best, May. So you got a bag to pick up?"

She took my arm and we set out for the baggage area. "A big one," she said. "I told you, honey, I'm here to party."

As we stood by the baggage carousel, waiting for May's suit-case to show up, I spotted Benny Wilder's mark. He was standing about ten feet away from me, his hands clasped behind his back and apparently also waiting. The little black eyes were focused intently on May, as if he were a butcher sizing up a succulent carcass. She was chattering casually away, feeding me stable gossip and racetrack news, and was unaware of his fairly intense scrutiny, but it annoyed me. "Hi, Ted," I said, "how'd you make out?"

His dark gaze focused on me. "What?"

I smiled. "I was sitting next to you in the Oasis," I said. "I got to talking to your pal Benny while you were in the men's room. I was wondering how you made out."

"He's one lucky prick," Ted said. "He took me for another four hundred bucks."

"You were bucking a tiger," I told him.

"Yeah? How do you figure?"

"The vigorish on that kind of bet runs to about twenty-six percent against you," I explained.

He didn't answer immediately but simply stared at me for a few seconds. "Says who?" he finally asked.

"Take my word for it," I said. "It's an old card hustle, one of the oldest. I'd stay away from Benny, if I were you."

"Fuck him and fuck you too," Ted said, his gaze once again focusing itself on May, who had suddenly moved away from us to inspect the name tag on a big gray Lark a few yards down the line. She was leaning over, her back turned toward us. "Your broad has got great buns."

"She's not mine, she's not a broad, and you're a jerk," I said as pleasantly as I could and smiling sweetly. "I'm sorry I told you anything. You're the kind of sucker grifters like Benny dream of finding. I should have kept quiet and let him take you to the cleaners."

I thought for a moment that he might make a move toward me, right there in public, with a hundred or so traveling revelers all around us, but his fierce, hostile gaze wavered as he noticed something behind me and his face broke into a grim attempt at a smile. "This way, sir," he said. "The car's out front."

A tall, elegant-looking, sandy-haired man of about forty swept past me, heading rapidly toward the exits. He was carrying a single small leather briefcase, which Ted tried unsuccessfully to relieve him of as he hurried along beside him. Finally he spurted ahead of him to make sure nothing would impede his progress. They disappeared through the exit doors just as May returned holding the bulky gray bag with both hands and grinning broadly. "Come on, honey, what are we waitin' for?" she said. "Let's party!"

For the next four hours or so, I forgot all about Ted and Benny the hustler. May and I spent the first two of them romping about our hotel room like a pair of lubricious gibbons, making up for some of the lost time of the past three months. By then it was too late to go downtown to see Vince, so I managed, by a judicious application of grease to the maitre d's palm, to acquire a couple of very good seats to the second show at the Xanadu, an elaborate musical revue featuring a horde of bare-bosomed showgirls and a couple of pots-and-pans magicians who, among other effects, made an elephant disappear and changed a female assistant into a black panther. I enjoyed myself only because of May, who spent much of the time either staring in astonishment at the elaborate production numbers or bouncing up and down in her seat at the magical feats.

When we finally emerged from the showroom at about twelve-thirty, May was showing no signs of fatigue, even though she'd been up since well before dawn. "That was great," she said, taking my hand. "Come on, Shifty, show me how you can dance."

We found a small club with two live bands a block off the Strip behind the Xanadu and stayed there till about two A.M. May turned out to be an untutored but wildly adventurous dancer, with a particularly good feel for rhythm and blues and country rock, which struck me as only natural, since she came from the South. I did the best I could to keep up with her, but some of her moves were way beyond me and all I could do was keep the beat while she gyrated around me, making her hips and shoulders perform in ways bordering on an X-rating. By the time we got out of there, I was turning gray. "Come on, honey, let's get some sleep," I finally had to say to her. "I've got to perform tomorrow morning."

"You perform real good," she said, throwing her arms around me and giving me a kiss. "I ain't been dancin' since I can't remember the last time."

"We've got four days."

"Right on," she said. "Okay, let's go." She took my hand and quickly led me out of there.

As we were moving through the Xanadu lobby toward the elevators, I spotted Benny Wilder. He was sitting at the corner of a bar just off the main gaming area, idly surveying the action at the tables. I hadn't intended to stop, but he noticed May first, which was only natural. She was wearing a black velvet jacket, a tight silver-sequined blouse, and a tiny black miniskirt, and her face, sporting only a trace of lipstick and mascara, was flushed with excitement. She looked sexy, wild, and desirable. It wasn't until we had skirted his position that the hustler recognized me. "Hey, how're you doin'?" he said. "Have a drink with me."

I would have demurred, but May, who was still looking for any excuse to go on partying, immediately sat down on the stool next to him, stuck out her hand, introduced herself and said, "You're one of Shifty's magician friends, ain't ya?"

I quickly told May that we had only met that same evening, while the hustler ordered a round of drinks, Kahlua for May and a light beer for me; he himself was drinking straight soda water. He then proceeded to concentrate totally on May, while trying to pass himself off as a rich businessman from Dayton, Ohio, in town for a convention. When, after about twenty minutes of this, I finally persuaded May to leave, the hustler said, "Hey, how about matching coins for the drinks? You know, just for the hell of it."

"You don't give up, do you, Benny?" I said.

The pale-blue eyes blinked innocently at me. "What do you mean? Back home, with the guys, we always toss." He reached into his pocket and produced two quarters. "Here," he said, pushing one at me, "it's a fifty-fifty proposition. Just for the fun of it."

"Okay," I said, glancing at the coin as I picked it up to make sure it was a real one.

"And we'll let the lady toss too," he said, producing another quarter and handing it to May. "If she loses, I'll pay the check anyway. Now you got two to one odds in your favor."

"That's right," I said, smiling brightly.

Benny winked at May. "On a count of three," he said. "Catch it and lay it down."

We all tossed our coins, caught them and slapped them down on the bar. "Three tails!" May said, with a giggle. "Hey, this is fun!"

"Well, what about that?" Benny said, as he quickly picked up his coin. "Again?"

"Sure, why not?" I said.

We tossed a second time and once more the coins came up tails. Benny's eyes blinked in mild surprise, but he quickly caught himself and laughed along with May, who hadn't a clue as to what was actually happening. After six tosses had obtained the same result, the hustler was ready to pick up his coins and quit, but May wanted to continue. "Hey, this is crazy!" she exclaimed. "How many times you figure this could happen, Shifty?"

"Once every two hundred sixty-two thousand fifty-three times," I said.

"You kiddin' me?"

"No." I looked at Benny. "Isn't that right, Benny? What

would you say the odds are against these coins landing tails up six times in a row?"

Benny forced himself to smile. "Just havin' a little fun," he said. "And I guess you ain't what you say you are either."

"Like you, Benny, I'm a master of hankypoo."

"What's goin' on?" May asked. "I don't get it."

"Look at your quarter, honey," I said.

She turned the coin over in her hand. "Hey, it's got two tails," she said.

"Show her yours, Benny."

He held the other phony quarter up for her to look at, then slipped both of them back into his pocket. "You're good," he said to me. "I was just having some fun."

"Right," I said, sliding my quarter toward him. "Here, Benny, you may need this one someday. It'll still buy a phone call to your lawyer. And you can pay for the drinks."

"Sure, sure," he said, hastily scooping up the coin and glancing nervously around. "You don't work for the casino, do you?"

"No, or I'd have had you out of here earlier, when you were hustling Teddy boy," I assured him. "But I wouldn't try too many of these hustles in Vegas. They might break your fingers here."

"Hey, it's all in fun, you know?" he said. "No harm done. It was only for quarters."

I stood up. "Come on, May, it's late."

"Bye, Benny," she said. "I still don't get it, but it was nice meetin' you."

In the elevator, on our way back to our room, she kissed me and held my hand. "I still don't get it, Shifty," she said. "If he had them two phony quarters, how come you always came up tails too?"

"I knew what he was doing," I explained. "When I caught my coin, I could feel with my thumb which side was tails and I just made sure tails came up every time. I don't need a fake coin, sweetheart. Not for a cheap hustler like our friend Benny."

She kissed me again as the elevator door opened. "Hankypoo," she said. "I'll show you a little hankypoo right now. You doin' anythin' important?"

"Nothing that can't wait till morning," I said, as I reached into my pocket for our room key.

2 / S *tiffed*

WE DIDN'T HEAR ABOUT CHARLIE until the next day. We got up at ten o'clock, had breakfast in the Xanadu coffee shop, then hurried over to the Ramada, about six blocks away, for the morning session of my little convention, scheduled to get started at eleven. We arrived a few minutes late, just as a young coin man from Montana named Tim Packer began moving fifty-cent pieces from knuckle to knuckle across the backs of his hands. May was immediately mesmerized. "What's he doin'?" she whispered, as we sat down in the back row of folding chairs.

"Backfire Reverse," Tim Packer said, as if to answer her. He was a tall, studious-looking young man with scraggly, dirty-blond hair that fell to his collar. I didn't know much about him, except that he worked as the night clerk in a motel on the outskirts of Billings and had apparently made himself into one of the finest coin men in the world. He now proceeded to prove it by executing not only his Backfire Reverse but a couple of other moves with quarters that I'd never seen before. He had big hands with long prehensile fingers, like those of a gibbon, and he could make his coins dance. "Wow," May said, as we all applauded.

This two-day magic convention, put on by a company that owned a chain of magic and novelty shops in the East, was the only one I liked to attend every year. It was limited to sleight-of-hand artists and brought together from all over the world a hundred or so of the best. It provided us with a chance to get together, do a little schmoozing, meet some new talent, catch up with each other, learn some new techniques. I had arranged it so May could attend this general session, in which we'd all have five or six minutes to show each other some moves. "Fantastic," May whispered, as Tim Packer returned to his seat. "How does he *do* that, Shifty?"

"Wait," I said. "You haven't seen anything yet."

Not everybody that morning proved to be a virtuoso, but May loved everything she saw. She was such a terrific audience that pretty soon all the magicians in the room began playing to her, and she ate it up. The guys who put out cigarettes into their clenched fists and caused rivers of playing cards to flow from their pockets only to make them vanish, who tore up twenty-dollar bills to reproduce them whole again out of sealed envelopes and plucked ice cubes for their drinks out of their pockets, May bought it all, every single effect, bouncing up and down in her seat, clapping her hands and squealing with delight. After I demonstrated a couple of my better card shuffles and followed up with a variation of mine on Three Card Monte, I thought she'd faint—and it actually made me blush. "May," I said, "my friends here will think I'm paying you to shill for me."

"Hey, Shifty, don't apologize for her," Vince Michaels said, as he followed me up to face this small gathering of our peers. "She's the kind of audience we all dream about."

"Watch," I said, as I rejoined May. "You haven't seen anything till you've seen Vince Michaels work."

He was a small citizen with spiky black hair that stuck out in small bunches here and there, bright black eyes and an enormous sweet smile that would occasionally spread across his face to warm an entire room. He loved magic the way Verdi must have loved music, with his whole being, and his delight in his own virtuosity was contagious, as if he himself couldn't quite believe what he was doing. He was the pure artist, the sort of person I knew I would never become, but an example to admire and emulate. He was a man obsessed.

"You know, this is a gambling town," Vince Michaels now said, holding up a pair of red casino dice between the thumb and forefinger of his right hand, "and it wouldn't exactly be unusual to own a pair of dice here, would it?" He went on to explain to us that all dice add up to seven on opposite sides, the six across from the one, the five from the two, the four from the three. "So if I put a pair of dice together like this," he continued, "then the opposite sides in a pair must total twice seven, or fourteen. Then if I have eleven on top, I have to have three on the bottom." He moved his hand in a tight little arc, but not his fingers, to illustrate his patter. "Now, if I don't want the three on the bottom, I can adjust it like this." He brushed his left forefinger lightly across the other side, then raised his right hand to show us what had occurred. "We have an eleven on the bottom and three on top and it still adds up to fourteen. But some guy said to me once, 'I think you've got eleven on the bottom and eleven on top.' " Vince then showed us an eleven bottom *and* top. "But if I show eleven on the bottom and eleven on top, when I really have three on top and three on the bottom, in order for it to add up to fourteen, you need one, two and then six and five . . ." As he continued to swing his right hand about in its tight little arc, the white dots on the surfaces of the dice changed in number without seeming to shift inside the grasp of his thumb and index finger. I'd known Vince for years, but I'd never seen him pull off this move.

"I don't believe him," May said, as my friend concluded his demonstration. "How does he *do* that?"

"Five or six hours of practice a day," I explained. "Not bad, huh?"

"Bad? He's almost as good as you are."

I laughed. "Forget it," I said. "I'm not half the artist Vince is."

After the performance, Vince joined us for a coffee at the bar in the outer room, where most of the magicians were milling around the tables displaying merchandise and printed material from the convention sponsors. I introduced him to May, who impulsively leaned over and kissed him on the cheek. "Shifty here says you're the greatest and I gotta believe him," she said, grinning broadly. "I guess you must have taught him everything he knows."

Vince blushed. "No, I didn't, May," he said. "Shifty's his own man." He glanced at me and winked. "If only he didn't love the ponies so much, he could be the best. Even now there isn't anybody at cards who can top him."

"I pay Vince a monthly retainer to say things like this about me."

"Knock it off, Shifty," he said. "By the way, that Three Card Monte is beautiful. But listen, I've got a move to show you. I've been working on it for weeks. You do it with two cards . . ."

And we were off and running for the next half hour, totally wrapped up in our magic and oblivious to everything else. Closeup is like that. You put a few of us in the same room and get us to comparing moves, it's like bringing chamber musicians together to discuss the nuances of interpreting Mozart or Beethoven, even down to the fingering of certain key passages. We both forgot all about May, who wandered away from us at some point to make a phone call. During her absence, Vince also introduced me to Sheigo Yamamoto, the elderly Japanese master who had invited Vince to return to Japan with him for a week. He was dressed in a shiny green suit and flowered necktie and he almost made an avian mating dance out of shaking hands with me, bobbing up and down so insistently that I found myself nodding in time to him. "I am going to Japan, Shifty," Vince informed me. "That is, if you can take over for me. Sheigo got the confirmation this morning."

"Sure, Vince, no problem," I said. "When?"

"Right after this is over. Can you work Monday night?"

"Absolutely."

"And you must come too," Yamamoto said, beaming at me through his thick spectacles. "Vince tell me you ahre hoss enthusiast."

"That's one way of putting it."

"We have many fine hosses in Japan," he continued. "You come too, one day, yes?"

"Yes, I'd like to," I said. "Perhaps when the Japan Cup is being run."

"Ah, yes, that is nice," the old magician said, still beaming and starting to bob his head up and down again. "You must do the cahds foh us one day, yes?"

"Yes. Tell me about magic in Japan, Mr. Yamamoto," I requested. "I really know very little about it."

"Oh, there are wonderful magicians in Japan," Vince assured me, "and they are revered as true artists. They're the most graceful in the world in all of their effects. You've seen what Sheigo does with his rings. Well, it's all like that. Magic in Japan has an aura of mystery and ceremony . . ."

Still smiling, Mr. Yamamoto stood quietly by as Vince continued to explain the status in Japan of magic in general. It was then that I spotted May. She was standing in the doorway leading to the casino lobby and she looked as if the blood had been drained out of her.

I quickly excused myself and hurried over to her. "May, what's the matter?" I asked. "Are you sick?"

She stared at me, her eyes wide with dismay. "It's Charlie," she said. "I just called the barn to find out how things were goin'. He's had a stroke or a heart attack or somethin'. He's in the hospital. It's bad, Shifty, it's gotta be real bad."

Two hours later I put May on a plane back to L.A. She drove straight to Arcadia Methodist Hospital, where she found Charlie isolated and under intensive care, with the usual modern complement of tubes plugged into him and his heartbeat being monitored by a machine. He looked very pale and still, obviously under heavy sedation. At first she was unable to get any information out of the medical staff around the nurses' station on Charlie's floor, but then had the happy idea of telling someone that she was his daughter and was eventually allowed to talk to the doctor on call. She telephoned me late that afternoon to fill me in. I had just stepped out of the shower, having left the last session of the convention half an hour earlier, when the phone rang. I wrapped a towel around myself and sat down on the bed to talk to her.

"Shifty, I thought he was dead," she said, going on to describe how she had found him. "Of course they wouldn't let me near him, but it didn't matter none 'cause he was still pretty much out of it. Then I got to talk to this doctor, who looked at me like I was a piece of shit, even though I told him I was Charlie's daughter and all. If I hadn't, he wouldn't have told me nothin'."

"Priests never like to explain the ritual to the lay folk," I said. "They get to feeling insecure."

"What does that mean?"

"Never mind. Tell me about Charlie. How bad is it?"

"Well, I had to write it all down, on account of I couldn't figure out what the hell it all meant." She paused for a few seconds to refer to her notes. "What he had, and this is how the doctor put it, was a 'major coronary occlusion.' That's like where a big vein into your heart gets blocked and you can like die on the spot. So as soon as they got him to the hospital they zapped him right into the operatin' room. This doctor said he'd have been dead in twenty more minutes. Then they did a cabbage on him."

"A what? Sounds like a vegetable."

"Ain't that the truth," she agreed, with a laugh. "And Charlie don't even like cabbage. Hell, he don't like vegetables. I never seen him eat nothin' but hamburgers, have you?"

"Steak and potatoes," I said. "So what's this cabbage mean?"

"My mouth kind of like fell open when he said that," she continued, "and I made him explain it to me, which kind of pissed him off. I guess he was in a hurry or somethin', but I started to yell at him. He looked at me like I was somebody's pet rock—"

"May, I'm sitting here on the bed in a towel and I'm wet," I said.

"Honey, I wish I was there to lick you dry."

"May, this isn't good for my health. So Charlie's going to be okay? They must have done a bypass."

"That's it, Shifty. It's a CABG, but they call it a cabbage, which is 'coronary artery bypass graft.' You know what that is?"

"Sure. I read about it somewhere."

"They crack you open like an old walnut," she explained, "and they take these veins out of your legs and use 'em to go around where it's blocked and all and then they sew you back up with chicken wire. I guess you hurt real bad for a while and you lose a lot of blood and all, but you're supposed to recover, I guess."

"How's he doing? Did the doctor say?"

"Oh, yeah, he says Charlie'll be goin' home and all in a week or ten days. Can you believe that shit? They open you up and mess around with your insides and put you back together, glue you all up, and throw you back out there. I mean, these medical guys are plumb crazy."

"I imagine he'll have to take it really easy for a while."

"Not accordin' to this doc," she said. "Charlie's gonna have to go through this whole program they got for several months, where he comes in three times a week for three hours and has to ride bicycles or some shit like that and he ain't gonna be eatin' any of that garbage he stuffs into himself. No salt, no fats, no this, no that. And he can't smoke. I mean, Shifty, they might as well have killed him. Can you imagine Charlie without a cigarette pasted to his mouth? He ain't gonna do that."

"It depends how badly he wants to live," I said. "I mean, Charlie's an old prick who's been smoking and drinking and fucking all his life and now they're going to try to turn him into Mother Teresa. Good luck. Anyway, the fucking part of it is all right. I don't think Charlie's been with a woman in ten years."

May laughed. "He don't like women," she said. "He thinks we come from some other planet or somethin'."

"What's going to happen to the horses?" I asked.

"I can keep things goin' for a while, at least a couple of weeks without him," she said. "Then I'll see what he wants to do. The doctor said I could talk to him when he comes out of it more, maybe in a day or two. Eddie and me, we'll keep things goin'. By the way, one of these Clarendon colts is a runner."

"Which one?"

"The roan."

"What's his name?"

"Old Roman, I think. He ain't ready yet, but he's workin' real good. Didn't I tell you?"

"We didn't talk much about horses while you were here."

"We didn't talk much about nothin'." She giggled. "You gonna give me a raincheck on our weekend in Vegas?"

"I might," I said. "But I can find other things to do here."

"I bet you can and if I catch you I'll kill you. What you gonna do tonight?"

"I don't know. Probably go downtown and watch Vince work," I said. "I'm taking over for him Monday, when he goes to Japan for a week. Will you call me tomorrow?"

"Sure thing. Or better yet, why don't you call me at the barn around nine-thirty, when the horses come off the track and we're pretty much done. You got the number."

"I'll do that."

"And don't you get into no trouble this week, hear?"

"Me? Trouble?"

"Honey, it's your middle name."

"When you talk to Charlie, tell him hello for me, will you?"

"Hello? Can't you think of nothin' better?"

"Okay, give him a kiss for me."

"Shifty, you're just bein' silly. I'll talk to you, hear?" And she hung up, leaving me feeling suddenly empty in that empty room. I realized to my surprise that our relationship had suddenly gone from friendship and casual sex to something frighteningly more substantial. I was in danger now of falling in love with her. That's the trouble with relationships; they evolve.

I spent most of the afternoon in the Xanadu sports book playing the horses at Santa Anita and managing to lose a few dollars, after which I drove downtown to have an early dinner with Vince prior to watching him work. We ate in the coffee shop at the Three Kings and talked magic, which Vince can do better than anyone else in the world, then at about seven we went upstairs to Luigi's, one of the two restaurants in the casino where Vince was employed as the resident master magician. "It's tough to work in here," he warned me. "You'll soon see why."

Luigi's was new and had taken the place of an elegant French bistro, all secluded nooks and crannies, in which Vince had performed his minor miracles for years. The private booths and curtained alcoves had been stripped away, the soft indirect lighting replaced by neon, and the area converted into a single large rectangular space with tables packed too close together for intimacy of any sort. It was noisy and geared to moving people in and out quickly. Worst of all from a magician's point of view, about every twenty minutes or so the waiters would group together to sing corny Neapolitan songs and classic Italian-American ditties of the kind popularized by Dean Martin. After a particularly distressing rendition of "That's *Amore*," bellowed off-key by a trio of untalented pizza hustlers, I grabbed Vince's arm as he was about to venture out into the sea of tables and pulled him aside. "How the hell are you supposed to work this room, Vince?" I asked. "Will the waiters shut up at least while you're out there?"

"Not a chance," Vince said, with a rueful smile. "Watch."

Somehow he got away with it, moving unobtrusively and purposefully from table to table, smilingly presenting himself as the resident magician, volunteering to show various groups of diners some of the simpler moves from his vast repertoire. Twice he had to stop in the middle of a performance to allow the waiters to massacre another song, but then immediately picked up from where he'd left off to finish with his customary panache and dazzling skill. I wasn't at all sure I'd be able to handle a situation like this and I told him so when he concluded his first stint, about forty minutes later. "You'll get used to it," he said, as we headed back down the escalator. "The atmosphere's tough, but I try to ignore it and concentrate on the magic. You stick pretty much to basic moves in here, nothing too complicated or subtle, mostly coins and cards. The great classics like Cups and Balls are wasted in here. When it gets too noisy, you freeze till you can be heard again. It's like trying to perform under a jet taking off."

"Whose idea was this?"

"Luigi's? Management, of course. With the recession the bistro was losing too much money, so they opted for fast and cheap, pizzeria style. At least the Mandarin Room is still okay. It's a Vegas tradition by now. I do two quick stints in Luigi's, early and late, but the good stuff I reserve for down here," Vince said, as we stepped off the escalator and headed across the casino lobby. "Hey, I can't complain. I'm the only closeup artist in all of Vegas employed to do just magic. Times are hard, Shifty."

We spent the next hour in the Mandarin Room, which must be the oldest Chinese restaurant in town. The decor is an odd blend of late Victorian and Chinese, with dark-red walls, tasseled hanging lanterns, and lacquered screens. The room is designed to afford a degree of privacy to large parties of diners, up to twelve, who may want seclusion. It's an ideal milieu for a closeup artist because you can work in an intimate space while commanding the concentrated attention of a small audience. And after more than a decade on the scene, Vince had by now acquired a devoted following, hundreds, perhaps thousands of people who came to the Mandarin Room every year just to watch him work.

I didn't hang around there too long after Vince began to do his stuff because I couldn't follow him about from nook to nook to watch him dazzle the folks and anyway I knew how to handle the Mandarin Room, having substituted for Vince quite a few times over the years. So I said good night and told him I'd bring my

bags over to his place about midmorning on Sunday, a few hours
before his departure for San Francisco and Tokyo. Then I walked
out through the casino lobby to the street and down a couple of
blocks to Binion's Diamond Horseshoe. It was early and I thought
I'd check out the action around the poker tables, where some of
the real heavy hitters in the game hang out. I'm a pretty good
poker player myself, but I haven't got the kind of money it takes
to play with the big boys and besides nobody wants to play with
me. There isn't anything I can't do with a deck of cards and, even
if I'm not dealing and don't even touch the pack, someone connected with the casino would be sure to recognize me and I'd be
asked to leave. This is too bad, because I really like the game and
I wouldn't mind being able to kill a few hours playing for modest
pots every now and then. The last time, however, I tried to sit in
on a few hands somewhere on the Strip a few years ago, I was
quickly whisked away from the table by a casino security guy who
told me I wasn't welcome at their tables. "It isn't that we don't
trust you, Shifty," the pit boss told me later, "but too many people
know about you in this town. We don't want any angry customers
complaining. They'd assume you're working for us and took their
money. You understand. Nothing personal." It's one of the iro-
nies of life that often the better you are at what you do for a living,
the less popular you become. I could have made a fortune hustling in card games all over the country by now, but I'd have had
to betray my talent and my skills. Corruption is an American specialty and cheating is a national pastime. But I also could have
wound up dead somewhere or with my hands smashed, so perhaps a life of dedicated but genteel poverty has its compensations,
after all. I had to content myself with kibitzing, which at least
keeps me in touch with the game.

There wasn't much action at Binion's this particular night,
perhaps because it was still early for the big players, so I lingered
at the tables for only a few hands before retreating to the bar,
where I ordered a Courvoisier and soda and killed another forty
minutes before heading back to the Xanadu. I missed May and I
was worried about Charlie. I didn't want to party, but I also didn't
want to go to bed. Like a horse after a good workout, I needed
cooling out.

I was just getting up to leave, when I suddenly spotted Teddy
boy again. He was still with the sandy-haired man and the two of

them were making their way across the casino floor heading toward the elevators. They were joined there by two other men, bulky citizens in their fifties who looked like ex-cops but were dressed in expensively tailored light-gray business suits, were also carrying briefcases, and had obviously been waiting for Ted and his man to show up. When the elevator doors opened, the four of them stepped quickly inside and disappeared from view. I remember being mildly interested in what they might be up to, since they obviously hadn't come to Vegas just to have a good time, but I attached no great significance to this encounter and thought no more about it. Teddy boy, I had decided, was merely some kind of security guard working for the sandy-haired man, while the other two were probably the latter's business associates in some perfectly respectable venture. I walked out of Binion's to the parking garage behind the Three Kings, picked up my car, and drove back to the Xanadu.

It wasn't until about an hour later, while I was lying in bed watching the eleven-o'clock news, that I was once more reminded of Ted. I was half-dozing and about to click the set off when I heard a male voice say, "The victim's name was Benjamin Wilder, also known as Snake. According to the police, he had a long record as a con man and hustler and was currently out on parole after serving three and a half years in Illinois for embezzlement and dealing in fraudulent bonds."

I opened my eyes and propped myself up against my pillows. A young reporter was doing a stand-up in front of an ambulance into which the body of Benjamin Wilder had apparently just been loaded. Lights flashing, the vehicle was about to drive away, but no one seemed to be in much of a hurry, probably because Mr. Wilder was already dead. His throat had been cut from ear to ear and he had been left, hands bound behind his back, to bleed slowly to death in an abandoned lot a few miles out in the desert north of the Strip. "What makes this crime particularly gruesome," the reporter continued, "is that Wilder was apparently tortured before he was murdered. His fingers were broken, probably one by one, by some sort of instrument, perhaps a pair of pliers. Police surmise that he may have been executed over a gambling debt or in a Mafia vendetta. This is Rip Kinsey reporting live . . ."

No, I told myself, Teddy boy couldn't have done it. Not that swiftly and brutally and totally for only a couple of thousand bucks. Benny must have been in way over his head in some other scam to have merited such a death. I found myself wishing, however, that I had kept my mouth shut regarding him. I didn't like the feeling I could have been responsible for his death.

3 / Keats

''BENNY WILDER? Yeah, I know the guy,'' Vince said. "We used to call him Snake."

"Why?"

"Because he was one." Vince leaned over to peer closely at the photograph of the victim, obviously a mug shot from an old police lineup, that accompanied the story of his demise in the *Las Vegas Sun*. "That's him, all right. I used to bump into him from time to time around the circuit. I think he used to work at Tannen's in New York, but that didn't last long. Nothing ever did with Snake. He'd show up somewhere, coil himself around something or someone, and slither away when things got out of hand."

"What did he do at Tannen's?"

"Worked there as a magic salesman, like me when I started out," Vince said. "He wanted to be a magician, too, he claimed, and for a while he worked at it. He mastered a few basic moves, but he was always looking for a way to make a quick buck. He might have done all right if he'd worked at it, but he had no staying power. The minute he picked up enough moves to work a few scams he'd be off somewhere. What did he do to get himself arrested?"

"Phony stock options, junk bonds, stuff like that." I told Vince how I'd met him two days earlier and about spilling the beans to his mark. "I don't think Teddy boy did him in, but he could have. I should have kept my mouth shut."

"I wouldn't worry about it," Vince said. "Snake probably had people all over looking for him. He must have been really down on his luck to be working small hustles on strangers in bars."

"He met this guy at the poker tables in Binion's," I said. "Beat him out of a couple of grand."

"And couldn't content himself with that," Vince added. "Just like a snake, always trying to swallow something a little too big for him. He was lucky to have lasted as long as he did."

"He wasn't more than forty," I said, "and having your fingers broken one by one before your throat is cut isn't my idea of luck."

Vince smiled and shrugged. "Want some coffee or a drink?"

"A drink, this early? Coffee."

"I didn't mean a real drink. You know me, a beer or two, but only after work," Vince said. "Make yourself at home, while I finish packing. The icebox is full of stuff and the coffee's plugged in." He walked up the stairs to his bedroom loft, while I poured myself a cup of coffee and sat down on the sofa against the far wall.

I liked Vince's place, probably because it reminded me of my own apartment in West Hollywood. We were both bachelors and both obsessed. In Vince's case, it was all magic. He'd begun his life in Las Vegas in a small duplex exactly like this one, then, feeling lonely, he had moved briefly into a larger complex full of young people nearer the Strip, but had found it too noisy and gone back to his old building into an apartment two doors away from his first one. "I guess I was hoping maybe to meet some girls, not be quite so alone," Vince had told me about his move, "but I couldn't stand all that confusion and the parties on their days off. You know me, Shifty, I'm a loner, even more of one than you are. I guess I'll always be alone, so I might as well resign myself. Anyway, this place has everything I need, except one other person in it. But I can't pay the price, I guess, for company and who could stand to live with me anyway? I've never found anyone who cares as much about magic as I do."

His quarters reflected this obsession. All the pictures on his walls, mostly framed prints and reproductions, had something to do with magic and magicians, spilled out of his bookshelves and into several cartons piled up in one corner. On his desk rested some of the objects—packs of cards, coins, bits of string, sponge-rubber balls and tiny animals, hoops, rings, wands, kerchiefs, thimbles, little boxes—that he used in his act, while on a small square table covered with green felt were the pieces he'd been practicing with most recently. Vince never let a day go by without working on some of his moves or devising new ones. I felt at home there and I looked forward to spending the week in his digs, if only because I'd be so immersed in the atmosphere his place exuded that I'd perform my own best work. It had happened to me before, when I'd substituted for Vince on his other out-of-town trips.

"Well, I see nothing's changed," I called out, as I sipped my coffee.

"What's to change?" Vince called back.

"You were going to put up more shelves, get the books out of the boxes, maybe acquire a cat to keep you company."

"Aw, hell, Shifty," Vince said, his head appearing over the loft railing, "I'll never get anything put away, you know me. I would like a cat, though. I think I will get one when I come back. Cats are an inspiration to me. What's more mysterious and magical than a cat?"

"A woman," I said, smiling.

"Ah, well, that's another matter entirely," Vince said, retreating out of sight again to finish his packing. "That's a nice girl you brought to the session. You serious about her?"

"I don't know," I admitted. "I like her more than I thought I would when we started seeing each other."

Vince's head popped up over the railing again and he peered down at me with those bright, glittery eyes. "Don't blow it if it comes along, Shifty," he said. "You blew it once with Dawn, remember?"

"How could I forget? I wasn't ready, Vince. Now maybe I am. But it isn't going to be easy. I live in West Hollywood and my place is too small and she's basically a gypsy. I don't think she's ever had a real home. She works at the track, which means getting up while it's still dark and being at the barn by sunrise and sometimes, if she has a horse running in the afternoon, not getting out of there before dark. If I'm working, it's usually in the evenings. What kind of a life together can we have?"

Vince grinned and waggled an index finger at me. "You know the old song, love will find a way." He laughed and went back to his suitcases.

Love will find a way—oh, sure, I thought. My affair with Dawn, a single mother who worked here in Las Vegas as a dealer at the blackjack tables, had broken up years before partly because I was too immersed in magic in those days, and partly also over my inability to commit to any living creature without a saddle on its back. Then, I didn't want to make the compromises a real relationship involves and we had sort of drifted apart between bouts of torrid sex until at last Dawn had mercifully put an end to it. As for my other involvements, they hadn't exactly been lucky. Amber, a poor little rich girl who had wanted to reform the world and thought of lovemaking as a "meaningful physical convergence," had been murdered. The other women in my life had turned out to be either crazy or betrayers of one sort or another. Maybe Charlie was right, after all; maybe they did come from a different planet. I remembered asking him once if he'd ever been married and his telling me that he had been, but that his wife became so angry at him one day that she chased him around their ranch with a meat cleaver. "I figured out I couldn't count on outrunning her the rest of my life, so I kept right on going," he said, "out the door, into the car, and back to the barn."

"A meat cleaver, Charlie?" I had said, figuring he was putting me on a little.

"That ain't the most dangerous thing they can do to you," Charlie had answered. "You ever see what a woman can accomplish with a credit card in her hand? She can chop you right into the ground, Shifty."

Well, that was old Charlie Pickard for you, and it made a good story for him and his redneck pals on the backstretch to guffaw over, but who could guess what the truth was? I knew from experience I wasn't easy to live with over a long haul and Charlie, with his nineteenth-century sensibility and cowboy outlook on life, had to be a minor nightmare to any female not trained to be a geisha.

"You ready?" Vince asked. He was standing at the foot of the stairs with a suitcase in each hand. "You look a little strange. Something wrong?"

"No, Vince, I was just daydreaming," I said. "I guess you got me to thinking about May and the whole big problem of women in my life."

"Problem? The only problem is not having one," he said. "I can't think of anything more wonderful than having someone to share your life with. I envy you, Shifty. Don't let this one get away." He started for the door. "I guess we better go. You sure you don't mind driving me?"

"Knock it off, Vince."

All the way to the airport in his car, as I wove through surprisingly heavy traffic, I kept thinking about what Vince had suddenly focused for me. I had a not very comfortable feeling that May would move in with me if I asked her, though I had ignored the whole question until this ill-fated weekend. Funny about guys like Vince. A fine artist, a sweet and gentle soul, he'd have made a loving husband and he longed to be one, but for some reason women didn't take him seriously enough. He had dated, of course, had lived briefly with one or two, had proposed to several, but nothing had ever worked out. He was doomed to remain a bachelor, living alone surrounded by his modest possessions and small treasures. His real love affair was with magic and perhaps this was what put potential partners off; the obsessed artist is never much fun to be around over the long haul. You either service his needs and submit yourself to his demands or you live a life of misery and frustration. Love is never enough.

Mr. Yamamoto, in another of his electric suits, was waiting for us by the check-in counter and Vince hurried inside to join him. "Be good, Shifty," he called back. "You don't have to meet me next Monday. I'll get a taxi. And don't blow all your money in the casinos this week."

Why do people worry about my gambling? I don't bet on anything except horses.

Sergeant Masterson, the officer on the front desk at the police station about eight blocks from Vince's apartment, obviously considered me another prime example of the foolish citizenry he had to deal with every day. He was a ruddy-cheeked bald man of about fifty-five with hard gray eyes and a thin mustache who looked as if he had heard and witnessed more idiocy in a month than any human being ought to be subjected to in a lifetime. I guessed that having to listen to the public was not his favorite pastime and that he had never found it rewarding in any way, but I plunged on regardless. I'm not sure why I had decided to do so, on my way back from the airport, but I think it was because I hadn't been able to get the picture of Benny Wilder's broken fingers out of my head. As a magician, I could appreciate the horror of it.

"So you think that this individual you saw at the bar with the victim could have committed this act?" the officer said, when I had concluded my account. "You think he picked him up, took him out into the desert, broke his hands and then cut his throat, is that what you're saying, Mr. Anderson?"

"Well, I'm not sure—"

"He would do this because the victim was hustling him at cards and took him for a few hundred dollars—"

"It was over two thousand, and no one likes to be hustled."

"No, of course not." Sergeant Masterson sighed and folded his hands together on the desk before him like a priest listening to a particularly boring confession from a middle-aged housewife. "And what makes you think he would do that, this man you saw with the victim?"

"I had a conversation with him at the airport when I went to pick up my girlfriend there," I said. "He's a pretty hostile citizen. I made the mistake of telling him what Wilder had been doing to him."

"Okay. Is that it?"

"I guess so."

"What do you expect us to do about this?"

"I don't expect you to do anything. I just thought you ought to know about this guy."

"His first name is Ted, but apart from that and what he looks like, you don't know anything else about him."

"That's right." I stood up. "I'm wasting your time."

"Oh, I wouldn't say that, Mr. Anderson. We got plenty of time here," Sergeant Masterson said, very sweetly. "We don't get more than four or five murders and two or three hundred felonies a week in here. What's time to us? We listen to everybody.

Where did you say you could be reached, just in case you have given us an invaluable lead?"

He wrote down my name, address, and phone numbers, in L.A. as well as Las Vegas, then looked up and smiled brilliantly at me. "You've been a great help," he said. "We'll be sure to call you if we need you to identify this person."

"Then you are going to try to find him?"

The officer leaned over the desk and fixed me with an intense, concentrated stare. "We are going to devote the entire resources of our department to bringing this individual to justice," he said. "If we can't do it alone, we will call in the F.B.I. How's that?"

"I think I'm getting the message," I said.

"Oh. And what message is that, Mr. Anderson?"

"That I shouldn't have bothered to come in here."

"Oh, I wouldn't say that, Mr. Anderson," Sergeant Masterson said, leaning contentedly back in his chair. "We want every public-spirited citizen to do his duty. We are here to serve."

"Are you pretty close to retirement?" I asked.

"Why?" He looked surprised. "What's that got to do with anything?"

"Just wondering."

"Five months, since you asked," he said.

"I'm certain you're going to enjoy it," I assured him. "I think you're ready."

"That is the most intelligent thing anybody has said to me all day," Sergeant Masterson said. "By the way, Mr. Anderson, if you see this individual you've told me about, don't make a citizen's arrest, okay? Please call us."

The week passed quickly. I settled into my familiar Vegas routine, which meant getting up in the morning around eight, exercising and jogging for an hour, then back to Vince's place for a good session at his little magic table. I'd begun to work some more with coins and I had put in some time at the convention with Tim Packer, so I spent much of the week mastering Backfire Reverse. It gave me a good feeling, being all by myself and able to spend all the time I wanted on my magic, free of the distractions of my life at home in L.A. To top off the morning, I'd always go back to cards, my first love, and end up with variations I'd worked out on the great classic shuffles. I'd finish up by midday, after which I'd shower and shave, then drive to the Strip to spend my afternoons in one of the sports books playing the horses at Santa Anita and, occasionally, Golden Gate.

After the ninth at Santa Anita, I'd have a couple of hours to get back to Vince's, wash up, change into my less formal working clothes—black pants, black shoes, a white silk shirt open at the collar, and a black velvet vest in the pockets of which I kept the small tools of my trade—and get down to the Three Kings by seven o'clock. I'd open in Luigi's, which, despite Vince's advice, I found to be a minor nightmare; I couldn't seem to make anything work in that noisy, crowded room. By the third day I'd narrowed my repertory down to about four basic tricks and a little patter, though I was able to get some comic mileage out of making fun of the atrocious singing by the waiters. But I couldn't get out of there soon enough every night and I dreaded having to come back for my second session. In fact, by the end of the week, I'd begun to cut down my stints in Luigi's to less than half an hour at a time. I concentrated on doing all my good work in the Mandarin Room and nobody complained, so I managed to enjoy myself quite a lot that week. There's something to be said for being on the road. The day-to-day responsibilities and preoccupations of normal daily life are banished and you live in a vacuum of pure pleasure, especially if you love what you're doing and are appreciated for it. I forgot about everything, including Charlie and May and my filly, and basked in being me—Shifty Lou Anderson, master magician and dedicated horseplayer.

I was also on a good streak at the track, which usually happens to me when I'm happy and working well and not under pressure. In fact, I was winning so much money on my action that I became extra careful about taking too much loot out of any one sports book. The people who run the casinos are not sportsmen and they're quick to cut you off at the betting windows if they realize you are knocking them over day after day. So I never went to the same book twice in a row, but divided my action between half a dozen of the major emporiums, even to the extent of switching from one to another in midafternoon. Which probably accounts for missing my pal Arnie Wolfenden, who had been in town for two days by the time he caught up to me at Caesars Palace.

"So here you are," Arnie said, coming up beside me as I was settling back to watch the fourth at Santa Anita. "Jay told me you were in town and staying at the Xanadu, but you checked out. I like Caesars better anyway. They aren't quite so chickenshit here about taking my action." He sat down at the empty space beside me and dropped his tattered *Racing Form* on the counter. "You got anything going here?"

"A small wager on the three horse," I said.

"Quitting speed," Arnie observed, with a sigh. "Will you never learn, Shifty?"

"I make a lot of money betting on quitting speed in California, Arnie," I said. "You're still thinking like a New Yorker."

"How true. Anyway, I'll root you in."

We sat facing the bank of video screens showing races from five or six different tracks and watched my speedball burst out of the gate at seven to one, lead until the last sixteenth of a mile, and fade to third at the finish. "Don't say it, Arnie," I warned him.

"What's to say, Shifty?" he answered. "You ever heard me knock a bet on a seven-to-one shot? Now if that had been some odds-on plodder, I'd have castigated you thoroughly. But you know better than that, so I keep my silent watch, that's all."

"You didn't bet, obviously."

"I have isolated only one legitimate contender from this herd of mediocrities today," Arnie said. "But I will sit here and favor you with the wisdom of my sixty-five misspent years. Jay sends his best and wanted me to tell you he heard that Pickard is doing okay."

"Yeah, May told me when I talked to her last night."

"Ah, May, the leggy frail who fills your nights with wonder, yes," Arnie said, smiling. "Shifty, you lead a life teeming with perilous distractions."

"And you're one of them, Arnie. What are you doing here?"

"My daughter's getting married," he said, "so I came in a couple of days early to indulge myself in the cornucopia of cultural wonders for which this burg is justly celebrated. Have you visited the Liberace Museum, the Louvre of the West?"

"No," I confessed. "In Vegas I lead a life of monastic simplicity, Arnie—magic and horses."

"What else is there?" Arnie said. "Anyway, I'm glad I found

you. I wanted to invite you to the wedding dinner tonight. Maybe you could do a few tricks for us."

"I'm working, Arnie. Where is it?"

"Someplace called Luigi's downtown," he said. "It's an Italian joint. Can you beat that? She's marrying an Irish guy and we're celebrating in an Italian joint."

"Hey, I work in Luigi's. Sure I can stop by. What time's the dinner?"

"Seven o'clock. They're getting married this afternoon at the Little Chapel of the Impossible Dream, here on the Strip." He glanced at his watch and bounced to his feet. "Four-thirty, shit. I have to get out of here, Shifty." He reached into his pocket for his wallet, extracted two hundred-dollar bills and dropped them on the counter in front of me. "Bet this on the nose for me on the six horse in the feature, will you? That's what I came here to do. I ought to get three to one or better and the horse is very live. Jay's making a major play on him." He started to move away from me, scuttling sideways behind the counter like an agile old crab, which is what he looked like in his baggy brown-checked sports jacket and light-gray slacks, his little beady eyes peering suspiciously out at the world as if it might one day catch up to him.

"Hey, Arnie," I called after him, "I thought you went to a Catholic boarding school."

"I did," he answered. "My mother was Catholic, my father was Jewish. I was raised on guilt. My daughter's Jewish, I think."

"What do you mean, you think?"

"I didn't raise her, my ex-wife and her second husband did and they're both Jewish. I'll see you tonight, Shifty. Thanks. It means a lot to me." He waved and disappeared up the aisle.

I didn't even know Arnie had been married and had a daughter, but that was typical of the racetrack, where people can know each other for years, see each other every day at the races, and know nothing about each other's lives away from the track. In any case, I hadn't known Arnie that long, since he'd only fled the New York racing scene a couple of years earlier for the kinder climes of the California environment. He was a survivor, an ex-pool hustler and shrewd, tight-fisted horseplayer, one of the chosen few who graced my friend Jay Fox's box at the L.A. hippodromes. I liked him because he was a philosopher of sorts, a gambler of surprising erudition who never made the mistake of underestimating the stupidity of his peers. It had kept him in action and alive for half a century.

I picked up my *Racing Form*, looked at the feature, and discovered that I'd also marked Arnie's horse as a potentially good bet, so I made up my mind to press my own action on the animal by another twenty dollars, then sat back to wait for it. The horses for the seventh race, an uninteresting sprint down the hillside turf course, were a couple of minutes away from the starting gate. I had no intention of risking money on this contest, since I had estimated that any one of six or seven horses in the field of ten could win it, so I got up to go and get myself a coffee. As I headed up the aisle, I spotted Ted again. He was standing at the back of the room looking at the TV screens, obviously studying the odds. He didn't notice me and then suddenly shot past me on his way to the betting windows.

I turned around and followed him, standing directly behind him and close enough to hear him bet five hundred dollars to win on a horse named Bellringer in the seventh. He went back to his post, still without noticing me, and I returned to my seat to check the animal out in the *Form*.

Bellringer was one of the horses I'd given a chance to win. Listed at twelve to one in the morning line, he was a lightly raced five-year-old gelding, obviously injury-prone or with physical problems of some sort, who had recently been shipped to California from the Kentucky racing circuit. He had won four out of seventeen races in his career, always in sprints, but he had never raced on grass before and his works were ordinary. Also, his trainer was a Kentuckian who had not raced in California before. What was interesting about him was that he always won at a decent price and after a series of two or three very poor efforts. In his most recent starts, he had finished fifth and seventh, well-beaten by several lengths. But here he was again, at a different track and on a different surface, inexplicably being bet down; he was going off as the third choice in the race, at odds of nine to two.

I had to force myself to resist an impulse to rush down to a window to bet on him, even though I've learned over the years almost never to risk money on a hunch or a tip. My mentor Jay Fox, the prince of handicappers, had taught me that valuable lesson; if the numbers don't add up, pass the race. So I sat there, nailed to my seat, and watched Bellringer break alertly out of the gate, drop back two or three lengths behind the speed in the race, and come on strongly in the stretch to win easily by a length and a half, paying $11.20 to win for every two-dollar ticket.

I looked around for Ted, but he was nowhere to be seen, then I checked my *Form* again and noticed that the horse was owned by Clarendon Farm, Charlie Pickard's most important new client. It didn't strike me as especially significant, if only because Clarendon was such an established and respected name in the world of horse racing. Still, somebody had known enough about this horse to bet heavily on him and knock the odds down on information not available to the average horseplayer. And Teddy boy, a sucker at card hustles, had obviously been in on it. That sort of action on a horse race always gets my attention, since making money on inside information represents the sort of edge Ivan Boesky went to jail for.

The O'Hara-Wolfenden wedding party, about thirty strong, was seated at a long table against the rear wall of Luigi's. I arrived there just after the waiters had finished mangling "Come Back to Sorrento" and Arnie, who was seated at one end of the table, as far away as possible from his ex-wife and her second husband at the other end, introduced me to the guests as "the greatest magician since Houdini." He made it sound as if he himself had personally arranged for me to be there, a special treat he had organized for his daughter, and I didn't betray him. Knowing Arnie, I figured he had consented to attend only because the bride and groom had been thoughtful enough to hold the affair in a casino. Arnie never stayed anywhere or went anyplace that wasn't within a half hour's drive of a pari-mutuel window.

I kept my act simple and to the point, with several card effects featuring a pairing up of kings and queens, which seemed thematically appropriate, then closed with Ring on a Stick. I used the bride's wedding band and popped it onto the groom's gold pen as he held it tightly at both ends with closed fists. It's a good move and always gets a good reaction. This time was no exception, with the groom, a pleasant-looking, freckle-faced Irish blue-collar type, looking amazed and his new wife clapping her hands in delight. She was cute, very small and with close-cropped curly

hair, a round face, dimples, and very large brown eyes as inno-
cent-looking as a doe's. She had to be at least in her early thirties,
I guessed, but looked much younger. "This is Sue's second marriage," Arnie confided, after I'd finished and sat down next to
him to share in a few toasts to the happy couple. "The first guy
was a bum who said he was a writer."

"What happened to him?" I asked.

"He disappeared in a cloud of rejection slips. She had to support him. I'd send her a few bucks from time to time, whenever I
was going good."

"Then you're close."

"Not exactly. She likes me, but she thinks I treated her mom
badly and that horses are more important to me than people."

"Well?"

"Shifty, horses are evolution's noblest achievement," he said.
"They don't lie, cheat, steal, or murder. They just give pleasure.
Let's drink to that." He grinned, raised his champagne glass and
took a swallow. "How did our champion run in the eighth?"

"Second."

"Horses will break your heart, but not because they mean
to."

I was getting ready to leave for the Mandarin Room and had
just paid my respects to the bridal couple when Arnie suddenly
rose from his seat to propose a toast "to the symbolic blending of
two cultures," as he put it. I saw his daughter's face blanch.
"Daddy, don't," she said.

Arnie beamed at her. "Sweetheart, I'm paying for this dinner
and I have composed a poem in celebration of it," he said. "I wish
to read it aloud on this most festive occasion."

"Sit down, Arnold," his ex-wife snapped from her end of the
table, but too late. Arnie had already started banging on his water
glass with a knife to get everybody's attention.

"Ladies and gentlemen, I have a toast," he said, "a verse epic
to commemorate this joyous day, from one who was known in his
time as the Keats of the pool halls."

"Daddy," his daughter said, "I'm so happy. Please."

The unsuspecting members of the Irish contingent laughed
and applauded as Arnie fished a crumpled piece of paper from
his jacket pocket and began to read. "Life is a wheel," he began.
"Death is a blow that we all must feel."

"I'll kill you, you sonofabitch," his ex-wife said.

"But if life was a thing that money could buy," Arnie continued, heedless of his family's distress, "the Jews would live and the Irish would die."

Arnie's ex-wife threw her glass at him as his daughter began to cry. I seized on the moment as my cue to exit.

4 / **P**ropositions

MAY HAD WARNED ME that Charlie might show up, but even so I couldn't believe it. He was actually sitting at his desk in the tack room when I arrived at his barn. It was eight o'clock on a Wednesday morning, two days after my return from Las Vegas, and I had driven out to Santa Anita to spend the day, first on the backside and then in the grandstand. I was planning to have dinner with May and then maybe whisk her back to my place for the night, but she hadn't been certain she'd be able to make it. "Charlie says he's gonna show up tomorrow mornin'," she'd told me, "so I don't know what-all's gonna happen. Hell, that old fool's either gonna die on me right on the spot, or he's gonna find a million damn things wrong with what I been doin' and he's liable to put me in the damn hospital. Shitfire, honey, we gonna have to play it as it lays, know what I'm sayin'?"

"I thought it would be another week or so," I ventured. "Are you sure?"

"That's what the man says," May answered. "I ain't gonna argue with him. You ever tried to argue with Charlie? Ain't but one way of doin' things, Shifty—Charlie's way. He'll be here."

And sure enough, when I turned the corner of the barn the next morning and walked down his shedrow, there he was. He was dressed, as always, in scuffed street shoes, work pants, an open-necked shirt, an old sports jacket, and with his brown cap pulled down over his bald pate. I'd have recognized him instantly from his costume, but even from a distance he didn't look well. He was pale, thinner, and seemed to have shrunk inside his clothes. I noticed, too, that he wasn't moving around, though his eyes were alert and he wasn't missing much of what was going on outside his open door. "Shifty," he said, as I came up to him, "what the hell are you doing here? I thought you was in Vegas."

"I was," I said. "I just got back Monday night. How are you feeling, Charlie?"

He smiled wanly. "I'm holding together," he said. "I guess you know all about it."

"Yeah, May told me."

"I can't believe I let them do that to me," he said. "They cut me open like some old turkey and messed around in there, then sewed me back up. I actually let them do that to me, Shifty. I must be getting senile."

"I don't think you had much choice, Charlie," I said. "You might have checked out on us. And aren't you back here a little early?"

"I can't risk any fuck-ups," he said. "I got a nice little string now and one big new client."

"Clarendon?"

He nodded. "That's the one."

"How did you land them?"

"Beats me, Shifty. I guess they took pity on a poor old down-trodden horseman." He smiled. "This guy Roger Baldwin called me out of the blue one day and wanted to know if I'd train a few horses for him. Said he'd wanted to send stock out to California for some time and that I'd been recommended to him as a good trainer. I couldn't turn him down, could I?"

"Who recommended you? I sure wouldn't have."

"Nobody would have asked you, Shifty," Charlie said. "You don't know shit about horses. What you know about is betting on them."

"That's more than most trainers know. I could get rich cross-booking bets with most of the trainers I know and that includes you, Charlie."

"I wouldn't try it."

"Why not? All you guys know is your own horses," I said. "You don't even read the *Racing Form*. You don't know anything about speed figures."

"Don't have to," he said. "I'm a trainer, not a damn diseased gambler like you."

"So who recommended you?"

He shrugged. "I still don't know," he said. "Baldwin wouldn't tell me. Said he'd asked around and heard about me. He didn't want to give his horses to some big stable out here, because he thought they might get lost in an operation with too many other animals. He was only planning to send out a few, five or six, mostly young ones. He'd heard I was the best with two-year-olds. Clarendon still races mostly in the East, you know, the New York and Florida circuits, also in Kentucky, their home state. Hell, it was a nice opportunity, so I just said yes. Didn't want to press my luck. The man could change his mind."

"Did he ever have horses out here?"

"A couple of years ago, with Gantry."

"He probably broke them down. Do you know Baldwin?"

"Never met him. First time I ever talked to him was on the phone, when he called to offer me the chance to train for him." He pushed himself to his feet and shuffled painfully to the open doorway. "May," he called out in a hoarse voice, as she came around the corner of the barn leading a big bay with a racing saddle on its back, "May, let Polo gallop the bay. The jock will work the two-year-old."

"Sure thing, Charlie," she called back.

"And tell the jock to breeze him three-eighths. Don't ask him for speed."

"Gotcha."

"Polo, a couple of turns on the bay, easy does it."

"Yes, sir, Mr. Charlie," Rodriguez said, as May gave him a leg up into the saddle; he was grinning broadly. "We get rich on this one, Mr. Charlie." He turned the big horse and rode off toward the track unaccompanied.

"That one of your new ones?"

"I just got him," Charlie said. "He won here the other day."

"Bellringer?"

"Yeah, that's him. Big, sore sonofagun, but he can run some."

"You put him over, Charlie?" I asked, surprised. "That was a nice little coup you guys pulled off."

"Me? I don't know what you're talking about, Shifty," the trainer said, easing himself back into his chair. "I told you, I just got him. Phil Hardin, who trains him back East, brought him out here for the race. They turned him over to me afterwards. Phil said the horse would really like these hard, sandy surfaces out here, so he talked Mr. Baldwin into leaving him with me. He's a nice horse, but he ain't all that sound. But the young horses, they're pretty nice." He looked up at me and winked. "I think you might have had something to do with this."

"Me? How? I don't know Baldwin."

"Mad Margaret," the trainer said. "I did a pretty good job with her. Somebody told Baldwin."

"Who would do that? Certainly not Gantry. He steals clients from people, not the other way around. Most of the other trainers out here would want Clarendon for a client, wouldn't they?"

"Seems like it, Shifty. Only they ain't been goin' too good the last couple of years. Anyway, I got 'em and that's what counts."

"Somebody from Clarendon must have asked around," I said. "You do have a pretty good reputation as a guy who doesn't abuse his animals. And you did a great job with Maggie, if I do say so myself, you ornery old bastard. Why don't you go home and go to bed? You got somebody to drive you?"

"I can drive myself. Don't worry about me."

"Aren't you supposed to be taking it easy?"

"I am. I'm sitting down," he said. "Now get out of here. You're blocking my view."

I went out into the stable area and caught up to May, who was busy doing up a nice-looking little roan colt tethered in his stall down toward the end of the shedrow. She was inside with him, working with a brush in each hand while keeping warily out of reach of the animal's occasional half-hearted attempts to bite her. She looked so desirable I wanted to jump into the stall with her and take her in my arms. Instead I leaned in over the door and looked at her. "How's the old fool?" she asked, without looking up from her work.

"He looks like hell," I said.

"That's what I told him," she said, "but you can't argue with him. Anyway, maybe it's better for him, I don't know. Seems like Charlie would just curl up and die if he can't be around horses." She suddenly jumped to one side as the colt's head spun around and his teeth snapped together only inches away from her arm. "Hey, sonny, shape up! You tryin' to kill me?"

"Mean, isn't he? Who is this?"

"Naw, he ain't mean," she said. "He's just playin' with me. He's so full of himself he thinks he can get away with anythin'. This sucker can run, Shifty."

"One of the Clarendon horses?"

"You bet. Name's Old Roman. He's a two-year-old. You won't see him till Hollywood Park, but he'll run quick over there. He's an early April foal, so he's pretty mature. And he's fast. We got him in twenty-two flat for the quarter the other mornin' and he went out the half in forty-seven and a tick just gallopin'."

"How about the others?"

"Oh, there's four other young ones, two colts and two fillies, all nice stock, and then there's Bellringer, you saw him."

"Yeah," I said. "I watched him win on a TV screen in Vegas. I thought they did a nice job of putting him over. He was coming off bad races and nothing works. I didn't think Clarendon pulled that sort of stuff."

She didn't answer me right away, but went on working on the colt. After a couple of minutes, she finished brushing him, gave him an affectionate slap on the rump, then stepped out of the stall to put her brushes away. "I agree with you, hon," she finally said. "I ain't gonna talk to you here about it, though."

"Am I going to see you later?"

"I don't know," she said. "It depends on Charlie, I guess. You goin' racin'?"

"Is God in His heaven?" I asked. "Will the earth spin on its axis? Will the moon wax and wane? Will the tides rise and fall? What kind of a question is that?"

She laughed. "If I don't see you over there, come back here after the ninth. I'm gonna try and get a nap after I finish up here and make sure Charlie's all right. But maybe we ought to stay out around my place tonight. Is that okay?"

"Sure. Say, who do you think told the Clarendon people about Maggie?"

"You got me, Shifty," she said, picking up a bucket of soapy water and a handful of rub rags and moving down toward the next stall. "I just work here. Charlie don't tell me nothin', the old prick. All he does is work me like a dog."

"I'll speak to him about that."

"It won't do you no good," she said, disappearing from view into the stall with another of the Clarendon two-year-olds. "Charlie don't know neither. I guess he's got a reputation. Word must have got around." She popped her head out the stall door and gave me a quick kiss. "Get out of here, honey. I may rape you or somethin'. I'll see you later."

I went back to the tack room to say good-bye to Charlie. He was on the phone, so I waited by the door, my back against the outside wall of the barn, and watched the goings-on. It was a day like any other, with horses and riders moving about the long, low stables, on their way to and from the track, cooling out and being groomed, the whole scene cushioned on an undercurrent of sound—voices calling, laughter, radios playing, commands, exhortations, curses, the early-morning choral symphony of the horse world.

There are few things as pleasurable as being in the backside of a racetrack at this time of day, especially when the weather is clear and the air crisp and clean. The men and women whose lives are bound to the fortunes and well-being of the expensive animals they care for work hard and for very modest pay, but they seem mostly to be happy and at ease in their circumscribed little world. Perhaps this is partly because they live for tomorrow, that golden day when one of these creatures they have nurtured and schooled and trained will explode out of a starting gate one afternoon to bring them fame and fortune and an exquisite moment or two of rapture. Racetrackers can survive years of frustration and misfortune because they are nurtured and warmed by memories of such moments and expectations of future ones. Good horses, and especially the great ones, are like comets; they streak across the leaden sky of your everyday existence, briefly lighting up your time, showering you in glory, and leaving in their wake memories and hope. It is this aspect of the sport that lifts the world of the racetrack above the gray mediocrity of routine, keeps all of us, participants and fans alike, clasped within its embrace, our eyes permanently focused on potential radiance.

"Shifty, come in here," Charlie called out, in that new, hoarse voice of his. "I got something to tell you."

I turned and looked at him from the doorsill. "You're going to give me a tip on one of your broken-down nags," I said. "Forget it. My ears these days are made of stone."

"Shut up and sit down," he said, "and close the door. I've got a proposition for you."

"It was a slip of the tongue," Angles Beltrami said, as I stepped into Jay's box over the finish line that afternoon, about twenty minutes before post time. "I'm telling you, just a slip of the tongue. And now she won't talk to me."

"I can understand that," Arnie said. "What I can't understand is why the woman moved in with you in the first place."

"Who are we talking about?" I asked, as I sank into the only empty seat, directly behind Jay.

"Beltrami's new girlfriend," Jay explained. "She moved in with him about a month ago. He picked her up in the clubhouse."

"The woman is evidently deficient in matters of taste," Arnie observed.

"Fuck you, Arnie," Angles snapped. "Ginger don't like you either."

"See? That's what I mean," Arnie said.

"She's okay," Jay explained. "She's a waitress at the Denny's on Hollywood Boulevard, but she wants to be an actress."

"Of course," Arnie said. "What else?"

"Angles gave her a couple of winners, they had a good time, and two days later she moved in with him."

"That was her second mistake," Arnie said. "Her first one was talking to him."

"She'd never dated, much less lived with a horseplayer before," Jay said. "She wanted Angles to take her to the beach the other day."

"Can you imagine?" Angles said, staring at me in disbelief. "When I got this six-to-one shot I been waiting a month for to come back, after he got a horrible trip last time and had to pull up on the rail just as he's starting his move, and she wants to go to the beach."

"Did you try to reason with her?" I asked. "Did you explain?"

"Of course," Angles said, "but it didn't do no good. She

couldn't see it. So I lost my cool there for a minute and now she won't talk to me."

"A slip of the tongue," Arnie said, smiling.

"What did you say?"

" 'You dumb bitch, you're ruining my life,' I said," Angles declared. "So she got mad and she won't talk to me."

"I can't imagine why," Arnie observed. "Can you?"

We all started to laugh and Angles bounded to his feet. "You guys," he said, "you got no fuckin' class." He started to leave the box.

"Where are you going?" Jay asked. "The horses aren't on the track yet."

"I don't have to see them," Angles said. "The four's a lock. I'm wheeling him to three pigs in the second. Besides, you guys don't get it. It was just a slip of the tongue." And he left us, still laughing, in his wake.

There are few things in life more pleasant than spending an afternoon at the races with your friends. Whenever I go to the track, which is as often as I can, I always look up Jay Fox, who never misses a day there. At whatever emporium is open, he occupies a box near the finish line that becomes a minor Mecca for the pros in the grandstand. Jay's a professional handicapper, the best one I know, and from his lair over the stretch he dispenses wisdom and expertise, much as I imagine any of the great philosophers in history must have to their coteries and acolytes. He never touted his selections to strangers or tried to talk others out of theirs, but he dispensed his wisdom freely to those who asked and hardly ever turned a supplicant away. I often marveled at his patience, not only with the innocents but with the aggressively opinionated self-styled experts who infest the game. Jay took them all in stride. And when his own action failed to produce the desired results—good winners at good prices—he'd merely smile, shrug his shoulders and resign himself to the realities the track imposes on the players. "If you have a good opinion in this game, there are still going to be days when you lose," he once explained. "What you have to do is not chase your money, but be poised for the moment it all turns around again and your selections start coming in like little trained monkeys, each one carrying its little sack of gold." Not even Descartes could have stated his mathematical principles more eloquently and succinctly. I admired him, even though we didn't always wind up on the same horse. My gift is for magic, not mathematics.

The rest of the afternoon passed pleasantly, with the horses pretty much performing according to expectations and all of us cashing enough tickets to make the day a success. No monster coups, no giant longshots, no spectacular endeavors—just the routine wonders of an afternoon at the races. I only made three bets, so I had plenty of time to ponder Charlie Pickard's odd proposal. At least, it had struck me as odd when I first heard it, but now the more I thought about it, the more sensible it seemed.

"You see, Shifty, I can't stay on top of things here like I should," Charlie had said. "Not for a while anyway. Look at me, I can just about make it to the door and back. I'm okay, they tell me, but I'm pretty damn weak. It's going to take a while."

"Sure it is," I agreed. "How long?"

"Maybe three months to build back my strength," he said. "I got to go over to this place and ride a damn bicycle for three hours three times a week. And I can't be here when the work starts, probably not before eight-thirty or nine o'clock. I been leaning pretty heavily on your girlfriend, but I guess you know that."

"Can't you hire somebody?"

"I got enough help," he said. "What I need is someone to take charge of the operation, make sure everything's running smooth."

"I don't know enough about horses, Charlie," I objected.

"Hell, I know that," he said. "You don't know one horse from another except on paper. I don't mean that part of it. I can still do that and May will tell the boys for me and she and Eddie will take care of the horses till I can get out here and when I'm gone. No, what I meant was, I need somebody who can talk to the owners for me, answer the phone, do the administrative shit."

"Cover your ass, right, if anyone asks about anything?"

"You got it," he said. "You're the greatest at fooling people."

"What you're saying, Charlie, is that Roger Baldwin and your other clients don't know how sick you've been and you don't want them to find out. How many owners do you have now?"

"Clarendon's the important one," he said. "They got the good horses and I don't want to lose 'em, Shifty. Then there's Abel Green and a couple of others with claimers. You know how to bullshit these folks. I'll pay you two hundred a week, just to be here when I'm not and to make phone calls. What do you say? You ain't working now, are you?"

"No, but if a job comes along—"

"I'll make it three hundred, but you have to promise me three months, till I'm back full-time. How's that sound?"

"I'll think about it."

"I need to know quick, or I got to find somebody else."

"I'll tell you tomorrow, all right?"

"Sure. I know it isn't much money, Shifty, I ain't a rich man," he said. "I got a couple of good two-year-olds here, though, and if one of them's a runner, I'll make it up to you. Besides," he added, with a wan smile, "you got May to keep you company."

"I'm taking that into consideration," I said. "I'll let you know tomorrow. And I have to call my agent, just to make sure he doesn't have anything lined up. Now why don't you go home, Charlie. You look beat."

"I feel like somebody's been standing on my chest for ten hours," he said, sinking back into his seat. "Don't ever let them do this to you, Shifty. These medical boys are a bunch of damn auto mechanics—cut this, splice that, weld this bit over here. Shit, they like to kill me, the sonsofbitches."

"Well," Jay said, rousing me out of my reverie as the horses began to file out onto the track for the last race, "no sense betting anything on these bums. I'm going to watch from downstairs and make a fast getaway. Shifty?"

"I'll join you," I said, standing up. "Arnie?"

"No, I'm poised to make a play on the favorite in here," he said. "No way it runs worse than second."

"By the way, what happened at your daughter's wedding?" I asked.

"It was a losing proposition," he said. "Everybody stopped talking to me. So I excused myself and went home to handicap next day's Aqueduct card. I hit the double the next morning for over a grand. Family, who needs it? All they do is cost you money and winners."

5 / Bodies

"How can you live like this?" I asked, as May stepped out
of the shower and stood looking at me from the bathroom door.
She had a bath towel wrapped around her and her hair was still
dripping wet, hanging in loose strands halfway down to her
shoulders. She looked about thirteen and so innocent, except for
the thin line of the scar that stretched from under her temple
down to her neck, the legacy of a troubled time back in Florida.
"How can you?"

"Like what, honey?"

I waved an arm around to take in the whole scene—the barren walls, the cardboard boxes piled up in the corners, the sagging
and soiled white curtains, the battered TV on its metal stand at the
foot of the bed, the open closet door with the rows of clothes
dangling from wire hangers or in a mound on the floor, the single
sprung flowery sofa against one wall, the lopsided table containing
her makeup articles and toilet kit, the row of shoes and boots and
sneakers all tumbled together by the bed, and the bed itself, a
mattress resting on a plain metal frame against the wall directly
opposite the front door. "This," I said, "this whole dreary scene."

"I ain't much at housekeepin'," she said. "You know that."

"I guess I did, but you're exaggerating."

"Honey, I ain't got time to be a lady, you know what I'm sayin'?"

"You could hang a picture or two," I suggested, "or a couple of posters."

"Where?"

"On the walls, May. You know, lend a touch of color and grace to the scene."

She smiled. "I'll give you a touch of color and grace," she said. "How's this?" She dropped the towel and stood naked in front of me.

"It's a start," I admitted, smiling back and propping myself up against the pillows to have a better look at her. She had a lean and hungry body, with great legs and a flat stomach, small knobby breasts with spiky nipples, long, stringily muscled arms and square shoulders. Not a lush or conventionally beautiful body, nothing soft or yielding, but it excited me, partly because I knew what she could do with it. "What did you have in mind?"

"Let me dry my hair and I'll show you," she said. "Meanwhile, buster, get naked, 'cause I want to see you lyin' there good and stiff when I'm ready for you, you hear me?"

"I hear you."

She went back into the bathroom and turned on the hair dryer, the buzz serving to cover the noise I made scrambling out of my clothes. When she came back to the doorway, I was ready for her. She laughed and lingered there for a moment, taking in the scene. "That's better, Shifty," she said. "You're some magician. You always got your wand with you, but you keep it in the damndest places."

"If you're going to make me laugh," I said, "we're not going to have a long and happy sex life."

"No?"

"No."

She came over and sat on the side of the bed, put her hand on me and stared into my face with large, dark-green eyes that seemed to burn through me. "You like this?"

"Yes, I like it."

"And how about this?"

"I like that, too."

"And this?"

"Yes. May—"

"Shut up, Shifty, you talk too much." She leaned over me and descended, her skin still damp from the shower. "Look," she whispered, "you see how open I am? For you, baby."

"Yes."

"Put your hand there, honey. Yes, like that. Now feel me, feel how open I am for you. You like it?"

"I like it."

"Here, kiss them. Yes, like that. Bite them. You feel how hard they are?"

I didn't answer because I couldn't and I felt no need to.

"Now look," she said, "I'm all open to you, honey. You gonna take me?"

"Yes."

"Not too quick, honey. Easy does it. In nice and slow, baby, nice and slow. Like that. Let me sit on you for a while. You like that?"

"Yes."

"Now I'll move on you, slow, real slow, like that. Ah, that's nice, sweetheart. You fill me up, baby."

"May—"

"Not yet, not yet. Easy. Slowly, baby, real slow now."

I rose to her from a well of longing and lust, as if I wanted to lift her, flaunt her before whatever gods dominate our destinies. We fucked as if it were a sacred ritual and would be immortalized by it.

"Yes," she said, "like that. Just like that, honey. Yes, give it to me hard, honey, let me feel you in there. Yes, like that. Oh, yes, yes . . . Oh, yes . . ."

"Now?"

"Yes. Find my clit . . . Yes, find my clit . . ."

"Shut up."

"My clit—"

"Shut up, we'll look for it later."

She laughed, we both laughed, but nothing could stop us, nothing, not laughter, not pain, not sorrow, nothing.

"Yes yes yes yes yes yes yes yes . . ."

"Now?"

"Yes."

"Now?"

"Oh, yes. Hold me, darlin', hold me tight. Now. Now. Now."

For that one tremendous moment we became one, clasped so tightly together that nothing, no one could have separated us. I remained inside her until I rose to her again, and so the night passed in celebration of the mystery and her dingy room became an enchanted palace in which together we explored the endless corridors of time.

"Honey, get up." She kissed me lightly on the lips and I opened my eyes to the darkness of the room. "Coffee's on."

"What time is it?"

"Time to go to work."

"It's dark out."

"Yeah, that's right. Get your ass out of bed."

She left me to see to the coffee. I tottered into the bathroom and stepped into the shower, letting the hot water pour down in a hard stream on the top of my head until I began to feel human. When I emerged, May was dressed and standing in the doorway, holding a mug of hot, dark liquid toward me. "Here you go, baby," she said. "I gotta run. You comin' over?"

"Later. I have to go home first. I have to pick up a few things, maybe call my agent. I'll probably be back no later than ten o'clock. Charlie going to be there?"

"I don't know. I guess." She kissed me. "I'll see you later, babe."

"May, we have to do something about this place."

"Like what?"

"Like clean it up a little, put pictures up, you know."

"You movin' in?"

"Part-time," I said, "if I accept Charlie's offer. Until the horses move to Hollywood Park next month."

"Then what?"

"Then maybe you can move in with me."

"Maybe."

"I'm twenty-five minutes from the track."

"Yeah, but a world away from me, honey," she said, blowing me a kiss from the door. "You don't know a lot about me."

"I'm not proposing marriage," I said, "just cohabitation during the meet. You can come and go as you like and you won't have to pay rent for a while."

"You'll just fuck me for it."

"Is that so bad?"

"Nope. It's the best offer I've had in a long time."

She let herself out into the night and I sat down on the bed, my back against the pillows, to finish my coffee and read the *Racing Form*. I hadn't had enough sleep, but I felt wonderfully refreshed.

I lingered around May's place for another half hour, though I knew I'd have to get on the freeway before seven o'clock or risk being caught in rush-hour traffic. She lived in a corner one-room flat on the second floor of an old two-story complex in Monrovia, behind a shopping mall and a couple of blocks from the freeway. The building, painted a dirty yellow and built around a dusty courtyard used as a parking lot, had all the charm of a third-rate motel. It was inhabited by people, many of them Mexicans, down on their luck or who worked long hours for the low pay that characterizes the world of the racetrack. I guessed it was a way of life that May had become used to, but it was new to me as a first-hand experience. I've never made much money and, until Mad Margaret came into my life, I'd pretty much had to scramble along myself on my gambling action and the modest fees paid to closeup magicians, but I'd lived better than May and the other backstretch employees. I found myself wondering how I'd like it, even for a few weeks, sharing May's life. It's one of the nasty little secrets of the game, a secret at least as far as the outside world is concerned, that in horse racing the animals are treated a lot better than the people who care for them.

The phone was ringing on Charlie's desk as I stepped inside his tack room door at about quarter of ten. No one else was around, so I picked it up. "Would you hold for Mr. Baldwin, please," a crisp female voice sounded in my ear.

"Sure," I said, sitting down on the corner of Charlie's desk and waving to Eddie, who was rubbing Bellringer a few stalls away from me.

"You *are* Mr. Pickard?" the voice inquired.

"No, Mr. Pickard isn't here right now," I said. "I'm his assistant."

"One minute, please."

I waited. To my right, between stables, Luiz was hot-walking one of the two-year-olds; Santos was riding another one around behind him; a large woman of about forty whom I'd never seen before was working on some other horse at the end of the shedrow. "Where's May?" I silently mouthed to Santos, who cocked a thumb back toward the track.

"Hello?" the woman said. "Could you tell me who you are, please?"

"My name's Anderson, Lou Anderson," I said. "I'm a friend of Charlie's and I'm also his administrator."

"When will Mr. Pickard be in?"

"I'm not sure, because I just got here myself. I had some business in town."

"One moment, please."

Again I waited, idly scanning the wall behind Charlie's desk where he had mounted half a dozen photographs of his more notable wins, including my filly Mad Margaret's tremendous victory at Del Mar the summer before. There she was, lunging magnificently for the finish to nose out the favorite, every ounce of her committed to victory, with Tim Lang, her jockey, flat over her neck, his arms stretched out full-length as if to push her beautiful head over the line in time. That image, I knew, would remain with me all my life.

"Hello? This is Roger Baldwin. Who is this?" He spoke in a deep, softly modulated baritone voice with a trace of a southern accent.

I introduced myself again. "I'm Charlie's administrator and assistant," I explained.

"He's never mentioned you."

"I just came on board a few days ago," I said.

"Where's Mr. Pickard?"

I took a deep breath and plunged in. "Charlie will be in later, Mr. Baldwin," I said. "He has to cut back a little over the next few weeks, doctor's orders, but he'll be here."

"Would you explain that to me, please."

I did so, omitting little but making it sound as if the trainer's heart attack had been a relatively minor matter, one that had to be treated and paid attention to, but not something to become alarmed about. In a matter of weeks, Charlie would be back full-time. Until then, his trusty assistant trainer, Miss May Isabel Potter of Tampa, Florida, would be in direct supervision of the horses in the early mornings, while I, Mr. Louis Anderson, trusted financial adviser to numerous nameless moguls, would be on top of administrative matters. I gave my spiel all the humorless, corporate sincerity I could muster, using the boardroom phraseology I had culled from the statements of tycoons and executives delivered to the press prior to being indicted by grand juries and public prosecutors. I wondered if I sounded as phony as I felt and I said nothing about Charlie's bypass operation. "So you see, Mr. Baldwin, things are fine here," I concluded. "Your horses are doing well. I believe a couple of them are still out on the track. Shall I have Charlie call you when he comes in?"

"No, I'm afraid that will be difficult," the voice said, "as I'll be on my way to New York for a few days. If you need to get in touch with me, my secretary Virginia will know where I am. I just wanted to check up on a few things, but they can wait. You can tell Mr. Pickard, however, that an associate of mine may be getting in touch with him during the next few days. His name is Aramis, Gene Aramis. He'll be in Los Angeles on business and may want to go racing. Anything you can do for him will be appreciated. I'll talk to Mr. Pickard myself next week."

"Sure thing," I said. "You can put Virginia on, Mr. Baldwin, and I'll give her my home number as well."

"Thank you. I'm sorry to hear about Pickard, but happy to know it's a minor matter," the cool voice said. "One moment, please. I'll put Virginia on."

After finishing with Virginia, I headed out toward the track and met May coming back with Old Roman. She was mounted on the stable pony, an ancient Appaloosa named Major, while Polo Rodriguez was up on the two-year-old, who seemed as feisty and ornery as when I'd last seen him. "You got back here pretty quick," May observed, as I stepped aside to let them pass.

"And you're a little late, aren't you?" I answered. "It's after ten."

"We ain't got the routine perfect yet," she admitted, "but we'll get it. Charlie never told me exactly what to do until yesterday."

"Did the colt work?"

"Naw, that's what's wrong with him," she said. "He's been bustin' down the walls to run and we won't let him. Just a gallop today. We'll breeze him a half tomorrow."

"If he breeze," Polo said, grinning. "This one, he want to

run. He see some horse in front of him, he want to catch him and he no like anyone going past him neither."

"Is that good?"

"It ain't bad, mister," May said. "You comin' back to the barn?"

"That's what I'm being paid to do," I said, falling into step behind them. "I was just coming to find you. Is Charlie going to show up?"

"Not today," she called back. "He wants you to call him at home around eleven."

I followed them back to the barn, where May set to work on Old Roman and I went into the tack room again. There were a few chores I had to take care of—rounding up the registration papers for two of the Clarendon horses; calling about a new set of silks for Abel Green, one of Charlie's owners and my partner in Mad Margaret; a call to Charlie's vet, Dale Hargrove, about an overdue bill from Green; a check to be made out for the farrier's recent work on the two-year-olds; and a call to the racing secretary's office to check on a race that still hadn't filled but in which Charlie was hoping to run the worst horse in his string, a ten-thousand-dollar claimer also owned by Green. These were all routine matters for a trainer, humdrum day-to-day stuff, but I had never dealt with them before, so it took me nearly an hour to take care of things, after which I studied the big chart on which Charlie had laid out the exact training routine for every one of his charges. I wanted to be prepared for any questions he might ask me.

Outside the door, as I worked, I could see May with Old Roman. The sun had broken through the overcast and in the warm, soft light the colt, still on his toes and full of himself, looked spectacular, his gray coat gleaming and his muscles rippling as he moved under May's patient ministrations. I suddenly had this odd feeling about him, that I was looking at a tremendous running machine, an entity vibrant with power that, if just set loose, would change the course of my life. I was caught up in this reverie when the phone rang.

"So May says you're comin' on board," Charlie's hoarse voice piped into my ear. "Glad to hear it, Shifty. I sure appreciate it."

I thanked him and filled him in on the morning's activities, then I told him about Baldwin's phone call. "Who's Gene Aramis?" I asked.

"Never met him, never heard of him," Charlie said. "But if he's a friend of Baldwin's, we'll take care of him. Get him Turf Club passes, seats, whatever he wants. You can handle it, can't you?"

"It's what you're paying me for, isn't it?"

"Yeah. May there?"

"She's working with Old Roman. You coming over, Charlie?"

"Not today. Got to see the sawbones."

"How are you feeling?"

"Better, I guess."

"But not great."

"I'll live, despite these bastards," he said. "I'll be in tomorrow about ten-thirty. Tell May to call me. I got to talk to her about the horses, which is one thing you don't know nothin' about."

"Except betting on them."

"Sure," Charlie said, "and what would you do if you didn't have me to get 'em ready for you?"

"That's what we count on you to do," I told him. "It's the one thing you ignoramuses know about. Make the horse, Charlie. You want May now? I think she's finishing up on the colt."

"Yeah, okay, but wait a minute," Charlie said. "I got something to tell you, Shifty. It ain't good. You sitting down?"

"What's the matter?"

"It's about your filly."

My heart froze. "What about her?"

"I got a call from the ranch last night," he said. "I was going to tell you in person, but I don't want you to hear it from anyone else."

"What's happened, Charlie? She sick?"

"No, she's okay," he said, "only I don't think she's going to make it back to the races, Shifty. The leg ain't been healing right, so they took some X-rays and found a slab fracture on her left knee, like a big bone chip. I'm going to have Hargrove look at the pictures with me, but if it's as bad as they say it is I don't think you'd want to risk running her again. You'd have to operate and put in a screw and it would be maybe another nine months to a year and still no guarantee she'd run again ever. I sure hope they're wrong, Shifty, and I'm sorry to have to tell you this on the phone."

"It's okay, Charlie, I appreciate it," I said. "I'll get May for you."

I guess I sounded all right, but I felt as if someone had stuck a knife in my gut and was slowly drawing it out, an inch at a time.

6 / Stories

"WHY DON'T YOU STOP LYING to me?" Gene Aramis suggested in his soft, pleasantly modulated voice, gazing unsmilingly at me through the thick lenses of his horn-rimmed glasses. "I really don't like the feeling I'm being lied to. Do you understand what I'm talking about?"

"I think I do," I said. "The thing is, I'm not really lying to you."

Gene Aramis smiled fleetingly and began tapping his right index finger on the white tablecloth in front of him. "But you're not telling me the full story," he said. "To me that's a form of lying. Wouldn't you agree?"

"I suppose I'd have to," I admitted, feeling foolish and more than a little inadequate.

"Then why don't you tell me the truth?"

"Ask me a direct question and I'll try to answer it."

"How sick is Pickard?"

"He's not sick," I said. "He's had a heart attack. I told Mr. Baldwin and you it was a mild one. Okay, it was more than that. But he's had a bypass operation and he's recovering. He has to pace himself for a while and that's why he hasn't been around much and that's why he couldn't make lunch with you today. It's my job to pick up some of the routine slack, like entertaining the out-of-town friends of his owners. Charlie's concentrating on the horses."

"How can he do that, if he's not around very much?"

"He's around enough," I explained. "He's on top of everything, but he has to pace himself. He's got good people working for him and he's got me. And in another few weeks, he'll be back full-time."

"I see," Gene Aramis said. "Why didn't you tell Roger this? Why didn't Pickard tell him?"

"For obvious reasons. Clarendon's important to him, Mr. Aramis. A fine old name in racing, a long history of great horses, a prestigious institution in the sport. When your friend Roger Baldwin turned over some of his stock to Charlie, it was a big deal. It *is* a big deal. Understandably, Charlie didn't want Mr. Baldwin to feel he couldn't take on the responsibility, especially as he's only had the horses a few weeks. It would be a shame if he lost them. He's the best horseman I know, Mr. Aramis, and I've been around the track quite a while myself. Charlie trained my filly, Mad Margaret, and he did a super job with her. He won a stakes with her at Del Mar last summer."

"Where's your filly now?"

"She hurt herself in that race. We had to turn her out. These animals are pretty fragile. I don't know how much you know about racing."

"Not much, but enough," Gene Aramis said. He now seemed to lose interest in the discussion and to be thinking over what I had revealed. He sat quietly in place and sipped his coffee, his eyes lost to me behind his glasses. He was a short, compactly-built man with small feet and hands. He had very blond, almost white tightly curled hair, neatly trimmed, and his fingernails had recently been manicured; they gleamed in the soft light of the Turf Club dining room. He was dressed in dark-gray slacks, a plaid cashmere blazer, and a red silk tie. His jeweled Rolex wristwatch had to be worth at least ten thousand dollars, and on his right hand he wore a diamond ring not quite as big as a boulder. He exuded the air of a man cushioned by a steady flow of loot, but I couldn't imagine its source. I was sure of only one thing: he hadn't inherited any of it.

I waited for him to reopen the conversation, but he didn't, preferring for the moment to ruminate on what I'd told him. The only indication of life was the idle movement of his index finger, up and down on the table before him. "Are you involved in the horse business too?" I finally asked.

"No, not directly," he said, without looking at me. "Roger and I have some other interests in common. Naturally, as a friend of his, I'm concerned . . ." He allowed the sentence to die unfinished.

"Look, I'm sorry," I said. "I guess we made a mistake. We should have leveled with Mr. Baldwin and with you. But I assure you Charlie's going to be fine. I hope you won't advise Baldwin to move his horses to somebody else. He won't do better with anybody else, especially with the two-year-olds. Charlie's great with young horses, the very best. Give him a shot, at least."

Gene Aramis smiled, but it wasn't very reassuring; it came and went as abruptly as if he'd touched a button. "It's not up to me," he said.

"I'll call Mr. Baldwin tonight and talk to him," I said. "Would that help?"

"No need to do that, Anderson," Gene Aramis said. "I'll see him in a few days. I'll tell him. Meanwhile, you people just keep doing what you're doing."

"Would you like to talk to Charlie yourself? I can call him or he can meet you."

"No, no need, no need," he said, glancing at his watch. "How much time before the races?"

"About forty minutes," I said. "Charlie's box is up above the aisle, over the finish line. You got the tickets? I left them at Will Call."

"Yes, thank you." He glanced at his watch. "Where is that bitch?"

As if summoned, the woman he had apparently been waiting for now appeared, walking languidly toward him in the wake of the maitre d'. She was a tall, very attractive brunette with a round face, huge brown eyes, a small scarlet mouth and a placid manner; she moved as if underwater or half-asleep. "Hello, my darling," she said, leaning over to plant a kiss on Gene Aramis's forehead, "you're lucky I am here."

Aramis made no effort to stand up or to respond; he merely sat in place and waited for her to settle. She turned to me as I rose out of my chair and extended a long, bare, very tanned arm toward me and smiled. "Hello there," she said, "I am Alma Glocken."

"Lou Anderson. Nice to meet you."

"Likewise, I am certain," she said, withdrawing her hand and paying no further attention to me; she descended like a coiled spring into a chair. "My darling, I found the most fabulous place." She thrust her left arm out toward Aramis, displaying a heavy silver bracelet encrusted with glittery green stones. "You like it?"

"It's fine," Gene Aramis said, motioning for a waiter. "What did it cost?"

"You would not believe it, so I will not tell you," she said. "It was on sale."

"I can imagine," Gene Aramis said. "Everything you buy is always on sale."

"You are lucky, Gino. If Teddy had not rushed me away, I could have bought many more beautiful things. He did not wish me to be late."

Again that smile flashed on and off. "That's what I pay him for," Gene Aramis said. "I could go broke."

"You said to do something for my birthday."

"Sure, fine. Don't tell me what it cost."

She laughed, revealing an absolutely perfect set of very white tiny teeth. "You will find out, of course."

"It's a beautiful design," I said. "Nice stones."

"Nice? Emeralds," she said. "You are not spouting the bullshit."

"Where's Ted?" Aramis asked.

She shrugged. "Out there somewhere," she said. "He is so bizarre. I can't stand him."

"It doesn't matter in the least what you think of him," Gene Aramis said. "He works for me."

"He is a pig."

The waiter appeared. "You want to eat something?" Aramis asked her.

"Of course," she said, picking up a menu. "You got salads?"

As she scanned the card and the waiter hovered nearby, I got up, thanked Aramis, and said good-bye to Alma, who ignored me. "I'm going to call Charlie and tell him we had lunch," I said, "and good luck today."

Aramis shrugged. "I don't bet," he said. "She does. I don't even like horses."

"I pick all the gray ones," Alma said. "I always win."

"Sure she does," Gene Aramis said. "If she loses, I pay. If she wins, she keeps it."

Alma looked up from her menu. "You wish to have your dick sucked while driving on the freeway at sixty miles an hour," she said sweetly, "you must pay for that, no?"

Gene Aramis looked thoughtfully at her for a second or two. "Someday I'm going to stuff something in your mouth you aren't going to like," he said. "Now shut up and order."

It hadn't occurred to me that Alma's driver, the Ted whom Aramis had referred to, might be the same man I had met being fleeced by Benny Wilder in Las Vegas. Not until I saw him sitting at the end of the bar on my way out of the dining room. He looked as surly and unpleasant as when I'd last seen him. He gazed straight through me as I walked past, with no hint of recognition.

"Why me?" Abel Green asked. "Why does this kind of shit always happen to me?"

"It doesn't always just happen to you," Charlie said. "It happens to a lot of people in this game, people who've spent a lot more money than you have. I know owners who've spent millions trying to come up with a Derby horse. You ain't alone in this, Abe."

Abel Green refused to be mollified. He sat slumped into his seat at Clockers' Corner, staring glumly out over the racing surface where the tractors were noisily raking the dirt to prepare the oval for the afternoon card. It was about ten-thirty and a gorgeous day, with a warm spring sun beating down over the infield and not a hint of smog yet in the air, though I knew it would build up later and cloud the afternoon. Only Abel Green seemed shrouded in gloom, as if it were raining on him alone. Until Clarendon, he had been Charlie's principal owner, a middle-aged, sloppy-looking restauranteur who had never invested in anything but cheap claiming horses until he had bought forty-nine percent of my filly, Mad Margaret, for seventy-five thousand dollars the year before. She had been turned out after her big win at Del Mar and now it looked as if she would never run again. The X-rays

Charlie had requested from the farm near Solvang, where the filly had been laid up now for nearly nine months, clearly showed the fracture and Hargrove, Charlie's vet, had confirmed the diagnosis. "You could put a screw in the chip," he had explained, "but there's no guarantee she'll run again. Fifty-fifty, I'd say. You couldn't do much with her before next winter." I had communicated this news to Abel Green and he had come out to discuss the matter with Charlie and me after the morning workouts.

"Charlie has a buyer for her," I said. "He'll breed her. We could keep her and breed her ourselves, but I can't afford to do that. Or you could buy her, Abe, and breed her yourself. I won't sell her to you if you want to try and run her again."

Abel Green weighed the options, but it continued to rain on his soul. "Why me?" he asked again. "What did I do I should have to put up with this aggravation?"

"Abe," Charlie said, "maybe there's just something about you that pisses God off."

"Yeah, very funny," Green said. He looked glumly at me. "I say we sell her. Put her in the next auction."

"No, I'm not going to do that," I said. "This filly has been very good to me. I'm not going to risk having her fall into the hands of some butcher."

"Who's the buyer? And what's he offering?"

"B. B. Weisbord," Charlie said. "He owns the farm where she's at. He's offering a hundred and forty thousand for her. Shifty here says he'll split fifty-fifty with you."

"I still lose money on the deal," Green said. "Two hundred."

"Not a chance," Charlie answered. "Maybe I can get a hundred and fifty, but that's it."

"She's a stakes winner," the restauranteur objected.

"One small stake," Charlie said. "She's a runner, we know that, but on paper that's what she's worth in this depressed market."

"Can we keep a small share of the foal?" I asked.

"No, I don't think so," Charlie said. "Weisbord is part-owner of a good stallion he wants to breed her to. They'll want to keep the foal to sell."

"What stallion?" Green asked.

"Promoter," Charlie said. "He was a top miler back East ten years ago. He stands for B.B. and his partners at Clarendon. If he buys the filly, he'll ship her out there in a few days."

"Why doesn't he breed her here in California?" Green asked.

" 'Cause the best studs are in Kentucky," the trainer explained. "You don't want to breed a real good filly like this to some so-so stud. Weisbord's a smart cookie. He'll probably sell her foals at the Keeneland yearling sales. You can buy one at auction, if you want."

"Great," Abel Green said, "terrific. They get you coming and going in this game."

"Why do you stay in it?" I asked.

"Because I keep thinking my luck will turn," Green said. "I thought maybe it had with this filly."

"He's hooked," Charlie said, smiling. "Abe thinks racing is like the lottery. You buy little bits and pieces and one day you hit a big winner. Only it don't work that way."

"It doesn't work the other way either," Green said. "I'm not dumb enough to lay out a million dollars for some well-bred yearling that can't run a step."

"But you're not smart enough to quit," Charlie said. "Cheer up, Abe. You get most of your money back. And this afternoon you're going to cash a good ticket. That old bum of yours is going to win today."

"Delmonico? You think so?" the restauranteur said, brightening slightly at the prospect of cashing a bet. "You really think so?"

"If he don't fall down coming out of the gate."

"With my luck, he'll probably do just that."

A few days later, on a Monday, May and I drove up the coast to see Mad Margaret. Now that we had decided to sell her, I wanted to meet her buyer and May had agreed to come along. It was an off-day at the track, so she had been able to get away after the morning chores. Traffic was light at that hour and we made good time. I planned to get there in midafternoon, visit with the filly and her new owner, spend the night somewhere, and then drive back the following morning. Charlie had been persuaded to hire two new grooms, Clara Wilson, the heavyset woman I had already met, and another Latino named Carlos, so May had finally been able to get a day off. She was reveling in it. I had the top down on the Toyota and we zoomed along the freeway heading north, with May sprawled out on the passenger seat, her hair loose in the wind and her arms resting against the back of the seat. She was dressed in sawed-off jeans, thongs, and a thin cotton T-shirt. We attracted a good deal of attention from truck drivers, to all of whom May waved and then gave a cheerful finger. "God, I love convertibles," she said at one point, as we swept past a busload of goggle-eyed Japanese tourists. "I'm sure gonna get me one someday, when I get rich."

"When's that going to be?"

"Oh, someday, when some big horse comes along. Maybe this colt of Clarendon's now."

"I know how you feel," I said. "If it hadn't been for my filly, I'd never have had this car."

"I never understood that," May said. "This old guy just up and died and left you his horse? How come?"

I'd been broke and between jobs when Charlie had introduced me to Lucius J. Bedlington, I explained to her, and I hadn't been winning at the track, either. Bedlington was old and rich and a true eccentric, a recluse horse owner who had become so disillusioned with life that at the time I met him he'd been planning and organizing his own suicide, as calmly as if he were simply throwing a big party for himself. It had stirred up quite a mess, including a couple of murders and an attempt on my own life, and it had ended sadly, too, with the old man finally going through with his scheme. But apparently he'd become fond of me. He'd left me Mad Margaret, his best horse, in his will and she'd bailed me out of the endemic poverty that afflicts horseplayers and closeup magicians. I now had enough money in the bank to cushion my losing streaks both at the track and in show business. And I also had a nice car. Was it any wonder I loved this filly? Of course, I'd have fallen in love with her anyway, just because of the way she ran. She was the sort of horse who'd put her life on the line for you every time, the kind of competitive athlete that ennobles any sport. There was no way I would have allowed her to fall into uncaring hands.

"Well, howdy there, folks," B. B. Weisbord said, stepping out onto his front porch as I turned into his driveway and parked in front of the house. "We've been expectin' you, but I sure didn't figure you'd get here much before sunset. How you doin'?"

"We're doin' good," May said, bounding out of the car on her long legs and shaking B. B. Weisbord's hand. "Shifty here drives like he's pilotin' a jet. I figured we might have to land somewhere. Sure is a nice spread you got here."

"Aw, shucks," B.B. said, not letting go of May's hand until he'd had a good, close look at her, "it's just a little old place Em and I fixed up a little. Boy, if you ain't a sight for sore eyes."

"Now, B.B., you keep your mind on your business," May said, "or I'll tell Emma on you."

"That'd be kinda hard," B.B. answered, "on account of poor old Em done passed away on me last year. Had the cancer, you know, where they can't do nothin' with it. Poor old gal, she suffered quite a bit, but I figure she's up there now bossin' God around and tellin' Him what to do, so I'll let Him deal with her for a while."

"Aw, gee, I'm awful sorry and all," May said. "Me and my big mouth. She must have been a nice lady. I sure am sorry, B.B."

"Don't think nothin' of it, honey," B. B. Weisbord said. "That's life for you, just a shitcan full of turds, if you know what I'm sayin'. But it sure makes a man feel alive just to look at you, sweetheart."

I was so stunned by this conversation I could hardly move. For a while I thought I'd blundered into some sort of pathetic Western sitcom, then I figured they had to be putting each other on and I was being entertained by a ruthless skit salvaged from a *Saturday Night Live* parody of rural folkways. To my amazement, however, neither of them cracked a hint of a smile; they went on talking cornball to each other, with B.B. holding on to May so as not to lose contact with those spiky little nipples popping up at him through her cotton shirt.

I decided I'd better get into the act. "Howdy there, B.B.," I said, smiling broadly and extending my right hand so he'd have to let go of May. "Shifty Lou Anderson, pardner. Sure is great to meet you."

"Goldang, but it sure was nice of you folks to come all this way," B.B. said, turning at last away from May and grasping my hand to pump it up and down. "I'm sure pleased to meet you. Come on in now. We'll get you a beer or a drink or an iced tea or somethin' and then we'll go see the filly. She's doin' real good, only I think you done the right thing to breed her and I'm sure glad to have her. She's a nice filly, no doubt about it, and we're gonna do right by her."

"Well, then, let's go in and talk turkey," I said, slapping May affectionately on the rump as we followed B. B. Weisbord into the house. "I got a powerful thirst on me, how about you, honey?"

"Shifty," May said, staring at me in horror, "what the hell's wrong with you?"

"Why, nothin', sugar," I said. "Just shootin' the shit here with you saddle dudes till we get out to see Maggie. What you talkin' about, honey?"

"You're so full of it," May said, as we followed B.B. into the house.

For the next hour and a half we sat in B.B.'s living room listening to his horse stories, in between phone calls and meetings with members of his staff, who dropped in from time to time to discuss procedures and problems relating to the operation of the ranch. They had about eighty horses they were caring for on a fifty-two-acre property that lay in a small valley with a stream flowing through it, about ten miles in from the coast and the town of Solvang. Large oak and pepper trees dotted the slopes and pastures and provided shade for the corrals and stables, as well as the house. Through the picture window behind B.B.'s head, I could see a herd of mares with new foals by their sides.

Despite his folksy manner, B.B. was clearly a smart cookie who was on top of everything that affected his operation. And he obviously didn't spend much of his time sitting around indoors. His living room was sparsely furnished, with a big leather couch, half a dozen chairs, a bar with high stools tucked around it, and a big table covered with pictures of B.B. and his late wife in various family group shots or posing with bigwigs from the racing world. The walls were plastered with framed winner's-circle photographs of stakes winners B.B. had had some connection to. "I used to race 'em, you know," he explained, when I asked about the pictures. "That was before I got smart and bought this here ranch and began to take care of other people's animals. It was Em who got me to buy this place back in the fifties. Best damn thing that old woman ever done for me. Now, let me tell you about this one time I thought I had me a Derby colt. That would have been Promoter, back in 1980 . . ." And he was off again on another story, a typical horse saga of early failures, sudden success, eventual heartbreak, when Promoter had bucked both shins three days before the Kentucky Derby and had had to be scratched.

" 'Course maybe we was lucky," B.B. said. "He come back in the fall and won some big races for us, but wasn't no classic distance horse, you know. About as good a miler as I ever seen, after Dr. Fager, and he could carry his speed a ways longer, if he don't get pushed early. He wouldn't have won the Derby, but he'd have given a good account of himself and I sure would have enjoyed it. That's the closest I come to havin' a Derby horse." He laughed and slapped himself on the knee. "Dang, but I sure run off at the mouth a lot. I bet you want to see your filly now."

I bounced to my feet before he could get started on another horse story, and he led the way out behind the house toward a couple of stables about fifty yards away. I immediately spotted Maggie. She was standing in an open pen directly behind the nearest barn and she looked fine, fat and sassy, her chestnut coat gleaming in the late-afternoon light. Her left front leg, however, was bandaged up over her knee. "Hi, Maggie," I said, in a soft, high voice as we came up to her. "How are you doing, sweetheart? Come on over here, it's old Uncle Shifty. And May. You remember May, don't you?"

The filly turned her head to look at us, then slowly ambled over to thrust her soft nose into my face. I reached up and patted her neck, while May went into the barn to look for carrots. "Well, I guess you folks will be all right here for a while," B. B. Weisbord said. "I better get back to the house. Got a couple of things still to do. She looks good, real good, don't she? We'll ship her out of here in about a week. It might not be too late to put her in foal this season, you know. I'm sure glad to have her."

"I guess you know Charlie's training for Clarendon now," I said.

"Sure, I heard that. I hope it works out. But I'm goin' to keep an eye on things back there," B.B. said. "Of course, my two partners and I own Promoter and we just board him there, but I still don't want to get caught up in nothin' bad goin' on."

"Like what, B.B.?"

He shrugged. "Aw, you hear stories," he said. "They got some problems. They kinda overreached themselves at the banks and all. Roger got in with some folks nobody knows much about. Just rumors, you know, but sometimes it's good to pay attention. What I heard is, if it wasn't for their one big stallion, they'd be in a lot more trouble than they are."

"Algonquin?"

"Yeah, sure. He's a really great stud, believe you me," B.B. said. "Got to be worth maybe twenty million now. I wish I could afford to breed your filly to him, but he's out of sight. A hundred and fifty thousand for a live foal these days. That's heavy and that ain't old B.B.'s style. Breed cheap, sell dear, that's my motto." He laughed and slapped himself on the thigh. "Come on by and say so long when you're through visitin'," he added, heading back toward the house. "And bring that little old gal with you. She sure is a doll."

It was dark by the time we left B.B.'s spread, mainly because it took us another hour and a half to say good-bye to him. B. B. Weisbord was a man with a thousand stories to tell and they all seemed to flow into one another like rivulets converging into a single mighty stream. At about the time that some of his hands began to stop by for a beer with him, I was finally able to extricate us, on the grounds that we were on our way back to L.A. that night and had to get up at dawn the next morning. Otherwise, there's no knowing how long we might have stayed, overwhelmed by B.B.'s torrents of anecdotes.

"How that man can talk," May said, as we sped out the gate and headed back down the winding country road toward the coast. "No wonder his poor old wife croaked. He must have talked her to death."

"You know, he talked so much I forgot to ask him for my check," I said. "But I guess he'll send it along."

"You still got the papers on the filly, ain't you?"

"Oh, yes."

"Then there's nothin' to worry about. Now let's find us a nice motel."

"Great idea. I'm feeling amorous."

"You mean horny, don't you?"

"Beautifully phrased, my sweet."

"Shifty, you know what your problem is? Too much fuckin' and not enough fresh fruit."

This woman could make me laugh, which is as good a reason as any to fall in love with somebody.

7 / Steam

I DISCOVERED THAT I LIKED my new life, especially after the horses moved over to Hollywood Park and I didn't have to spend two hours on the freeways whenever I wanted to go home. Two or three nights a week I'd been staying with May, which was a much easier commute and a lot of fun and games, but I could never get comfortable there. May was a slob and not inclined to waste any time or money making her place more livable or attractive, so I made myself think of the arrangement as a sort of occasional camping trip, like staying at a bad Club Med with a good deal of cheery sex to compensate for the inadequate living conditions.

My biggest problem had been finding a place to work on my moves, since being a closeup artist entails the daily discipline of practice, at least several hours a day a minimum of five days a week. It's the price I willingly pay to be able to call myself a master magician. But because living with May made it impossible to do that, I'd have to linger at the barn after the workouts, shut myself up in the tack room, and work on Charlie's desk. I had no time to relax between my administrative duties for the stable and the racing in the afternoon.

This all changed once the horses moved across town and I

was back in my own digs, less than half an hour away from the
stable gate. My new routine allowed me plenty of time to get back
and forth, and I didn't have to deal with May's disorder. As for
my administrative chores, I found them easy to carry out, especially as I was in daily contact with Charlie, at least by phone.
What I liked best about the deal was being around the backside
every day, an intrinsic part of the world of racing; I even began to
think of myself as a horseman, not just a bettor who didn't fully
belong back there, where the real work of the game takes place. I
loved that feeling. I loved the sights, the smell of it, the sounds,
the impression I got every day that everything could change, for
better or for worse, at any second. And I never let a morning pass
without putting in a half hour or so up in the guinea stand, a hot
carton of coffee in my hand, watching the horses go past my position, each one of them, even the lowliest plater, a miracle of grace
and beauty in my eyes.

Only two aspects of my new situation troubled me. The one
that bothered me the most was Charlie's slow recuperation from
his surgery. Some days he seemed to have made real progress.
He'd show up around nine or so, toward the end of the workouts,
and take over from us. He'd look fairly well and seem to have
some of his old energy. Most days, however, he looked drawn and
he moved like a very old man, painfully and breathing with his
mouth open, as if not getting enough air. And there were the
times he'd fail to show up at all and we'd have to talk to him
exclusively by phone. On those occasions, he'd sound raspy or
hoarse, exasperated by his weakness but unable to overcome it. I
asked him on one of these bad days whether he'd been to see his
doctor and what the prognosis was. "They don't tell you nothin',"
Charlie had answered. "These guys are like lawyers. They got a
lock on their own racket and they're not about to let it get away
from them."

"What does that mean, Charlie?" I said. "When you ask your
doctor how you're coming along, what does he say?"

"What do you expect him to say?" the trainer answered.
"The usual vague bullshit about how I've got to be patient. I told
him I know how to be patient, that I have to take care of racehorses. Ain't nothin' more patient-making than that. So he just
smiles and tells me to think the same way about myself. Give myself time, he says. Shit, I don't mind the time, Shifty. What I do

mind is feeling a thousand years old. But I'll be okay. Stop worrying about me." And he dropped the subject to ask me about what was going on and to go and get May for him.

Less troubling to me, but puzzling, was May's refusal to spend much time at my place. She loved it, she said, but she didn't want to move in with me, even for only the length of the meet. She wanted to be nearer the track, so she and Clara Wilson rented adjoining rooms in a seedy motel on Century Boulevard, only a few blocks away from the stable gate. May would come to me on Sunday or Monday night and stay, but the rest of the week she preferred her motel room.

During her second overnight at my place, I asked her again why she wouldn't move in with me. "I'm not that far from the track," I told her, "and isn't this nicer than living in a motel?"

"It sure is," she answered. "It just ain't convenient. And anyway, it's your place, you know what I mean? It don't have nothin' to do with me."

I knew what she meant. I liked my apartment; it represented everything I stood for, everything that mattered most deeply to me. It was located on the ground floor of a shabby two-story building a couple of blocks below the Strip in West Hollywood. The architectural style was California Tudor, but built around a patio and a swimming pool shaded by ancient palm trees. Most of the other residents were either young people hoping to move up in show business or aging losers clinging to faded hopes. I kept my distance from them all, because I fitted into neither category; my one big room was a sanctuary, a place to which I could retreat to rest, to practice my craft, and to nurture my own dreams.

Apart from my queen-size bed, a single padded armchair, a large TV set, a couple of stools, a chest of drawers, a large wooden table and my kitchen furniture, all I had was my magic props, my pictures of horses (including a great blowup of Mad Margaret's last win), and my large framed posters of Houdini and Giuseppe Verdi, two of the greatest magicians who ever lived. "That's old Joe Green," I had explained to May, when she asked about the composer, "one of the all-time greats in opera."

"Opera?" May had said, reacting with as much horror as if I had revealed myself to be a secret child molester. "You can listen to that stuff?"

"I can lose myself in it totally," I assured her. "Verdi knew more about life and human passions than any other great artist I know. I'll take you to hear him sometime."

"No, you won't," she said. "Country, that's my style. And for passion, baby, I don't need no Wopera. And you don't neither. I'll give you all the passion you can handle."

She was right about that. I also enjoyed being around her. What I had to accept was that, for some reason I couldn't yet figure out, May was determined to freeze our relationship at its present stage of evolution. We'd see each other every day at work, but on most nights she'd go off to her own room and I'd go home. Even during the times we were together, we never achieved a degree of intimacy that went beyond sex and palship. Any attempt by me to find out about her and what ultimately she might want out of life was fended off on some pretext or other. She'd had a tough time as a kid and I suspected she'd been abused, perhaps by her father. I also knew she'd been married once, when she was sixteen, to a journeyman quarter-horse jock who'd abandoned her after six months, when she became pregnant. She'd tried to have the baby, apparently, but had miscarried. And then I knew, too, how she'd acquired the scar on her neck—from a boyfriend in Florida who'd slashed her with a knife in a jealous rage. But apart from these few facts, I knew nothing about her. "You don't want to know, Shifty," she said to me one night at my place, after we'd made love and I'd tried again to sound her out about her past. "Most of it ain't good and I don't want to talk about it."

"It's hard to fall in love with people you don't know much about, May," I tried to explain to her. "I'm only asking because I really care about you."

"Don't, Shifty," she said, propping herself up to look at me very intently. "Don't do that, honey. I ain't up to it. Let's just enjoy what we got, okay, and not worry about nothin' else. I'm probably not the kind of person you think I am. Let's just have us a good time and let this other stuff go. The lovin's good, ain't it?"

"The best. No complaints."

"Then don't spoil it, mister," she said. "I ain't no saint."

"Sainthood has very little to do with sex, May," I said. "I've yet to see a picture of the Virgin Mary in a bikini."

"Shifty, don't you take nothin' serious? Is everythin' in life a joke?"

"Mostly, yes. If I had to take life seriously, I'd either have to become a terrorist or join some sort of revolution."

"Well, I guess you got that right. Now stop talkin' and come over here, honey. We ain't hardly started yet."

Old Roman ran in early May in the very first two-year-old race of the meet, at four and a half furlongs on the dirt. There were ten entries in the race, the fourth on the card, and the colt drew the worst post position possible, the very outside, which meant that he'd have to break quickly and use his speed to get over toward the rail in order not to lose several lengths being carried very wide on the turn. He couldn't take back and tuck in behind horses, because the race was so short he'd run out of ground by the time the leaders reached the finish line. Also, he'd get too much dirt kicked up in his face and young horses are not used to that and sometimes pull themselves up. I thought Charlie might scratch him and wait for the next race but, partly on May's advice, he decided to run him. "She says he's kicking the barn down," the trainer said, "so we might as well let him run. These two-year-olds can go sour real quick if you don't let 'em fire when they're ready."

I had no idea what the morning line on the colt would be, since his works did not indicate early speed. Charlie rarely asked his charges to do more than breeze in the early mornings and Old Roman's two works out of the gate had not been impressive; on each occasion he'd broken a step or two slow and posted indifferent times. Not one of the professional clockers had singled him out or taken note of the fact that he'd run under wraps, with the boy on his back keeping a tight hold on him and letting him run just enough to let him use up some of his pent-up energy. Nevertheless, when the line was made, I wasn't too surprised to note that he'd been listed at five to one, the fourth choice in the race. It's hard to fool everybody at a racetrack; somebody must have noted that the colt wanted to run and that every time he'd worked in company, no one had passed him, even with Polo, who weighed over a hundred and twenty pounds and had arms like a blacksmith, on his back, trying to choke him down. And when I arrived at Jay's box that afternoon, about forty minutes before post time for the race, I found my friends in a high state of excitement.

"Hey, Shifty, what's the story?" Jay asked, as I joined them. "Is it a go?"

"Of course it's a go," I said. "Charlie always tries with every horse he has, you know that."

"I got information that says this horse is a runner," Jay said, "that he's always worked well and he's on a fit and ready list. What do you say?"

"Exactly right. Whether he can win from way out there, I don't know. But he'll run his race."

"Charlie here?"

"Not yet, but he said he'd be here."

"I see where Charlie ain't using Tim Lang, his usual speed jock," Angles said. "How come?"

"Because Wib Clayton is one of the world's great riders and he's very strong," I explained. "This colt needs a lot of handling. He's got a mind of his own."

"That puts him one up on Clayton," Arnie observed. "Wib has no mind."

"But he can ride," Jay said.

"That he can. I'm going to bet on him, but very small," I said. "There are a couple of speed horses inside of him and these two-year-old races are awfully short. Charlie just wants him to run well."

"Better Clayton than Lang," Jay said. "Tim's only fifty percent honest."

"For a jockey, fifty percent ain't bad," Angles said. "I figure you got to beat the two horse in here, The Swinger. He's got nothin' but black type in his works and Chino's a bootin' and scootin' rider."

"Unfortunately, he has a trainer who couldn't teach a dog to piss on a fire hydrant," Arnie observed.

"Anybody can train a horse to run half a mile," Angles said. "I figure the angle is The Swinger busts out of there, opens up maybe two, and just lasts. He'll be the favorite, so I'll put him on top of your colt and the four horse, Letmego, good breeding and a good trainer."

"A risky proposition," Jay said calmly. "This is a race to watch. All I can do is wish you well, Shifty."

I thanked Jay and went down to the paddock, which at Hollywood Park is behind the grandstand, to wait. Charlie was standing under the tree where Old Roman would be saddled and I went over to join him. He didn't look well. His face had a grayish tinge and he seemed thinner than when I'd last seen him a few days earlier. His clothes hung loosely on him and he looked old, the lines on his face carved deep into his skin. I said nothing about any of this to him, because I knew from experience that he'd react impatiently to it. I'd made my peace with it by this time; you can't save people from themselves. "Hi, Charlie," I said, summoning as much cheerfulness as I could manage, "how's the colt doing?"

Charlie shrugged. "We'll soon find out," he answered. "May and Eddie are with him in the receiving barn. Did you call Baldwin?"

"Yeah, I couldn't get him. But I told his secretary the colt was running and that we'd call him after the race."

"That man sure moves around a lot."

"Seems like it," I said. "Who do we have to beat in here, Charlie?"

"Who knows? Who cares? I don't bet."

"Just making conversation," I said. "One thing I do know, this beast can run."

"Yeah. I guess it'd be nice if he does show us something," Charlie said. "It's my first Clarendon horse. I wish I wasn't feeling like shit. They're killing me with their damn therapy. And I got to go in again tomorrow for a checkup."

"What kind of checkup?"

"I guess they think maybe I ain't doing as well as I'm supposed to," the trainer said. "I told 'em it's this damn exercise routine they got me on, but they want me to come in anyway. So I'll be out for a day or two, I guess."

Our conversation was interrupted by the roar of the crowd rooting home the horses in the third. After it was over and people began to arrive at the paddock for the fourth, I looked up at the odds board to see what was happening to our horse. On the first click after the money began to come in on him, he immediately dropped to two to one. Charlie noticed it too. "I suppose you've been shooting your mouth off," he said.

"Not me, Charlie. I told a couple of my friends that he can run some but hasn't worked too well out of the gate, that's all."

"Tell the owner anything?"

"More of the above and only to his secretary."

"That's it?"

"That's it."

"Well, somebody sure got a message."

"The track is full of wiseguys, Charlie," I said. "A lot of people like the way he looks in the A.M. and the connections. You've got a reputation with young horses."

"Hell, everybody knows I'm a genius."

"Yeah, especially you."

When May and Eddie led Old Roman into the paddock to be saddled, I was immediately struck by how terrific the colt looked. His coat gleamed with health and he was bouncing on his feet, full of himself. He was looking all around, taking it all in, but not nervous or apprehensive. He reminded me of a fighter in prime condition about to go for the title and I felt a surge of confidence in him. I didn't care what the odds were, I was going to make a bet. When May began to put the saddle on him, I took another look at the board. He'd dropped another notch to nine to five, but I didn't care. By that time I knew he was going to win.

Charlie's instructions to Wib Clayton were characteristically terse. "This colt can run," he said. "He might be a little slow out of the gate, but he's fit."

Clayton nodded, said nothing and stood silently next to us, his whip tucked under his left arm. He was short, like most jockeys, but solidly built, with very strong hands and a serious, pointed face set off by a pair of deep-set brown eyes. He was in his early forties, still one of the world's great riders, but fighting every day to keep his weight at a hundred and seventeen pounds, the maximum for any American rider with an active career. He had no plans to hang up his tack anytime soon, he had informed the press, and no one could finish on a horse any better than he at any weight. I thought he'd suit Old Roman perfectly.

By the time the field headed into the tunnel under the grandstand, Old Roman had dropped to eight to five. I fell into step beside May. "I'm going to go up and make a bet on him," I said. "Where are you going to be?"

"Bet fifty on him for me," she said. "I'm going to wait for him down by the weigh-in scales, where I usually stand."

"The odds are pretty low."

"It don't matter, honey," she said. "He's gonna win."

I bet two hundred on him myself, then joined Charlie in his box, about four rows back over the finish line. I focused my glasses on Old Roman, who had begun to move around the turn toward the starting gate, and liked what I saw. Clayton had put him into a slow gallop away from the escort rider on his pony and the colt was moving easily under the jockey's guidance, his head bowed against the pressure of the bit. He was giving Clayton all he could handle, but not fighting him, just getting the message across that, once the race began, he'd give whatever was asked of him. "He looks good, Charlie," I said.

The trainer nodded but didn't answer. He looked old and tired, but I was too excited to pay much attention to him. I kept my gaze focused on the colt. Then, at about two minutes to post time, Angles Beltrami came charging up the aisle toward our box. "Shifty," he shouted, "what the hell's going on?"

I lowered my binoculars. "What do you mean?"

"Look at the goddamn board!"

The odds on Old Roman had plunged to three to five, so quickly I hadn't even been aware of it. "What's going on?" Angles asked angrily. "You been hiding this horse?"

"Get him out of here," Charlie said quietly. "I'm sick enough already."

"Angles, I don't know from where or why the money's coming in on him like this. Nobody's hiding anything."

"It's got to be Vegas money," Angles said. "Steam, that's what it is. Somebody bet your horse huge in Nevada and they're laying it off at the track."

As if on cue, the tote board blinked again and Old Roman went to one to two, an incredible underlay on a first-time starter with a reputation for breaking slowly and in a bad post position. Angles went charging back down the aisle and I stood up, intending to turn in my ticket before the race; at one to two, I wouldn't bet on the sun rising. But it was too late. The horses had reached the starting gate and were being loaded into their stalls.

The board blinked one more time before the start and the odds dropped to one to five; somebody had rammed another twenty thousand on him into the tote. Just then the gate opened and Old Roman broke last. It was a few seconds before he got his feet under him and by that time he was already five or six lengths back, with The Swinger out in front by two and the rest of the field bunched up behind him.

"Blinkers next time, Charlie?" I asked, my eyes focused on the colt.

"No," the trainer replied softly, "he's just green."

I had already given up any hope of winning the race and I was feeling like a fool for having thrown money away on an odds-on favorite. All I cared about now was seeing whether Old Roman would run at all, because I knew how important Clarendon was to Charlie. I didn't have long to wait. By the time the horses began their run around the turn, Clayton had Old Roman in gear. The trouble was, of course, that he'd have to go at least five or six wide.

It didn't matter. I've seen some weird and wonderful races in my time, but nothing to top this one. Old Roman put his head down so low that he seemed to be sniffing the ground and then he began to move past horses as if they were wallowing in quicksand. By the time The Swinger reached the head of the lane, still two lengths in front and running strongly, Old Roman had passed everyone else and now took off after the leader.

It wasn't even a contest. Old Roman caught The Swinger just past the sixteenth pole and blew him away, coming in by two lengths in 51.1 seconds flat, tying the track record for the distance. "My God, Charlie, I guess he can run a little bit after all!" I said, bounding out of the box. "You coming down?"

"No," the trainer answered. "Go ahead, Shifty. I'll be all right."

I arrived at the winner's circle just as the horses came back, Old Roman bringing up the rear. The colt hadn't even worked up a sweat and was tossing his head back and forth against Clayton's tight hold. "We could have gone around again," the jockey commented, as May led the horse and rider into the ring to get our picture taken, "and we'd have won by twenty. This is one nice little horse you got here, let me tell you. I'll ride him back for you anytime, anywhere."

"You mean to tell me none of you had any idea this colt could run that fast?" Jay asked me that night, when he and I met for dinner at a fancy Chinese restaurant, all silk screens and spotless white tablecloths, on Melrose. "I find that hard to believe, Shifty."

"And I'm telling you it's the truth, Jay," I said. "We knew he had ability and that he was eager to run, but Charlie doesn't work them fast."

"Yeah, I know, but—"

"All he wanted to do was put a race into him because he was ready to run."

"An understatement, if ever I heard one," the handicapper said. "If this colt stays sound and can stretch out to a mile, you're going to the Breeders' Cup this year. Where is it?"

"In Louisville, on November 2nd. It's a long way off."

"Sure enough. Is he nominated?"

"Oh, yes. All the Clarendon horses are. And don't worry about the distance," I said. "This colt is bred to go long on both sides, even though his daddy was primarily a sprinter."

"Speed and stamina," Jay said, "a tremendous combination."

"Let's just hope he stays sound. All these young horses come up with some ailment sooner or later," I said. "You have to be lucky."

"Sooner or later, the luck evens out," Jay said. "The winners are the ones who know when to take advantage of the good streaks. Hey, look at that!"

I was sitting with my back to the entrance, so I hadn't seen whatever had caught Jay's attention. When I turned to look, I found myself gazing at Ted, who was standing by the maitre d's stand with a tall woman who seemed to be wearing no clothes. She was in her mid-thirties, I guessed, with a nondescript face hidden by too much makeup under a wild mop of dyed red hair, but she had a voluptuous body that had somehow been stuffed inch by inch into a very tight pink minidress that was all but invisible in the soft light of the room. "I'm laying even money she's not a virgin," I said.

"A working girl, right out of the ad pages of the *Free Press*," Jay said.

The maitre d' led Ted and his date across the room to a booth against the rear wall. "It's like an ad for the twenty-minute motel room," Jay said. "I wonder what she charges?"

I stood up. "I'm going over to say hello."

"You know her?" Jay asked, in astonishment.

"Him."

Ted apparently again failed to recognize me and he was

clearly not pleased to see me. "We met in Las Vegas," I reminded him. "You were being hustled by a grifter named Benny Wilder and I tipped you off."

"Yeah? So what?"

"So I just wanted to congratulate you."

"Yeah? What about?"

"Our colt's race today," I said. "You must have been there."

He leaned back and really looked at me for the first time. "What are you, a wiseguy?"

"Me?"

"Yeah. What do you want?"

"Nothing, Ted. I know you work for Mr. Aramis, who's a friend of Roger Baldwin's," I explained. "I work for Charlie Pickard, who trains here for Clarendon. I guess you saw the race today."

"Sure. Good race. Now beat it."

"Gee, that's not nice," the redhead said. "Hi, I'm Verna." She smiled and stuck out her hand.

I shook it. "Hi, Verna, nice to meet you. Who's your rude friend?"

"I don't know. I just met him tonight," she said, smiling. "Usually, I do phone sex only, on account of my boyfriend gets mad if I go out with the clients, but Teddy here was like, so demanding and all, you know? So here we are. I'm not sure about the karma in this place, are you? I mean, why are we fighting and all? It's such a ponderosity trip. Be nice, Teddy."

He ignored her. "I said beat it," he snapped. "I don't want to talk to you."

"No, I guess not." I nodded to his date. "Good night, Verna. Take care of yourself." I smiled at Ted. "Funny thing about poor old Benny Wilder," I said. "He was just a small-time hustler. I guess you heard somebody killed him. Broke all of his fingers and cut his throat. It seems an excessive price to pay for a couple of crude scams. The police told me about it, in case you're interested."

"What is this?" Ted said, standing up. "You want something, fella? I'll give you something."

"Nothing, nothing at all, Ted," I assured him, backing away. "Sorry to have bothered you. Give my best to Mr. Aramis and Alma." And I retreated back to my table.

"What was that all about?" Jay asked. "The guy looked pissed off. You made a move on his bimbo?"

"Not at all," I said. "I just tried to get you her phone number. That's her specialty."

"Shifty, you're weird, you know that?"

"I guess I am. Maybe I just don't like goons."

8 / Pounded

CHARLIE CALLED ME at the barn the next morning, sounding more cheerful than he had in a long time. "It's this damn medication they got me on," he explained, "something called Inderal, which I never heard of, have you?"

"No, Charlie, I haven't. You allergic to it?"

"Something like that," he said. "It's some drug that slows down your muscle functions or some crap like that. You feel weak, it affects your brain, too, which is why I'm feeling so dumb these days. And it makes you impotent, though that ain't exactly a problem. I gave up women a long time ago on account of the aggravation and all. Anyway, that's what's been making me feel half-dead."

"Is it something you have to take?"

"They're going to try putting me on something else, which is okay except the doc says it can make you constipated," he said. "Now impotence, like I said, is no problem, but constipation, that's real. At my age, taking a good crap is something you can build your whole day around. Anyway, Shifty, they want to keep an eye on me for a few days. I got to take it real easy. After that, I ought to be okay. I mean, I'll still have to go to therapy and all that, but I'll be on my way back."

"Well, that's good news. You want to talk to May?"

"Yeah. How's the colt doing?"

"Great, Charlie. The race took nothing out of him. May told me he ate everything in sight and he's just full of himself. What have we got here, a Derby horse?"

"Hey, Shifty, after you've been around as long as I have, you stop thinking like that," the trainer said. "You take them all one day at a time."

I put May on the phone to him and walked over to the track kitchen to get a cup of coffee, then went outside to watch the workouts while I drank it. I got back to the barn a half hour later and found a message on the desk asking me to telephone Roger Baldwin at Clarendon. He was not in his office when I called him back, but Virginia tracked him down somewhere on the property and I soon had him on the phone. He was his usual cordial self. "Mr. Anderson, thank you for calling back," he said. "I understand our little colt put on quite a show yesterday."

"It was terrific," I told him. "I think you've got yourself a real nice one. I know Charlie's going to call you about him."

"He did so, last night," Baldwin said. "We're very pleased, of course."

"He had a terrible trip, too," I elaborated. "He broke poorly and went wide, but he can really run."

"So I understand. Yes, very gratifying, always," he said. "In this business, any success is to be treasured." He sounded about as excited as if he'd been informed that some over-the-counter stock he had a hundred shares of had just risen an eighth of a point. I wondered if being cool was an affected style with him or if, after having spent all of his life in the game, he had simply taught himself not to become too enthusiastic too early; horses were such fragile creatures, prone to flash like comets across the firmament and burn themselves out so quickly. Better to be laid back, he must have figured, so as not to be disappointed later. Still, he was depriving himself of pleasure and that, in my flawed book, is a cardinal sin. "But I didn't call you about that," he continued. "And I didn't have time to discuss this with Mr. Pickard last night. It's about Bellringer."

"He's running in a couple of days."

"Yes, I'm aware of that. You've been very efficient about keeping us informed. I appreciate it."

"That's what I'm paid to do. What about the horse, Mr. Baldwin?"

"We have a rider our trainer here, Phil Hardin, would like you to use."

"Tim Lang rode him last time," I said. "I imagine Charlie would want to ride him back, since he just won with him."

"Yes, of course, that's a given," Baldwin said. "But we'd like you to put up Daryl Spencer. He rides quite a bit for us back here."

"He's coming out to California for this race?"

"No, he's moving out there," Baldwin explained. "He's a friend of Phil's and we'd like to help him get started on the California circuit. We'll be putting him up on some of our horses. Not all of them, but some. We'd like you to ride him on Bellringer, sort of to get him started, you know."

"I'll tell Charlie."

"Would you? Thank you so much. Daryl left here yesterday. He'll be contacting you today or tomorrow."

"Does he have an agent?"

"No, he's never had one. He's very selective about his mounts and he rides mainly for us and one or two other stables," Baldwin said. "We'll be using him quite a bit. In any case, I know he'll contact you, tomorrow at the latest. When is the race?"

I checked the overnight sheets. "Friday, day after tomorrow. I think we may have already told Lang's agent that he has the mount. He'd certainly expect to get it, after winning with the horse."

"Yes, well, I'm sorry about it," Baldwin said, not sounding in the least afflicted, "but we owe Phil Hardin a great deal and also Daryl, so we'll expect you to handle the matter as delicately as you can. I'm very grateful."

"Sure. Anything else?"

"No, just keep doing a good job," he said. "We're very impressed."

"Thank you. Oh, I did have a question for you."

"Yes?"

"Has my filly Mad Margaret been doing all right?"

"*Your* filly? I thought Mr. Weisbord and—"

"I sold her to him. I still think of her as mine."

"Oh, yes, well, she's doing just fine. We're going to breed her to Promoter in a week or two, I think. She's taken a little time to get adjusted, but she looks wonderful."

"That's good news. I don't want anything bad to happen to her."

"Nothing will, Mr. Anderson, I'm sure. Good-bye now. Thanks again."

When I told May about this conversation a few minutes later, she looked as surprised as I had been. "I know that jock," she said. "He ain't much, believe me. You say he's movin' out here? He's gonna ride this circuit, where we got maybe the ten top jocks in the world? Shifty, it don't make sense."

"Who is he? I never heard of him."

"I know him," Clara Wilson said. She'd been hot-walking one of Abel Green's old platers and had come by where we were standing, outside Old Roman's stall. Now she paused in her rounds and led the horse over to us, out of the path of the other animals being cooled out. "He's bad news."

"What do you mean?"

"I mean he's got a reputation for stiffing horses, that's what," she said. "He used to ride the Maryland circuit, then came down to Florida for a while, but he left so many horses in the gate they got to calling him Old Iron Hands. Then he moved to Kentucky about eight or nine years ago and he was just an exercise boy for a while. He was drinking and using stuff and nobody'd give him mounts. Then he found Jesus and started riding again five or six years ago. I guess he wins his share. He's like in the top ten or twelve riders back there. Always did real good at the smaller tracks, don't you know. But hell, that's the minor leagues. It's funny he'd move out here, ain't it?"

"How old is he?" I asked.

"Early to mid-forties," Clara said. "I guess he must have an in with Clarendon."

"He's a friend of Hardin's, Baldwin says."

Clara shook her head, as she started to resume her walk with Green's animal. "People sure do dumb things at racetracks," she said. "I wouldn't put that guy up on a goat, much less a horse I want to win a race with."

"Maybe that's the point, hon," May said. "Maybe this time they don't want to win with Bellringer."

The phone rang again in the tack room and I went back to

complete my morning administrative chores, but I kept thinking about May's remark. It seemed to me, as I sat at my desk trying to recall Bellringer's past performance record, that Daryl Spencer had ridden the horse several times back in Kentucky. I couldn't remember whether he'd won with him or not and I wondered what Charlie would have to say about this turn of events.

Waldo Pierce, Tim Lang's agent, was very unhappy about his being taken off Bellringer, but I told him that I had talked to Charlie and that he felt the same way he did, only there was nothing we could do about it. "Baldwin owns the horse, Waldo," I said. "He wants Spencer up, so that's it."

"Hey, I could understand it if it was some top boy, like Singer or Clayton, but Spencer? Don't they want to win?"

"Waldo, I'm just carrying out orders. You know Charlie would never do this, if it were up to him."

"Yeah, well, shit," the agent said. "You got to ask yourself what that's all about. Old Iron Hands, shit."

"He's a friend of Hardin's," I explained. "He's moving out here and I guess they want to help him. That's the way it was explained to me, Waldo."

"I hope the horse breaks its fuckin' leg," the agent said, angrily spitting into the dirt at my feet. "It's hard enough in this fuckin' game to get a win."

"I'm sure Charlie will make it up to you, Waldo," I said. "And if you're going to spit again, aim away from me, will you?"

Waldo was angry and I didn't blame him, but I wasn't going to let him work his frustrations off on me. He was a fierce little citizen, an ex-jockey himself, with a touchy sense of self-importance and a large chip on his shoulder. As a rider he'd been mediocre and had always had to struggle for mounts, so he identified strongly with his clients. I admired him for it, but on this occasion I found it annoying. "Waldo, I promise we'll make it up to you," I assured him to get him off my back. We were standing outside the cafeteria, where I had tracked him down after Baldwin's telephone call. It was late, and I was anxious to get home to wash up and change before post time. "Now just take it easy."

"You'll make it up to me?" he said, grinning maliciously at me. "Okay, just give me the mount on Old Roman."

"Waldo, take Clayton off to put up Tim? Come on."

He spat again not too far from my feet and left, still in a fury, without another word. I contemplated giving him a quick boot in the rear to speed him on his way, but settled for a swift departure myself. One thing about being an administrator, I had discovered, was that it was not unlike martyrdom; every day somebody shot an arrow or two into me.

I had forgotten all about the mild unpleasantness with Waldo by the time I settled into Jay's box that afternoon, half an hour before the first post. I loved the card, I had done some serious handicapping the night before, and I was looking forward to a profitable afternoon cushioned by the company of my track cronies.

"No tonguing, she tells me," Angles was saying, as I sat down beside Jay. "Can you believe that?"

"It was your first date, what did you expect?" Jay said. "You might have frightened her."

"Frightened her?" Angles said, indignantly. "I had her tits out by that time."

"Did you get laid?"

"No," Angles said. "I mean, I think I could have, if I'd pushed it. But that remark kind of put me away. I mean, I couldn't figure the angle on this broad. She comes on to me at the bar like I'm the king of the universe, you know, and we're doing great and then she ices me with this no-tonguing bullshit. I mean, what did she think we were doing, discovering the beauties of nature?"

"With you, Angles? Hardly," Arnie said. "I imagine she was fighting for her virtue."

"What virtue?" Angles snapped. "There I am with this big diamond cutter in my pants and she's letting me feel her tits and all and now I'm supposed to kiss her like she's my sister."

"You have a sister?" Arnie asked. "The poor child."

"Angles, you rushed it," Jay explained. "All women have a cutoff button they push when they think that things are moving too fast. You have to respect it. It's up to them whether you get laid or not. You have to back off and be nice. They'll let you know when they're ready."

"Who are we talking about? Ginger?" I asked.

"No, that's all over," Angles said. "I stopped seeing her when she started complaining all the time about how I'm wasting it at the track every day. The broad is a sickee. No, this is a new broad, Shifty. I met her last night over here at the Cockatoo. She's a cocktail waitress there. Anyway, I freeze up and go home. It's real depressing, I tell you. I can never figure the angles with broads. They all got some crazy set of rules they expect you to play by, only they don't tell you what the rules are until you're halfway through the game. Fuck 'em, who needs 'em, right?"

"You do, obviously," Jay said. "We all do. It's the dance of life."

"Yeah? Well, I'll sit this one out."

"I'm glad those unhappy days are behind me," Arnie said. "I recall my own youth as a series of unfortunate encounters and misunderstandings with the opposite sex. But who can blame the women? They have everything to lose. When you're a bachelor and you're young, your basic attitude to women in general is a period of sexual harassment to be followed by attempted date rape. I mean, gentlemen, we have a Supreme Court justice who couldn't keep his pecker in his pants. How are we mere mortal slobs expected to behave? Women are to be commended for their tolerance."

"Arnie, for Christ's sake, all I wanted to do was get laid," Angles explained. "What's so terrible about that? I had a rubber and everything. And it wasn't as if she gave me no encouragement either. She liked it when I'm playing with her tits."

"Spare us the unseemly details of your courtship," Arnie said. "You are disrupting my concentration on the double."

"Send her flowers, Angles," Jay suggested. "Send her a nice bouquet, apologize, and take her out again. This time don't touch her, don't even lay a finger on her. And next time you ask her out, she'll be more truthful and more willing."

"Yeah," Angles agreed, "but it costs money and meanwhile my balls are turning blue thinking about her. And you know how much time you waste? I mean, it really cuts into your handicapping."

"All the more reason to withdraw from the fray," Arnie commented. "Only in quiet, monastic contemplation can winners be isolated from the great mass of misleading statistics before us. Now, gentlemen, it is nearly post time. Let us confer on the conundrum at hand."

We did pretty well, winning two of the first five races at decent prices, and we had a nice triple coming up, so I had pretty much forgotten about Daryl Spencer when he suddenly materialized outside our box. "Anderson?" he said. "They told me I'd find you here. I'm Daryl Spencer."

He was tall for a jock, but thin and wiry, with big hands. He had a long narrow face with very pale-gray eyes and hair plastered to his skull by some sort of fragrant cream. He was neatly dressed in black jeans and a blue western shirt open at the collar, but there was something unsettling in his appearance, as if he were in disguise from himself. We shook hands and I introduced him to my friends. "Daryl, welcome to California," I said. "Did you find a place to live?"

"Oh, sure, with the Lord's help," he said. "Mr. Hardin made a couple of calls for me. I've got a nice place in West L.A., over by Rochester. Kind of a furnished room, really, but it'll be fine, I expect, till I can get really settled, come fall. That is, if I can get some mounts out here." His smile was sudden and abrupt, as if he'd switched it on by command. "I sure appreciate what you and Mr. Pickard are doing for me. It'll help to get me started. Well, I don't mean to interrupt anything, so I'll be on my way. See you in the morning, the Lord willing. Nice to meet you boys."

"What in the hell was that?" Angles asked, as soon as he'd gone. "Your new exercise boy, Shifty?"

"That was Daryl Spencer," I explained. "He's moved here from Kentucky and we're putting him up on some horses to help him get started."

"Daryl Spencer, I know about him," Jay said. "He was a crook and a drunk and then he found Jesus. At his best he was never much rider. What's going on, Shifty?"

"He's ridden for Clarendon quite a bit and he's a friend of Phil Hardin's, their trainer back there," I explained, "so Baldwin is making Charlie use him. There isn't much we can do about it."

"What does Charlie say?"

"Pretty much what I just told you. I guess he feels we can live with it as long as they don't tell us every time who to ride in every race."

"Hey, they're at the post, you guys," Angles said, raising his binoculars to focus on the start of the sixth. "Let's get this triple in."

"A born-again rider," Jay said. "Well, maybe finding God has turned him around. I think he used to be known in Florida as Old Iron Hands."

"Right," I said. "Clara Wilson, one of our grooms, told me about him."

"Ah, if only the human soul could be cleansed like a stained sheet," Arnie observed, his eyes also focused on the impending start of the sixth. "But think of the evils committed in this vale of laments by people acting in God's name."

"Yeah, right," Angles said. "If Jesus had been a jock, he'd have pulled his share. Believe me, the only jocks that don't cheat are dead jocks."

The race went off, our triple came in, paying a little over three hundred dollars, and I forgot all about Daryl Spencer.

I didn't see him again until the Friday morning of Bellringer's race, when he came around the barn during the workouts. He was dressed to ride, with a helmet on his head and boots on, and he immediately apologized for not having shown up the day before. "It took me longer than I thought to get settled," he said, "and then my car broke down on the freeway and I had to get towed to a service station. It was quite a day. But everything's fine now, thank the Lord. Where's old Bellringer at? Just thought I'd get reacquainted with him."

I walked him down to Bellringer's stall, where the gelding was standing with his back to us and muzzled to keep him from eating anything before his race. "He sure looks fit," Spencer said. "I'm looking forward to this, though a mile may be a little far for him."

"Well, Charlie wanted to keep him on the grass and this is as short a race as we could find for him," I explained. "There's very little speed in there and we drew a good post, the four hole, so you should be able to get him out on the lead and give him a breather down the backside. You ought to have plenty of horse under you for the drive."

"Is that what Mr. Pickard says?"

"Yes, he told me to tell you. He may not be out today. He's on some new medication and he says he's feeling better, but they want to monitor him another day or two."

"Sure thing," the rider said. "Well, we'll give it our best shot, won't we? And we're all in God's hands."

I took him around and introduced him to everybody, after which he left, invoking Jesus and saying that he had a couple of horses to gallop for another of Phil Hardin's friends, a trainer named Lipton, and that he'd see us in the walking ring that afternoon.

I had a busy day on the phone and with various chores, as well as a long conversation with Charlie to bring him up to date on everything. The trainer hadn't been out all week and was becoming impatient about having to stay away, so to keep him in check, at least until he felt better, I filled him in on matters in considerable detail. Then, when I'd concluded, I put May on and she gave him a rundown on the condition of the horses. It was nearly eleven o'clock when we got through and I had to rush home and then rush back in order to make the third, Bellringer's race.

I don't remember now exactly what I had expected from it, but certainly not what happened. Because Charlie couldn't make it, Eddie Graham, who had an assistant trainer's license, was on hand to officially saddle the horse, but Eddie, a withdrawn and self-effacing man who had worked for Charlie for over twenty years, offered no opinion on the race. I had already told Spencer earlier what Charlie expected the horse to do, so I added nothing to his instructions and all May said when she gave the jock a leg up into the saddle was, "Good luck, Daryl. Just get us the money." Spencer had given the horse a nice pat on the neck as the field headed out of the paddock toward the tunnel and I think we were all feeling fairly confident. So confident, in fact, that on my way upstairs I stopped off to bet a hundred dollars to win on him. Ten minutes before post, the horse had been backed down to five to two, half his morning-line odds, but that didn't strike me as unusual because he'd run such a good race last time on the turf and an animal with speed always gets a lot of support from bettors, especially in California where speed is the name of the game.

Even Spencer's past record on the horse reassured me. He had ridden him his last four times in Kentucky, twice each at two different tracks, won once and finished second once with him. There was nothing in these past performances to indicate that he might not have tried to win every time and I decided that perhaps the jockey had been unjustly maligned. Or perhaps snuggling up to Jesus had really turned him around. The only thing I did notice was that Bellringer's one win had been at long odds, twelve to one, and that both his losses had come when he was the favorite and in the wake of his strong second-place finish. But then bettors are notoriously fickle and prone to false enthusiasms. I dismissed these negative inklings from my mind and went outside to watch the race from Charlie's box.

At about three minutes to post, the odds on the horse began to drop. A huge chunk of money had come in on him and the board suddenly blinked him down to eight to five. A minute later, he was six to five. As the horses reached the gate, he went to even money. And by the time the race went off, a couple of minutes later, Bellringer had become another overbet, odds-on favorite, at four to five.

I sat there, watching this action in disbelief, but unwilling to make myself go back to a betting window to sell my ticket. I was too interested in what would happen in the race itself to want to risk missing the start of it, so I just sat there, watching the money come in on our horse as the animals were being loaded into the gate. What made the happening even more improbable, aside from the fact that the horse had never run this far before either on dirt or turf, was the presence on his back of Daryl Spencer, an unsung journeyman with a dubious past who had never ridden in California before. The money pouring in on Bellringer in bunches was obviously not local money, but coming from somewhere else, probably Las Vegas. Whatever or wherever, the horse, as the gamblers say, was being pounded.

The race was nearly as improbable as the betting action. Old Iron Hands popped Bellringer out of the gate on top and quickly opened up two lengths with him as they hit the first turn. Running easily at this point, the gelding hugged the rail and opened up to lead by four as they reached the backstretch. The first quarter mile had been run in twenty-two-and-three-fifths seconds, fast time for the distance, but one that could be defended on the grounds that, with a speed horse, you'd need to use some of it to get to the front. At that point in the race, a good jockey would have taken hold of the animal and tried to slow him down, thus conserving his energy and saving something for the drive. He had four lengths on the rest of the field, plenty of margin to adopt this standard front-running strategy.

To my amazement, Spencer made no visible effort to slow his mount down. Given his head, Bellringer simply kept on running as fast as he could. The half mile went by in forty-five flat and the lead grew to nearly eight lengths, with the field bunched up behind him. The crowd began to roar in excitement and disbelief. Halfway around the turn for home, Bellringer still had about five lengths, but now, inevitably, he began to tire and shorten stride. By the head of the lane, his lead had shrunk to a length and a half. His nearest pursuers caught him at the eighth pole. Spencer was whipping and pumping hard, but to no avail; Bellringer had already run his race. He finished next to last, with nothing left, and Spencer was greeted a couple of minutes later with a rousing chorus of boos when he came jogging back toward the finish line.

I ran down to the track to meet him as he headed toward the weigh-in scales with his tack in his arms. Before I could say anything, he shook his head and smiled ruefully. "I couldn't hold him out there today," he said. "He was rank and trying to get out on me, so I gave him his head, hoping he'd settle down. I guess the good Lord didn't want us to do it today. I sure am sorry."

I didn't answer, but went over to where Eddie and May were getting ready to lead Bellringer back toward the barn. "He's okay," Eddie said. "He just thought the race was over after he'd run so hard."

"Spencer told me he was rank and lugging out," I said.

"Bullshit, honey," May said. "He wasn't doin' neither of them things. There's more than one way to stiff a horse."

"Why would he do that, with all that money coming in on him?" I asked. "That had to be inside money being bet on him."

"They're gonna be pretty unhappy with old Daryl," May said. "If I was him, I'd get out of town, maybe to another country."

"Well, that was a very interesting race, Shifty," Jay said, when I bumped into him and Arnie in a betting line a couple of races later. "One or two more efforts like that and Spencer's going to go back to Kentucky or wherever in a pine box."

"It was too blatant," I said. "And why would he stiff this horse?"

"All my life I've wondered about jockeys," Arnie said. "I think they do these things to get even with us."

"For what, Arnie?"

"For having been born short."

9 / Poison

ALMOST THE ONLY MOUNTS Daryl Spencer was able to acquire during his first two weeks in California were for Clarendon. On each occasion I received a phone call from Baldwin's office and Virginia would tell me to engage the jockey. Baldwin himself was usually out of town or not in his office, but there was little doubt that the instructions came from him. Virginia would recite them as if she had taken them down verbatim and they left little room for argument. For my part, I'd simply pass the information on to Charlie, who never liked what he was hearing but had to go along. Clarendon was paying the bills and Charlie was in no shape to put up a fight. He was feeling better, but it would still be a while, he thought, before he could begin to resume some of his on-hand morning activities.

There was no repetition of the Bellringer incident. Spencer rode four of the Clarendon two-year-olds and made no mistakes, finishing in the money with all of them and winning one race, on a nice little filly called Sweetheart. No one else gave him live horses to ride, but he seemed to know what to do, at least, and I began to wonder whether he hadn't been right about Bellringer.

The chart of the race, published a couple of days later in the *Racing Form,* had stated that the horse might have been rank, though there was nothing indicating he had tried to lug out. Still, Spencer had ridden the horse before and knew him well. Who was I to second-guess him? All I knew about horses was what I'd learned over the years of betting on them. Even Charlie, when I showed him a videotape of the race, grudgingly admitted that the horse might have been a little rank. I decided not to become paranoid about Spencer.

What was unusual, however, was the betting action. Every time a Clarendon horse ran, it was bet heavily, well below its morning line. There was nothing subtle about it either. The money would come slamming in in big chunks, early and late, and all the wiseguys noticed it. Somebody even commented on it in the *Form.* Nobody knew, however, whose money it was or where it was coming from. Jay was certain it had to be from Las Vegas. "They're obviously betting these Clarendon horses at the sports books there," he said, "and Vegas is so chickenshit nobody will book such heavy action. The result is, every time a horse gets pounded, they lay it off through their on-track contacts. You know Vegas. The casinos will take any amount of action on their slots and games, but racing scares them. They're not in the business of losing money on gambling action they can't control, so when they see somebody plunging on a horse, they run."

"Yeah, but who's doing it and why?" I asked. "It's dumb. Whoever's betting the money is running it into the tote so clumsily that everybody notices it. So even when one of their horses wins, the payoff is well under what it should be. It's a losing strategy. I don't get it."

"I don't either," Jay said. "Of course, the Vegas guys want everybody to notice. The happy jack squirrels out here jump on that kind of action, figuring the horse is a cinch to win. The lower the odds, the less the risk for the part of the action Vegas does book. They obviously aren't laying it all off."

"It's stupid at every level."

"Oh, yes," Jay agreed, "but racetracks and casinos are not run or patronized mainly by Nobel Prize winners."

Charlie was upset by what was going on every time we put a Clarendon horse into a race. He showed up at around ten one morning, after most of the work was done, and we sat in his tack room with the door closed to discuss the situation. "It stinks," he said. "The word is out that I'm running some kind of gambling stable here. A couple of my friends have called me at home to kid me about it, but I don't think it's funny. What the hell's going on, Shifty?"

"I haven't a clue," I admitted. "Say, you're looking pretty good, Charlie." He was, too; his face had some color in it and he had put on a couple of pounds.

"Yeah, I'm feeling better," he said. "I'm going to be showing up more often around here pretty soon. This new medication they got me on is working, only I have to take a laxative every two or three days to take a crap, but I can live with that. At least I'm not dragging around like a goddamn corpse. I was going to give myself another week, maybe, but this Clarendon business is beginning to get to me. What do your junkie friends say?"

"What everybody's saying, Charlie—that it's Vegas layoff money. Somebody's hammering these horses and the casinos are passing it on into the tote."

"I don't like it," the trainer said.

"Baldwin must be a big gambler."

"He isn't, as far as I know. It's somebody else, maybe somebody connected to him."

"Maybe this guy Aramis," I said, "but he doesn't even like the horses. At least that's what he said to me. His girlfriend bets."

"No, this is a lot bigger than just one person, Shifty," Charlie said, shaking his head. "This isn't good."

"It's not illegal to bet heavily on your own horses, is it?"

"Don't be funny," Charlie said. "This nutty kind of heavy betting is bad news. There could be an investigation."

"On what grounds?"

"I don't know. Money laundering?"

"Whose dirty money? Clarendon's?"

"You tell me. Whatever it is, I don't want to be connected to it. I've never been involved in anything shady, you know that." The trainer began to grope in his pockets, as if searching for a cigarette."

"You haven't started smoking again, have you? What are you, crazy?"

"Crazy? Yeah, to be in this business," he said. "You think a sane man would do this for a career? No, I'm not smoking. It was a reflex action."

"Maybe you ought to talk to Baldwin."

Charlie thought that one over for a few minutes. "He probably knows about it," he said. "Spencer would tell Hardin and Hardin would probably tell Baldwin. Obviously, he ain't too concerned about it, or he'd have contacted me." He lapsed into silence again, trying to think his way through what he clearly saw as a serious problem. "You know what, Shifty," he said at last, "if it weren't for this colt, I'd tell these people to take their horses elsewhere."

"You're kidding."

"No, I'm not," he said. "I've been around this game a long time. I've always stayed clean. I've never been part of any operation that looked shady in any way."

"Shady? Clarendon? I thought they were a fine old name in racing."

"So was Calumet," Charlie said. "Look what happened to them. The most famous stable in America, with a great history and a great tradition, all down the tubes in less than two years. The name is nothing. It's who you've got running the show. I don't know much about Baldwin. His father created the stable, made the reputation. After he died, ten years ago, there was a fight over who would get the business between Roger and his older sister, Betty Ruth. Old Joe was a widower and he left two different wills. There was going to be a court fight, only they made a settlement at the last minute. Roger got the farm."

"What happened to the sister?"

"She's around, I guess. Lives in Louisville, I think. She got half the money, which meant that Clarendon had to sell off some land and some of the breeding stock to buy her out. That's all I know about it, except that Clarendon's been doing okay. They held on to Algonquin and some of the broodmares. I didn't hear anything bad about them, not really. A few rumors."

"What kind of rumors?"

"Nothing much, nothing too specific," Charlie said. "Just that they're in fairly deep with the banks. Everything was okay as long as things were booming, but the bottom just about fell out of the horse business at the time Clarendon was expanding again. The stable did real good for a while, but with the Bush depression they had a couple of real lean years and that's when you started hearing the rumors. I don't generally pay attention to that crap. I just try to do my job and let other people worry about the other stuff.

But I have to tell you, Shifty, I don't like the smell of this much. Something's going on and I'm damned if I know what."

"But you wouldn't want to give up Old Roman, would you?"

He shook his head. "No way, Shifty. You can wait a whole lifetime for a horse potentially as good as this one. I haven't got too many more chances either. I just wish I knew what was going on."

"You want me to find out?"

"How?"

"Mad Margaret's back there," I said. "They're going to breed her to Promoter in a couple of days. Why don't I just get on a plane and drop in on Clarendon? Maybe I'll get a chance to talk to Baldwin."

Charlie thought it over for a few seconds, then nodded. "Not a bad idea," he said. "You can even tell him I suggested it. Tell him what's going on and that it looks funny, okay? Let's see what his reaction is."

"You want me to say you sent me for some reason?"

"No. You're there on your own, all right? Make up something."

"I'll dazzle them with misdirection. It's one of my specialties."

"And I've got a guy for you to call back there, a fellow named J. B. Tender," Charlie said. "He used to be a breeder, but he's back training again. Mostly he works with yearlings, breaking them and all. He's in Lexington and he's a pretty sharp old boy. You call him, tell him you work for me, but don't do any magic stuff. J.B. ain't got much time for show folk."

"I need the money, Kenny," Rainbow was saying, as I came up beside him under the TV monitor in the clubhouse. "Come on, Kenny, baby, I *need* the money."

The horses were being loaded into the starting gate and Rainbow had his eyes glued to the screen. He was an old black man who'd acquired his track name because, he said, he'd been looking for years for the pot of gold at the end of the rainbow and one day he'd find it, in the form of a giant pick-six or some other exotic wager. He worked for Tim Loftus, a moderately successful trainer with a string of about twenty animals. Rainbow's style was to play jockeys, which is not usually a winning strategy, and every meet he'd select some new champion who'd waft him to wealth. This time he'd apparently settled on Ken Otay, a Canadian rider who was always in the top ten in the jockey standings, but who often lost races by going too wide on the turns. When he did win, it was usually at a decent price. I liked Rainbow, because I have a weakness for dreamers, and someday, I suppose, I'll learn his real name.

"Hey, Rainbow, what race is this?" I asked. "I just got here."

"The fourth," he answered, without wavering from his intense concentration on the screen. "Kenny's gonna bring this one in for me and pay the rent, you watch."

"Why don't you go outside and look at it live?"

" 'Cause some mother stole my glasses last week," he said. "I got to win me a couple of races to buy another pair. Now, Kenny, my man, you gonna make my day. You just watch this, Shifty."

When the horses broke from the gate, Rainbow went into his routine root, which I always derive pleasure from hearing. "Ah, that's nice, Kenny, you broke just right," he said. "Yes, now don't get fanned here on the turn. Tuck in, Kenny, tuck in. That's good. Now just sit there behind that speed, just let 'em go out there and kill each other off, baby. Good. That's good. Now don't get boxed. Don't get trapped in there along the rail. You know better than that, Kenny, baby. Okay now, just sit there, my honey boy. Yes, like that. Okay now, on the turn don't move yet. Hey, it's too soon. You got the fractions in front of you. Kenny, I *need* this money. Don't go fuckin' up on me, you hear? Okay, now you can move. Yeah, *now!* Hey, that's a little wide, baby. Where you goin'? You comin' home through the parkin' lot? That's wide enough, Kenny, baby. Okay now, set him down, Kenny! You bring this mother home to me, Kenny, baby! I *need* this money, Kenny!"

As the horses charged three abreast for the finish line, with Rainbow's contender pulling gradually away foot by foot, the old groom really turned it on. He dropped to both knees and raised his arms in supplication toward the screen. "Oh, you Kenny, baby, you bring him on home to me now! Yes, yes, yes, that's the way to do it, Kenny, baby, 'cause I *need* the money, Kenny! Yes, you done fine, sugar! You made this old man rich! Oh, you Kenny, baby, you the king! Yes, you made me rich and I *need* this money! Oh, you Kenny baby!"

Rainbow's winner paid $12.60, more than quintupling his

twenty-dollar bet. "Hey, Shifty, my man, let me buy you a beer," Rainbow said. "Come on!"

"It's okay, Rainbow. I'm happy for you."

"No, no," he said, grabbing my arm and leading me over to the bar, "you don't want to bring me no bad luck, do you? One beer, that's all, on my man Kenny Otay, yes indeed!"

We stood at the bar and nursed our beers, while Rainbow went on singing the praises of his new champion. "You see, Shifty, that boy, he can think and ride at the same time," he said. "There ain't many can do that."

"He tends to go a little wide occasionally."

"Oh, yeah," Rainbow said, "but that way, you see, he don't get into no trouble inside. He don't get shut off, you see. You ever seen him get shut off? And anyway, a lot of horses, they don't run inside, you know. Get all that dirt in their faces. But they'll all run outside. That Kenny, he knows that, Shifty. He's a smart little mother. He's gonna make old Rainbow rich, he is."

"What about Daryl Spencer?" I asked, on an impulse. "What do you think of him?"

"Oh, sure, I know him. I was workin' down in Miami at Calder when he come down there one year," the old man said. "Say, you want to watch yourself with that boy. He can ride, but he's a cheatin' motherfucker. Hey, I notice your man Pickard is ridin' him a lot. You tell him to be careful. I mean, that boy, he can pull a giraffe's neck down to its shoulders. I wouldn't bet no serious money on that dude, no, sir. They probably done chased him out of Florida."

"Yeah, that's what Clara said."

"Who?"

"Clara Wilson, that new stablehand we have working for us."

"Oh, yeah, Shifty, I know her, too."

"You do? From Florida?"

"Sure. Big, strong lady, right?"

"Yeah."

"She been around a while. She come from up the coast, up in them piney woods up there. She's got quite a story."

"What kind of story?"

"Her daddy, I guess, he run a place up there on the old coast road, where they had them gambling games. You ever heard of razzle-dazzle?"

"Yes, I have. It's an old carnival game, really crooked."

"You got it, Shifty, that's it. Well, that's where she come from. And I think that that other gal that works for you—"

"May?"

"Yeah, that good-lookin' one."

"She's a groom for Charlie."

"Yeah, she's a groom and a half, Shifty."

"I know what you mean. What about her?"

"I think she come from back there also. She and that Clara, they used to be around together, if you know what I'm sayin'."

"What exactly do you mean, Rainbow?"

"They like each other a lot, Shifty. A lot of guys was hittin' on her, but they was a team, them two. It kind of discomforted the boys, if you know what I'm talkin' about."

"I guess I do," I said, but before I could ask old Rainbow any more questions Angles came charging up to me.

"You won't believe this, Shifty," he said. "I swear to God you won't believe this."

"What won't I believe?"

"You remember my girlfriend Ginger?"

"The one you broke up with?"

"Yeah, only that was her fault. She didn't want to come to the races with me. She said I was wasting too much time here."

"What about her?"

"She's here and you know who she's with?"

"I have no idea."

"That old man Pickard trains for, that's who."

"Abel Green?"

"Yeah, that's him. Can you believe that? Not only is she at the track, but she's with this old man, Shifty. Can you believe it?"

"Maybe she's doing it to make you mad."

"Well, if she is, it's working."

"Where are they?"

"In a box right behind us. Wouldn't you know? Can you believe that?"

"What happened to the cocktail waitress from the Cockatoo?"

"She wouldn't go out with me no more. She said I tried to rape her. Another one. They're all cunts."

"You're lettin' life aggravate you, my man," Rainbow said. "You got to loosen up and lay back or the demons gonna devour your soul. You got to think positive thoughts. Agitation and aggravation demean the spirit and close off the life juices. How you gonna pick a winner with all that poison inside of you?"

"You know, he's right," Angles said. "I haven't had a horse in the money all day."

"You see? The poison is in your soul," Rainbow said. "You got to get cleansed to have a winner. You got to purify the spirit to climb the heights."

"You sound a little nuts," Angles said, "but you got an interesting angle there. Maybe I'll go sit somewhere else where I don't have to look at 'em."

"The view is important," Rainbow said. "You got to feast your eyes on the good things, not the bad ones. Beauty and harmony, that's the key."

Angles rushed off again, still in a state of high agitation, and Rainbow left to cash his winning ticket. I lingered at the bar, nursing the dregs of my beer and trying not to allow Rainbow's revelation regarding May and Clara Wilson to upset me. I wasn't succeeding very well and I was still standing there when Abel Green and Angles's ex-girlfriend walked past me. She was hanging on his arm and staring adoringly up at him as he talked to her. Abel, I guessed, was in his late sixties or early seventies and she was in her mid-twenties, rather sweet-looking, with a trim little body, innocent blue eyes, and a mop of brown curls. I wondered if she knew that Green was married and had grandchildren. Whether she did or not, I found myself beginning to think like Angles. Women were duplicitous and exploitive, full of secrets and surprises, committed to a private agenda and embarked on some lonely quest hidden from men. I decided not to make any bets and to go home. I could feel what Rainbow called the poison beginning to invade my soul.

10 / Revelations

I ARRIVED IN LEXINGTON, Kentucky, the day before Mad Margaret was to be bred to Promoter, rented a cheap compact at the airport, and checked into a motel a few miles west of the town, about halfway to Keeneland which, I had been told, was the prettiest racetrack in America. It was closed, but I drove into the grounds anyway and walked around, soaking up atmosphere. From the outside, the grandstand looked like an Ivy League football stadium, all rough stone and ivy in a bucolic setting of lawns and old trees, and to the north, away from the old highway, the countryside seemed to stretch endlessly away, a tapestry of rolling hills and clumps of forest crisscrossed by dark fencing and peppered with stables and farmhouses. The famous so-called blue grass looked green to me, but as rich and dense as thick carpeting and good enough for humans to browse on.

It was a hot, humid day, more like summer than late spring, and it didn't take me long to work up a sweat, so I was glad to get back into my air-conditioned car and just drive around. Everywhere I went, whether along the main roads or the narrow back-country lanes that followed the contours of the gentle hills, I passed farms large and small, with acres of fenced pasture where herds of horses grazed—mares with leggy new foals by their sides, yearlings, stallions enclosed in solitary splendor in their own private domains. From time to time I'd stop the car and get out, walk over to the nearest fence and lean on it to take in the view. This was the world of the Thoroughbred I had never seen before, the place where it all begins, and about as far from the bustle and uproar of a racetrack as could be imagined. For some reason it moved me, perhaps because I knew that all this beauty and tranquility rested entirely on the shoulders of Jay and Arnie and Angles and all of us who frequent the track with any regularity. These glorious animals owed their very existence, in fact, to the desire of one man to bet on his horse against another's in a race that took place so long ago and in so foreign a locale that we could only guess where that seminal event might have occurred. It was humbling to think about, especially because so few people do. To politicians the sport is simply a means to gouge money out of the public; to the people who run the game it's a livelihood and little else; to most of the fans it's a gambling proposition, pure and simple. The Thoroughbred is not a wild animal; he was created largely by man for a specific purpose—to run fast and be competitive. No one who has watched racehorses in training in the early mornings can doubt for a moment that they exist to run, that the desire is as ingrained in them as the will to live. Still, it takes a visit to the horse country, I reflected, to remind us that this animal is also one of the miracles of evolution, a creature so noble in its beauty that artists have immortalized it in stone and bronze and wood and paint. The concept of a pari-mutuel machine seems a desecration in such a setting.

When I got back to my motel in the late afternoon, I called Clarendon and caught Virginia just as she was leaving the office. "Oh, Mr. Anderson, how nice to hear from you," she said. "We were wondering when you'd call. Your filly is scheduled for ten o'clock tomorrow morning."

"Exactly where are you?" I asked. "I've been driving around for a couple of hours and I thought I'd kind of blunder into your place during my wanderings, but I didn't find you."

"Oh, we're out on the Old Frankfort Pike, about eight miles from Keeneland. Do you have a map?"

"I do, but I didn't look at it," I confessed.

"Well, once you're on the main road, go about four miles and watch on your right for a sign that says 'Clarendon.' It's pretty big and painted in our colors, green and gold, so you won't miss it. Turn right and about a quarter mile in you'll come to the main gate. The office is another quarter mile beyond the main house and the breeding shed is to the right, but please come to the office first and we'll arrange to escort you. Will that be satisfactory?"

"Oh, yes, thanks so much. Will Mr. Baldwin be around? I'd like to meet him."

"He's due in late tonight, sir, and I imagine he'll be in the office tomorrow morning. I'll tell him you wish to see him. Is there anything else I can do for you?"

"Know a good restaurant anywhere?"

She gave me the name of two places in downtown Lexington and I thanked her, then I called J. B. Tender. "Well, hell, what are you doin' right now?" he asked, when I invoked Charlie's name and told him who I was. "You want to grab some dinner?"

"I was planning to do that," I admitted and mentioned the names of the two restaurants Virginia had recommended.

"Aw, they're just little old phony joints servin' up frog and Eyetalian food and chargin' a dollar a bite," he said. "I'll meet you at Buffalo and Dad's in half an hour. I was goin' by there anyway. Say, how is old Charlie? We heard he was sick."

"He's doing a lot better," I said.

"And I hear he's got a real fast two-year-old."

"How'd you know? Charlie tell you?"

"Aw no, word just gets around. I'm glad to hear the old fool's feelin' all right. I ain't talked to him in a couple of months or more. I'll see you over there."

"Where exactly is this place?"

"Aw hell, ask anybody. Everybody knows where it's at." And he hung up.

He was right, everybody did know where Buffalo and Dad's was, though the two middle-aged women behind the counter at my motel seemed surprised that I'd want to go there. "It's kind of a rowdy place, if you know what I mean," one of them said. "Country and horse people, you know."

"They had a big brawl in there last week," the other one added. "The police came and all."

"Sounds like my kind of people," I said, smiling. "How's the food?"

"Well, it depends what you like to eat," the first one answered. "They have real spicy burgoo and the hot brown's real good. It's not exactly health food, if that's what you're used to."

"I'm not. Health food can kill you."

"Then you'll like Buffalo and Dad's," the second woman said. "I guess it's all right, though it can get pretty rough. I wouldn't go in there alone, if I was you."

"I'm meeting someone."

"Oh, then it'll be fine. Have a nice time now."

Buffalo and Dad's was located in downtown Lexington and consisted of three dark rooms with two bars, a jukebox, and enough old racing pictures and track paraphernalia on the walls to stock a museum. It was crowded and noisy and dense with smoke, so I stood briefly just inside the main entrance to get my bearings. Before I could take a step, a large man of about sixty rose up out of a nearby booth and beckoned me over. He had a stomach like a barrel, arms as long as those of an orangutan, and a red face with a long nose and small, dark eyes. He was dressed in jeans, boots, and a tight black shirt, and he wore a straw-colored cowboy hat that looked as if it grew out of his skull. "Hi there," he said, extending a paw in my direction. "I'm J.B. Sit down. Want a drink?"

"They serve wine in here?"

"You don't want to drink the wine, Lou. Have a bourbon."

"Okay."

"You want water?"

"A splash of soda."

Without waiting for the waitress, he lumbered over to the bar, bellowed his order, and came back three minutes later with a tall glass full of what looked like very strong iced tea. "I forgot about the soda," he said, "but that's real good Kentucky sour mash. You don't want to thin it out too much." When he sank back into his seat, the booth shook. I decided it would be important to keep on the friendly side of J. B. Tender; he looked strong enough to take on the whole room by himself.

It was difficult to carry on a conversation at first, because of the jukebox and the bar noise, but we eventually moved, after ordering dinner, to a quieter corner in one of the adjacent rooms. "Hard to hear, wasn't it?" J.B. said. "Thought you'd like to get a feel of the place, so I started us out in there. This way we can talk and you'll like the food."

I did like it. I ordered burgoo, a hot local dish of unknown ingredients that tasted not unlike chili, and a salad. Both orders came in gargantuan proportions that I washed down with bourbon and a couple of bottles of beer, while J.B. devoured a ham and told me about his work. He had a small horse farm of his own not far from Clarendon, where he owned a few broodmares, now in foal, and boarded some others. But his main source of income was breaking yearlings. He had a team of riders who worked for him and they'd drive all over the state and as far as the Virginias and up into Ohio to "contract-break" yearlings. "I don't ride myself anymore. I'm much too big and fat and old, but I know what it takes," he said. "And I got a bunch of top boys workin' for me. I guess I'm just about the best there is at it. It's a livin'.'"

"You're a breeder, too."

"Yeah, but I had to cut way back and pick up this other work, on account of the business is in pretty bad shape these days," he explained. "I started out breakin' horses and I guess I'll end up breakin' 'em. I guess you know enough about the horse business to know what happened to it these last few years. When the tax laws changed back in the mid-eighties and then the Japanese and the Arabs began cuttin' back, the price of horses just dropped through the bottom. We was breedin' damn near sixty thousand foals a year, I guess, and now we're down to maybe forty-five thousand. We put a lot of cheap stock on the market and we're payin' for it. Lot of those farms out here are in big trouble. You can buy just about any property you want these days, and pretty cheap, too. Maybe it'll come back, but I don't know. The whole industry's in poor shape."

"What about Clarendon?"

"Well, nobody really knows for sure," he said. "They seem to be all right, but then you hear these rumors."

"Like what?"

"That they're in hock up to their ears with the banks," he said, "but can't nobody pin it down. The *Lexington Herald-Leader* did a story a couple of months ago about it, but in it the local banks all denied they had anythin' at all to do with Clarendon. In the interview with Roger, he said the farm was doin' fine and they'd made some kind of deal with overseas investments or somethin' like that and there wasn't no problem. But the story just won't die down, especially 'cause Roger won't tell nobody what the overseas connection is and all. He says he can't say nothin' about it, on account of his investors don't want their names in the papers. So you don't know what to believe. What's Charlie say about it? He's trainin' for 'em, ain't he?"

"Charlie doesn't know any more than you do, J.B.," I said. "He's not especially happy with what's going on. Every time one of these Clarendon horses runs, it gets hammered at the betting windows. And then there's Daryl Spencer. You know him?"

"Sure, everybody knows about Daryl out here," J.B. said. "He's always got Jesus ridin' on his shoulders. He ain't good company."

"Anyway, we have to ride him. He's moved to California."

"Don't go bettin' on no horses ridden by Daryl," J.B. said. "That man probably pulled up comin' out of his mother's womb."

"He claims that God has turned him around."

"You know why he's out in California, don't you?"

"No."

"He walked out on his wife and boy," J.B. said. "They was livin' in Louisville, but he started foolin' around with some chippie he met at a church social. There was some kind of hubbub over it, especially after he moved in with this gal. Then, after about a month, he dumped her and come runnin' back to his wife, only she wouldn't let him in the house. So he packed up and went to California. He made a big deal out of confessin' his sins and all, but people was kind of disgusted with him. I guess he figured he could maybe start over in California."

"He's a friend of Phil Hardin's, the Clarendon trainer," I said. "That's why we're riding him."

"They used him a lot," J.B. said. "Daryl's pretty good with young horses. He's got good hands. In fact, he's got a lot of talent. He could have been a real good rider, only he's got the soul of a thief."

"Maybe Jesus will turn him into an honest man."

"I wouldn't bet on it," J. B. Tender said. "Most of the biggest thieves I know go to church on Sundays."

The horse people go to bed early and J. B. Tender was no exception. He had to get up before dawn the next day and drive with his team into West Virginia to break some horses for a farm in the eastern part of the state, so we were out of Buffalo and Dad's by eight-thirty. I spent the next couple of hours working on my moves and shuffles, then lay down on the bed and stared glumly at some witless television movie for an hour or so. After that, I lay in the dark, listening to a thunderstorm boil up out of the west and replaying in my head my getaway dinner the night before with May Isabel Potter.

"What do you mean, Shifty?" she asked me. "What are you gettin' at?"

We were sitting in a booth at the Tanqueray, an overpriced but comfortable restaurant in one of the big hotels along Century Boulevard, near the airport. It was the middle of our working week and May had told me she didn't want to get home too late, so we had settled at the Tanqueray as a compromise. "You got to get up early too," she said. "You can stay at my place, if you want."

And that was when I had dropped my little bomb. "The bed's pretty small for the three of us," I had said, regretting it the moment the words had spilled out of my mouth.

"So what are you gettin' at?" May had asked again, when I hadn't answered immediately.

"Tell me about razzle-dazzle," I said instead.

"Why? What about it?"

"You never heard of it?"

"Sure, I heard of it," she said. "It's a dumb bettin' game they used to play up the Florida coast when I was a kid. It's a sucker game. But what's that got to do with us sleepin' three in a bed?"

"I found out today that you and Clara go way back. You want to tell me about it?"

She smiled and bounced back into her corner of the booth, looking at me as if she had never quite seen me before. She was wearing one of her tight T-shirts, with no makeup and only a pair of large gold-hoop earrings for decoration. I wanted to sweep her into my arms, but sat frozen in place instead. "What the hell is this, Shifty?" she asked. "Sure, me and Clara go way back. So what?"

"I'd like to know about it."

"Why? What difference does it make?"

"It does to me," I said. "I can't help it. I guess it's because I care about you."

"You think it's gonna make a difference?"

"I don't know. I'm sorry I said what I did. I shouldn't have said it."

"Well, okay, honey, if you want to hear about it," she said. "I usually don't like to talk about it."

"You don't have to. It's okay."

She ignored me and plunged ahead. "I ran away from my folks when I was fourteen," she said. "I couldn't take it no more. My daddy was a drunk who used to beat up on my mom awful bad and I couldn't do nothin' about it. When I tried once, he like to kill me. Broke my cheekbone and a couple of ribs. But my sister and me, she was younger, we just had to take it. He was workin' for a fruit rancher up there and we was all in one small trailer and I just couldn't take it no more. So I ran away one night and hitched up the coast. Clara and her folks took me in and gave me a job, paid me five dollars a day and room and board. I wore these little tight shorts and a halter and I pumped gas, mostly. I was cute and innocent, so the folks drivin' by would look at me. The fathers'd get all hot and bothered and the moms thought I was cute and I had this patter. Clara worked with me on it, 'cause she was out there helpin' me. Only she didn't look cute or sexy, she was always kind of big and clumsy, you know. But she had the patter down."

"What kind of patter?"

"Oh, we'd ask where the folks was from and tell 'em that for what they was spendin' they could go inside into the store and have a free roll of the dice," she continued. "They had these dice, eight of 'em, and a little bucket full of dollar bills. Well, the first roll was free, so everybody just about rolled at least once. And once you got 'em rollin', they couldn't hardly stop. See, they'd get points for every roll and if they could get up to forty-eight points they'd win a lot of money. I never saw nobody win nothin' and I was there over a year. I guess it's about one in a million you can win somethin'."

"To be an instant winner, one in one point seven million times," I said. "To make forty-eight with more than one roll, just about impossible. It's the most vicious gambling game in the world."

"Yeah, I guess," May said. "I never seen no one win. People lost thousands tryin'. Well, one night this fella came back and he had a gun on him. And he shot Mr. Wilson dead and the police came and we was all arrested. Clara and me was sent off to a camp together for six months. And that's when me and her became—well, more than friends, I guess you'd say. And we stayed together for a while."

"So when she showed up here a few months ago, you persuaded Charlie to hire her."

"Yeah, I guess I did. Shifty, we go back a long ways and we been through a lot. We was both raped in that camp and when we ran away from there, we stayed together. I didn't want nothin' to do with men. Clara, well, she was always that way, you know, and I guess she always really liked me. But then I got married and it stopped. We been friends ever since, Shifty, and we ain't gonna stop bein' friends. That bother you?"

"It did. It bothers me less now."

"That's good. What do you want from me, Shifty? Ain't we got enough goin'? Clara and her folks was always real good to me. I ain't gonna turn my back on her. You're gonna have to live with that."

"I can live with it."

Yes, I could, but I had to admit it bothered me. I finally drifted off to sleep with the rain hammering down on the roof of the motel and lightning flashing off to the west somewhere.

11 / Romance

IT WAS STILL RAINING when I got up the next morning, but outside it looked as if it might clear later in the day. I felt drugged, as if the burgoo and bourbon had congealed into a sludge to clog my capillaries. I stood under the shower for twenty minutes and drank two cups of strong black coffee, then ate what passes in Kentucky for a health-food breakfast—eggs over easy, ham, grits, biscuits, and gravy, all washed down with more coffee. I found myself wondering what the life expectancy was in this state, but for some reason I was feeling fine by the time I showed up at the Clarendon office a little after nine.

"Oh, you're Mr. Anderson," the woman at the front desk said, as I walked in the door. "It sure is nice to meet you. I'm Virginia Corcoran." We shook hands. She was about forty, tall, big-boned, with long dark curly hair and very white skin; a hand-some woman, but soft and overweight. "Mr. Baldwin came in early this morning. He wants to see you. Did you have a nice evening?"

"Fine, thank you. I had dinner with a friend of Charlie's at Buffalo and Dad's."

117

"You did?" Her eyes opened wide, as if I had admitted to a fondness for bungee jumping. "And how was it?"

"A little noisy, but all right," I said. "I survived."

"It must have been one of the quiet nights," she said. "It can become very active, you know."

"So I heard."

"Mr. Baldwin's on the phone, but I'll tell him you're here as soon as he's off," she said. "Can I get you anything? Coffee?"

"No, thanks." I sat down, my eyes beginning to take in the decor, which, apart from standard office furniture, evidently consisted almost exclusively of large framed photographs on the walls of every important horse Clarendon had ever raced or bred. Then I picked up a handsome illustrated brochure toasting the exploits of the farm and providing relevant statistics: nearly thirteen hundred acres, eighteen barns, a stallion complex with fourteen stalls, a main office building, a main house and two smaller ones. A brief history of the farm revealed that it had been built in 1938 by the original proprietor, Stormy Joe Baldwin, on three hundred and twenty-six acres, since added to over the years. Clarendon had produced over four hundred stakes winners, including twelve national champions, and bred an average of thirty stakes horses a year. It had once sold a yearling at the Keeneland July sale for two and a half million dollars and another one at Saratoga for a million two. Currently, eleven studs were on hand and several hundred broodmares. Algonquin, the most important stallion on the grounds, had alone sired four national champions and a couple of dozen major stakes winners. The statistics trumpeted tradition, solvency, success. I was in the heart of the Kentucky racing establishment. What could possibly be going wrong here? Maybe we were all imagining things. No wonder bettors knocked the odds down on these animals; they were all potential champions.

"Mr. Anderson? I'm Roger Baldwin."

I looked up and he was standing there, smiling, with his hand out. I stood up and shook it. He was tall, with sandy-colored hair, probably in his early forties, with a wide lower jaw and pale-blue eyes. I had first seen him in the Las Vegas airport, while I was waiting for May's luggage and Ted was there to pick him up. He was dressed informally, in jeans and a windbreaker, but his clothes looked as if they'd been custom-tailored for him; he exuded an aura of casual, landed wealth that I had always associated with the aristocratic Old South. "It's nice to have you here," he said. "What brings you our way? Do you still have an interest in that filly of B.B.'s?"

"No, I came out on my own, but I love that filly and I'd like to see her," I said. "Anyway, I've never been to the horse country before, so I thought I'd take a week off and look around."

"Well, let me be your guide," he said, turning to Virginia. "I'll be back in an hour or so. Now, Mr. Anderson, let me give you a quick tour, then I expect you'd like to see my breeding operation. Ten o'clock, I believe."

We hurried through the drizzle outside and into Baldwin's green Jaguar sedan, in which he proceeded to drive me slowly around the farm, past rows of stables and pastures full of mares with foals by their sides and fenced enclosures containing yearlings, much the same sights I'd been looking at ever since my arrival. The farm, however, was one of the loveliest I'd seen, rambling over gently rolling hills and crisscrossed by streams; the structures were immaculately maintained. "If there is a life after death," I told him, as we headed for the breeding shed, "I guess this is where I'd like to come."

"I gather you're from the city," he said.

"Yeah, essentially just a sidewalk dude, originally from New York."

"How did you get into the horse business?"

"I'm not really in it," I explained. "I've been helping Charlie out on a temporary basis. I got interested in horses because I like to bet on them."

He laughed. "I presume you don't make a living at it."

"I wouldn't want to have to," I said. "It's a tough racket, but I do okay. It's given me a lot of pleasure and I love the game."

"So do I," he said. "I grew up in it, as I guess you know. I've never wanted to do anything else from the time my daddy put me up on my first pony."

He parked in front of the breeding shed, a one-story building as big as a barn, with rows of stalls for the stallions and a large circular area for the breeding activity itself. The place was spotless, scrubbed clean and hosed down. I had very little time to take in details, because, as we entered, a gray stud, obviously Promoter, with a penis as large as a club, was being guided toward a waiting mare. With a start I recognized Mad Margaret. She was obviously not happy, but had been rendered helpless. Her left front leg had been lifted clear of the floor by a harness and her head was being held in place by a clamp around her upper lip. She was wild-eyed and washy, as eager to be made love to as a sorority virgin about to be assaulted by a gang of drunken frat boys. I felt I was about to witness a rape.

Which was pretty much what it amounted to. The stallion rose up on his hind legs and thrust into her. He never would have made it if Maggie hadn't been practically immobilized and two men on either side of him hadn't forcibly guided his penis into her vagina. The act was accompanied by much stamping and neighing and snorting and was absolutely devoid of delicacy. It was all over in a matter of a few minutes, after which Mr. Wonderful was led away, back toward his quarters, and Maggie was released from her bondage and calmed, before being led off in her turn toward a waiting van. "It went just fine," one of the five men in attendance said to Baldwin. "It was her first time, so she was a handful."

"It'll be easier next year," Baldwin told me. "They learn what it's all about."

"Does it get a little more gracious?" I asked. "I didn't expect candlelight and soft music, but there wasn't even foreplay."

Baldwin laughed. "Not much time for that," he said.

"Where's Algonquin?" I asked.

"He's back here. Come on, I'll show you. Lawlor?"

"Yes, sir," one of the men answered. He was a short, muscular black dressed in a white jumpsuit and rubber boots.

"Is Algonquin back there?"

"Yes, sir," Lawlor said. "He's got a Jonabel mare to cover at eleven."

"Mr. Anderson would like to see him."

"Sure thing. This way, sir."

Lawlor led us back toward the stalls, about half of them occupied by the Clarendon stock. The others, I was told, were in their outside pens. At the very end of the aisle, in the biggest corner enclosure, I suddenly came upon Algonquin.

You don't have to know much about racehorses to recognize greatness. I had never actually seen Algonquin run in the flesh, only on television screens, but I remembered him vividly. He was a huge dark bay who ran like an express train, not quick or agile, but simply overpowering. Once he got into gear, he'd charge down the lane in one awesome, overwhelming move. Because of his size, he had never run as a two-year-old and at three he had not competed in the Triple Crown races, because it had been late spring before he was ready to make his debut. He had lost his first race, a sprint, by a length, then had been immediately stretched out to a mile and had broken his maiden by eight. He'd won every race he competed in later that year, including the Travers at Saratoga, then had gone on at four to win three more before losing the Jockey Club Gold Cup at Belmont. In that one he'd fallen to his knees when the gate opened and had still managed to pick himself up and run fourth. He won twice more before breaking down, with a pulled suspensory in a workout. He'd ended his racing career with eight victories in ten starts. If he'd stayed sound, there's little doubt that he'd have become one of the immortals, another Secretariat or Seattle Slew.

As a stallion, however, he had eclipsed his record as a runner and established himself as the most successful American sire since Alydar. And he looked it. He was a mass of gleaming muscle, several hundred pounds heavier than when he'd been on the track, and looked as serene as a Greek statue. He stood quietly at the back of his stall, eyeing me with only mild curiosity. "Wow," I said, "he looks unbelievable."

"Yeah, he's doin' good," Lawlor said. "He's coverin' sixty mares this spring."

"That's a lot, isn't it?" I asked, glancing back at Baldwin.

He shrugged. "There's a big demand for him," he said. "We accommodated as many as we can, the market being what it is."

"How is the horse business these days?" I asked.

"It could be worse," Baldwin said. "But if it weren't for Algonquin, we'd have to close up shop."

I looked around. "Really?"

"No, just kidding, of course," Baldwin said, but he wasn't smiling.

The big, red-haired woman turned into her garage, sat in her car until the security gate slid safely shut behind her, then stepped out, locked the car door and headed for the elevator. The man waiting for her appeared out of the shadows where he had been hiding and walked up to her. She wasn't overly surprised to see him, or perhaps he had already pulled a gun or a knife on her. Whatever the case, no one in the building heard an outcry or even loud talk of any kind. They went upstairs together. It was well after midnight, probably closer to one o'clock, and she had just come home from the phone and escort service where she worked, an old Hollywood bungalow just off Santa Monica Boulevard.

She lived on the top floor of the four-story building, a large apartment complex in West L.A., one of many in the area. She had been there less than three months and had no friends on the premises, only the sort of acquaintances one makes around a swimming pool. Several of the men who lived there had noticed her and one, a young lawyer for an insurance company, had asked her for a date. She had turned him down and he had not asked her a second time. "She had a great body and she seemed okay," he said later, "but she looked kind of cheap and I thought she might be a working girl."

She and the man who picked her up in the garage had gone into her apartment. What happened once they got inside, whether he immediately attacked her or later, after some sort of disagreement, was still open to conjecture. The police report seemed to favor the former, if only because there was no sign of a struggle. He made her undress, after which he tied her wrists to her ankles and raped her. It's possible, of course, that she consented to the initial sex acts; she was, as the young lawyer had suspected, a prostitute, but her boyfriend and pimp, a black man named Spider Landon, claimed that she had given up most of her live customers to specialize in phone sex, at which she was reportedly a virtuoso. She had only recently gone out with no more than half a dozen major clients, well-heeled middle-aged males willing to pay up to a thousand dollars for a date. The police were tracing phone calls made to her recently, hoping to track down the names of the men she might have dated. Spider Landon had informed investigators that she had had an appointment book, which she carried in her purse, but it was missing. No one at the house in Hollywood had kept a record of the calls made to her, nor had she ever mentioned the names of any of her clients. They were reportedly all foreigners, businessmen visiting the States. The police were, of course, checking phone company records and trying to track them down.

The attacker must have spent a long time with her. Her body was covered with bruises, burns, and small cuts. Her nipples had been pierced with pins and she had been sodomized with a hard object, perhaps a gun barrel. At the end, with her wrists still bound to her ankles, he had dragged her or carried her into the bathroom, slit her throat with a razor or a very sharp knife, and dumped her into the shower stall to bleed to death.

Her body had been found two days later, when her boyfriend had come looking for her. He had fled in a panic without notifying the police, but had called the escort and phone service and talked to one of the girls there. It was she who had called the cops. The story made the late news and the newspapers, leading immediately to speculation that a new serial killer might be on the loose, but the police report stated that no similar killings had occurred in the area within the past year or so. The best scenario seemed to indicate that she had run afoul of a sadistic customer, probably a foreigner.

It was Jay who filled me in on the story. I called him the evening after my visit to Clarendon, because I had heard from May earlier that Charlie was planning to run one of Abel Green's old claimers in a race the next day. He was expected to win and I wanted to get a bet down on him. I didn't understand at first why Jay was telling me about the murder. "Don't you remember, Shifty? I think it's the woman we saw that night in the Chinese restaurant," he said, "when you went over and almost got into a fight with that guy she came in with. Wasn't her name Verna?"

"I think so. Jesus!"

"This woman's name was Verna, Verna Under-something," Jay said. "Anyway, it struck me, because it's an unusual name. Who was that guy she was with? Could he have done it?"

"I don't know, Jay. Maybe."

"Whoever did it is some kind of monster. You know what else he did to her?"

"What?"

"He broke her fingers, all of them, one by one. Can you imagine?"

• • •

"You're a magician," Maddison Baldwin said, as I entered the house. "Can you make my husband's business friends disappear?"

"Not right away," I answered. "Maybe later."

She was a tall, slender woman, blond, with a good figure and a deep tan, but also a slightly ravaged look, either from too much alcohol or too many disappointments, or perhaps a combination of the two. I had the impression of a restless, angry animal in a cage and I instantly decided to be wary of her. "Come on in," she said. "Let me introduce you to Roger's little friends."

She led me past a formal dining room, where two black uniformed maids were laying out a lavish buffet supper, and a library, packed from floor to ceiling with books, then into the living room. Roger Baldwin came over from the bar, where he was mixing drinks for his guests, and greeted me warmly. "I'm so glad you could come," he said. "I should have thought of inviting you yesterday, when we met. Just a gathering of friends, you see. It was Maddie who reminded me I was being a poor host. I was afraid you might have left already."

"I'm going tomorrow morning," I said. "I'm heading for Louisville for a couple of days."

"Whatever for?" Maddie asked. "It's a horrible place."

"I've never been to Churchill Downs," I explained. "I figure that as a dedicated horseplayer I owe it to myself."

"It does have a great tradition," Baldwin said. "You should come to a Kentucky Derby sometime."

"I loathe that place, especially on Derby day," Maddie said. "You can't even take a pee."

"Maddie, really," her husband objected, forcing a smile.

"Well, it's true, Roger," she said. "You big boys just open your pants and let fly anywhere, but the rest of us have to stand in line for hours. I can't even have a drink there, for God's sake."

"Maddie, introduce Lou around, please."

"Why not? Whom haven't you met?" she asked.

"Just about everyone."

"Of course. Come on, then." She took my hand, curling her fingers into mine.

"What can I get you?" Baldwin asked.

"Bourbon, with a splash of soda."

"A barbarous drink," Maddie Baldwin said, "but it suits the locals. Come meet the barbarians."

"You're not from Kentucky, then?"

"God, no. Can't you tell? I weigh under three hundred pounds. No, darling, I'm from Virginia." She turned to address the room at large. "Quiet, everybody!" she barked. "I want you to meet our new friend from California, Mr. Lou Anderson. I'm told he's quite a magician." She looked at me quizzically. "You *are* a magician, aren't you?"

"Yes, when I'm not at the track."

"Mr. Anderson works for my husband in Los Angeles," she continued, inaccurately, "which must be a bit like working in a snake pit."

There were ten or twelve other guests, mostly middle-aged couples, all obviously horse people. They talked almost exclusively about the business and were no more interesting about it than bankers or dentists or, I suppose, magicians are about their own occupations. Put people from the same profession all together into one room and inevitably they talk shop. Among them was Phil Hardin, a lean, angular man with long arms and big hands like those of a cowboy. I never saw him smile, but once, as he brushed past Maddie Baldwin on his way to a bathroom, he jumped. I realized with a start that she had just goosed him. After he'd moved away, she put her head back and laughed, but it had the harsh sound of anger in it, as if she'd made an idiotic bet or a stupid prediction and lost.

Half an hour or so after my arrival, we drifted into the dining room and loaded up our plates from the buffet. I managed to get in line behind Phil Hardin and, as I reached over for a piece of corn on the cob, I said, "Phil, what do you make of all this wild betting going on?"

"What kind of betting?"

"All this action on the Clarendon horses."

"You said 'wild betting'?"

"Yes, I did."

"What do you mean by that?"

I told him. "That doesn't happen here?" I asked, when I'd finished.

"No, or anywhere else. Have you told Roger?"

"Not yet."

"Every Clarendon horse, you say?"

"That's right. I've never seen anything like it."

"There must be some guy around with a screw loose."

"It's an awful lot of money for one person to be shoving into the tote," I pointed out. "I'm talking tens of thousands of dollars at a pop."

"That much?"

"Yes. It's not even smart money. It's too obvious and too clumsy. Charlie's worried about it. He thinks there might be an investigation."

"On what grounds?"

"The same grounds they must have used in New York a few years ago, when so many trainers were obviously cheating, using elephant juice and other drugs," I said. "Remember? When horses claimed by certain trainers suddenly improved ten lengths overnight? Of course it didn't stop the practice, but it slowed it up some."

Hardin didn't answer, nor did he make any further effort to talk to me. We carried our plates of food and glasses of wine back into the living room, but he waited until I sat down, then settled himself in a corner safely across the room from me. I found myself in a group of breeders and their wives, who pretty much ignored me and spent most of the time talking about prices at the most recent yearling sales. It wasn't until dessert and coffee that anybody paid any attention to me and then only because Maddie Baldwin suddenly went to the center of the room and clapped her hands loudly to shut her guests up. "You folks may not know it, but we have with us this evening a very famous magician," she said, slurring her words a bit. I glanced at her husband; he was standing by the bar next to Hardin, a bemused smile on his face. "So here is Mr. Magic himself," Maddie Baldwin concluded and sat down abruptly on a corner of the sofa.

I hadn't known exactly what to expect from this gathering, to which I'd been invited by Baldwin as a casual afterthought, and I had wondered all evening how he had found out about me and my profession, but I was prepared. No self-respecting closeup artist ever goes anywhere without at least a pack of cards in his pockets. So now I stood up, pretending to a degree of modest confusion, and walked uncertainly to the center of the room. "Well, I don't know about magic," I said. "Let me see what I've got in here."

I reached into my side pockets and made a pretence of groping in them. "I can't seem to find anything," I said. "Oh, what's this?" I pulled out a card fan in my right hand, looked at it in amazement, then dropped it on a coffee table. "That's not it," I said, as another fan appeared in my left hand. "Damn," I said, dropping that one, too, as somebody giggled.

For the next three minutes, looking ever more confused, I proceeded to pull perfectly arranged card fans out of my pockets and throw them away. Then, suddenly, I lit up and exclaimed, "Ah, at last!" I came up with two shiny silver dollars and showed them to the room at large. "This is what I was looking for," I said, holding them out, one in each hand. "Now let's see what happens." I closed my fists over the coins, held my hands out toward the room and asked, "Okay, now where are they?"

No one answered. I opened my hands to reveal that the two dollars were both in my left hand. I pretended to be surprised. "How did that happen? I guess I'd better start over." I again made a couple of fists and passed the coins from left to right. I looked dismayed. "That's not right," I said. Two more closed fists, but this time the coins vanished. I was annoyed. "What was that all about?" I clapped my hands to my side pockets. "Oh, oh. Maddie?" I asked. "Would you be so kind as to look in my jacket pockets and see what's in there?"

She came up behind me, pressed in close and reached both hands into my jacket pockets, where she found the silver dollars and showed them to her guests. They laughed and several of them applauded. I turned, smiling, toward Maddie just as she dropped both coins down the front of her dress. "Now how will you find them?" she said, with one of those hard laughs of hers.

"I have no idea," I admitted. "That's not magic. That's paid sex, which is something quite different."

The smile froze on her face. She reached into her bosom and flung the coins on the floor. "What do you think I am?" she snapped. "Another Croatian bitch who performs for money?" She whirled around, clearly intending to leave the room, but the swiftness of the move made her dizzy and she almost fell. Phil Hardin caught her; then, with his arm around her waist, he led her from the room.

"I'm sorry," I said. "I didn't mean to offend."

Roger Baldwin looked grim, his eyes following Hardin and his wife as they left the room. "It's quite all right," he said calmly.

"My wife has had a little too much to drink. My apologies, Lou. That was a splendid performance, really."

The evening broke up quickly after that. I lingered until I found myself the last to go, alone for a moment in the front hallway with Baldwin. Neither Maddie nor Hardin had reappeared, but we had all tactfully chosen to ignore their absence. "Thanks for a great dinner," I said. "Again, my apologies to your wife."

"Nothing to apologize for, Anderson," Baldwin said. "Very nice of you to come."

At the door, I turned back for a moment. "Do you have a man who works for you named Ted something or other?"

Baldwin looked puzzled for an instant, his eyes wavering, as if he were anxious to get back inside the house, perhaps to find his wife and trainer. "Ted? No, I don't—oh, *Ted*," he said, turning back to look at me. "You must mean Ted Mendoza. A short, swarthy fellow?"

"Yeah. He's about forty or so, lots of hair all over, very bulky."

"Yes, that's Mendoza. No, he works for Gene Aramis. Why?"

"Just curious. I see him around a lot. I was just wondering who he is."

"Ah, yes, well. Good night, Lou."

He shut the door on me before I could ask him anything else.

12 / Family

LOUISVILLE IS A GRACELESS TOWN. It is ringed by freeways and partly cut off from its waterfront along the Ohio River. Like so many American cities, its inner core has been decimated by the flight of the affluent, largely white middle class to the suburbs, leaving behind a wasteland of office buildings, parking lots, and rundown residential areas soon to become bona fide slums. I took one look at the city in a quick swing through the heart of it and checked into a motel near the airport, only a few miles from the racetrack. My room was dismal, but had a comfortable king-size bed and anyway I had no plans to spend much time in it. A few minutes after checking in and dumping my two bags inside the door, I was on my way to the track.

My first sight of the twin spires of Churchill Downs, arising out of a sea of junky one-story family homes, had the same effect on me as my initial view, during my only trip to Europe, of the cathedral at Chartres, in France, a Gothic marvel that ennobled its humdrum surroundings. And, as at Chartres, the minute I stepped inside the premises, the cares and troubles of the outside world faded from my consciousness; I was in a sanctuary, in touch with immortality and feasting my eyes on beauty. Playing the horses is a religion like any other, but has an added advantage over most of them. It produces for its true believers tangible rewards; the virtuous and the scholarly benefit, while the ignorant, the greedy, the cruel, and the dogmatists perish, drowned in seas of losing tickets. I'd swap what I know of paradise, at least as envisioned by the fanatics of every creed I've ever heard of, for an eternity of afternoons at a well-run hippodrome.

I spent the first hour at Churchill just looking around, strolling past the paddock, then up into the cavernous grandstand and clubhouse. The dominant color motif was green and white and the ornate architecture had a Victorian feel enhanced by a ground-floor pavement of red bricks. Inside the Kentucky Derby Museum, I passed a pleasurable half hour watching a slide show, with brilliant sound effects, detailing the history of the Derby, during which I had a chance to glimpse the Clarendon colors, twice winners of the race. I also came upon a still photo of Algonquin, galloping all alone toward the finish line in the Travers. He hadn't won the Derby, but as Kentucky's leading sire the big black horse obviously merited local recognition.

At about twenty minutes to post time, I went back to the paddock to look at the entries in the first, a sprint for cheap claimers. I didn't know the local horses and I had no intention of risking any serious money on them. I was planning merely to enjoy the scenery and bask in the atmosphere, but no sooner had I taken up a post by the rail than I spotted J. B. Tender. He was standing in a group of several other heavyset, red-faced men, who looked as if they spent a considerable portion of every day scraping manure from their boots. I strolled toward them and J.B. immediately spotted me. "Hey, Lou, how are you doin'? Come on over here," he said, then introduced me to his friends. "You boys know Charlie Pickard. Lou works for him."

The boys all nodded and mumbled greetings and shook my hand. They all either knew Charlie or knew about him and so I was immediately accepted, although I don't think any of them mistook me for a horseman. "So how was West Virginia?" I asked.

"Aw, same old stuff," J.B. said. "Most miserable bunch of scrawny, crooked-legged little old yearlings I ever seen, but what the hell, a dollar's a dollar. We broke every one of 'em, took our money, and got out. I got a couple of days off, so I ran on over here to have a little fun. You by yourself?"

"Yeah, just looking around."

He took my arm and pulled me aside. "Hogan over here owns the four horse in this race," he said. "Go make a bet on him. He's gonna run good." I started to reach for my *Racing Form.* "Don't look at that sheet," he said. "The horse ain't won in six months, but Hogan's got him cranked up today. He's gonna pop. Go put somethin' on him. I wouldn't bet the family jewels."

"You're going to bet on him?"

"Already done it. Go on now, the horses are leavin' the paddock," he said. "We'll meet up by the bar, second floor of the clubhouse, or in Hogan's box." And he gave me the number.

I left him and headed for the clubhouse without looking at my *Form.* On the escalator, however, I turned to the race and decided that Hogan's horse, a seven-year-old gelding named Strunk, had no chance. In his last four races, against the same sort of company, he had run no better than fifth in slow time and he showed no works. He had been one of the horses I had quickly eliminated as a possible contender. I decided not to bet on him at all, even though he was seventeen to one on the board and ordinarily the only time I ever even consider listening to information is when the animal being touted is at least ten to one. Who needs tips on favorites?

I went outside and watched the race alone, because I didn't want to feel like a fool in case the horse did win. When the gate opened, Strunk, a compact gray running in front bandages, popped out of his stall like a jackrabbit and opened up two lengths. On the turn he widened it to four. I was beginning to regret my caution, when I noticed he'd begun to shorten stride at the head of the stretch. By the eighth pole he was switching his tail wildly about like a flag, a clear indication that he wanted to quit, and in the last few yards he was caught and passed by two closers. He finished a well-beaten third.

J.B., Hogan, and the boys didn't seem at all dismayed when I rejoined them at the bar. "Hell, he run good, Hogan, and you picked up a piece of the purse," J.B. said. "Ain't nothin' wrong with that for a sore-legged old hard knocker, is there?"

"He don't run good today," Hogan said, "he was goin' to the killer."

J.B. looked at me. "You didn't bet too much on him, did you, Lou?"

"Only a couple of dollars," I said. "I thought he'd win it. Where'd he get all that speed?"

"Aw, he's got speed," J.B. said, "only he don't use it too often, if you know what I'm sayin'. With these old cripples you can only pop 'em a couple of times every few months and try to make a hit, otherwise you got to turn 'em over to the killer."

"For pet food?"

"It's a cruel business sometimes, Lou. You know, you been around a while. At the end of the road, the killer's always waitin'."

I wanted to tell J.B. that in California, with its bigger purses and high-quality racing, the kind of obvious maneuver his friend Hogan had just tried to engineer was harder to get away with. You pull that stuff too often and the stewards would haul you in for a little chat at which they might want you to explain just how it was that a horse that had shown no speed for six months and no workouts could suddenly run like a cheetah, even though it didn't win. I kept quiet, but I decided that in Kentucky, where these good old boys were in residence and had a firm grip on the game, I'd content myself with betting only on the better animals, the ones in allowance and stakes races.

The rest of the afternoon passed pleasantly enough and I even cashed a couple of tickets, providing myself with a modest profit. The eye-opener was a race for maiden two-year-olds in which J.B. and his friends made a small killing, betting heavily on an unraced colt with modest breeding credentials and routine works. The animal was backed down from a morning line of eight to one in a field of ten to go off as the favorite, at four to five. He won by six, well in hand, as the horsemen say, meaning that he hadn't had to extend himself. I had, of course, not bet, since it's against my religion, as I explained to J.B., to risk large sums on anything at less than two to one, especially on an animal I knew nothing about. "You know what we told you," J.B. said. "You don't want to pay no mind to them numbers in that paper. Clockers ain't paid enough in this state to be honest, especially on these two-year-olds."

I smiled and congratulated them, but I was secretly proud of myself for not having gone along. These old boys had invented their particular version of the sport and they weren't about to let it get away from them. But the game was changing drastically and it was leaving them behind. I thought of Jay Fox, back in L.A., handicapping expertly off his numbers and statistics and I knew that that was where the truth ultimately resided. "You can't beat every race," Jay liked to say, "but you can beat the races." I couldn't explain that to J.B. and these hardboots, who lived at the track to put over their little coups, but in my book they were as extinct as the dodo bird.

Toward the end of the day, as we stood at the clubhouse bar, toasting our success in beer, I told J.B. about my evening at Clarendon and about the episode with Maddie Baldwin. "Oh, Maddie, that gal sure likes her liquor," he said. "She probably started boozin' at breakfast. She can hold it pretty good, but sometimes it gets out of control and then things happen."

"She and Hardin having an affair?"

J.B. laughed. "That what you call it? Aw, she and Phil been foolin' around for years, but he ain't the only one," he explained. "Maddie's got hot pants. There was a time a while back she was playin' the field. Old Hogan over here, he nailed her a couple of times. I never did, but I guess I could have, if I'd have wanted my wife to shoot me, which she sure as hell would have done. No, Maddie's been quite a story for a long time now. She was one good-lookin' woman when she and Roger got married twenty years ago, but I don't think she wasted any time bein' faithful to him."

"Why does he put up with it?"

J.B. scratched his head and looked thoughtful. "Well, I'll tell you," he said, "I guess it has somethin' to do with old Stormy Joe, his dad. He was a great horseman, but not so good as a father. I mean, that old boy was tough and he had some kind of temper. He was a hillbilly, one of the few who came out of them mountains to amount to anythin'. He started as a gypsy, takin' horses all over the circuit, breedin' and racin', and he done pretty good. Then he married this gal Marge Busby from Lexington, who had a farm and a little money. And old Joe just took off from there. He didn't have much schoolin', but he was one smart old boy. Seems like everythin' he did just turned to money. Ten years after he started Clarendon, which he named after some schoolteacher who was good to him when he was in high school, he won his first Derby. And I'm tellin' you, there was no stoppin' him after that. He made that farm a showplace and he bred and raced nothin' but winners. He never got real big, like Calumet or Greentree or any of them other big outfits, but horse for horse he had the best operation goin'.".

"It must have been tough on Roger, growing up with a hugely successful father like that," I observed. "Sort of like being the son of Giuseppe Verdi and wanting to be a composer."

"Who?"

"Never mind, J.B. So what about Roger?"

"It was okay so long as his mamma was alive," J.B. continued. "Marge was pretty tough herself and she had a lot of class, which Joe didn't. She sent the boy off to good schools in the East and all that and she kind of acted like a wall between Roger and old Joe. Roger was the youngest, see, and he was born pretty late, kind of by accident. Betty Ruth, his sister, she was ten years older, and she and old Joe didn't get along good, but it didn't matter much, on account of she was a girl and Joe didn't give a shit about no girl. So she kind of stayed clear of him and had nothin' to do with the horses or nothin' about the farm. She loved art. She went off to Paris, France, to study art and all and then she stayed there for a number of years. Never got married or nothin'. Fact is, there was some talk about her not likin' men, if you know what I mean."

"I guess I do. So why didn't she stay in France? Why come back here?"

J.B. shrugged. "I don't know," he said. "She come back after Joe died. I guess it was to get the estate settled and all. And she stayed. She does a lot of charity work and she's head of the art museum and real active in culture and shit like that. She lives by herself. I guess she always has. She's homely as sin. She was pretty tough about the money with Roger. They never got along too good either."

"So when did Marge die?"

"Oh, a long time ago," J.B. said. "That was when the trouble started between old Joe and Roger. He come out of college and went to work for his dad, but Joe treated him always like he didn't know what he was doin', didn't give him no responsibility or nothin'. He used to dump on him in public, tell everybody what a fool and a sissy his son was, made fun of his accent and his eastern ways. It was embarrassin' sometimes. About three years before the old man died, Roger left and started up a farm of his own, only he didn't have no money. That was when Joe wrote him out of the will and made Betty Ruth his heir. But that didn't last neither, on account of Betty Ruth wouldn't have nothin' to do with the business. I guess what saved Roger was when he started seein' Maddie. He met her at some kind of society event in Lexington when she was in town and he fell crazy in love with her. He couldn't make a go of his farm, so it was said that Maddie helped him patch it up with the old man. Roger sold his place and went back to Clarendon. That was about a year or so before old Joe died. He wasn't no easier on Roger, but Maddie knew how to handle him. She teased him and joked with him, buttered him up and all, and he just loved her to death. He called her his golden girl, Goldie, for short. He even started treatin' his son like a human bein' and the story was, he was rewritin' his will again when he died."

"Suddenly?"

"Just like that," J.B. said. "One moment he was ridin' his horse around the property and the next he was dead on the ground. Heart attack, they said it was. That's the way to go, ain't it? Out like a light doin' what you love to do."

"So after his death, Roger and Betty Ruth got together and settled the estate," I ventured. "Roger got the farm and the horses and she got money."

"Lots of it," J.B. said. "It wasn't settled right away. I mean, there ain't much love lost between them two. I guess it was old Marge kept the family together. After she was gone, what you had was three people who didn't have much in common. And Betty Ruth hated Maddie on sight. They kept the lawyers busy there for a while. You know, even if Roger did want to split from Maddie, he probably couldn't afford to."

"You think that's what keeps them together?"

"That, maybe, and the fact that Roger's kind of soft."

"Weak, you mean?"

"Well, he ain't Stormy Joe, that's for sure."

"Are you ever going to work again?" were Happy Hal Mancuso's first words to me, when I returned the phone call I found waiting for me at my motel.

"Hello, Hal, how are you?" I said. "It's nice to hear your cheery voice."

"Don't give me that shit. I've had a hell of a day."

"I'm sorry to hear it."

"No, you're not, you lousy degenerate," he said. "I've been in court all day trying to bail out one of my other clients and then I got to chase all the way to fucking Kentucky to find you. So don't give me any of that 'I'm sorry' shit."

"What are you doing in court?"

"I got a diseased ventriloquist with a penchant for flashing."

"Women?"

"What else? He runs down San Vicente Boulevard in Santa Monica in his raincoat and when he sees some jogger he likes he runs up to her and opens his coat. So they arrested him and I got to bail him out."

"Is he a good ventriloquist?"

"Yeah, why?"

"Maybe you can get the dummy to take the rap."

"Very funny. Jokes I need now. As if my whole day isn't a joke. My life is a joke. And then, when I'm leaving the courthouse, some asshole says to me, 'Have a nice day.' Can you beat that? What the fuck business is it of his whether I have a nice day or not!"

"Hal, what's going on?"

"I just told you."

"Why did you call?"

"Oh, that. You mean you really want to work again?"

"I have been working."

"Don't give me that shit. I know what you've been doing. It's sickening."

"Hal—"

"Okay, okay, okay. I got a Vegas gig for you, but you aren't going to like it."

"Why not?"

"Because it's in August, the first two weeks. You'll miss some of Del Mar."

"I'm listening, Hal."

"Sure you are. Okay, it's two weeks at the Nirvana, in the lounge. It's a small stage, intimate room, seats maybe two hundred. You do twenty, twenty-five minutes, three shows a night, fifteen hundred bucks. It's a living."

"What's the Nirvana?"

"A new hotel, small, big emphasis on family holidays, so no smut or off-color stuff, no naked girls, big sports program. You play golf?"

"No."

"Too bad. They got a nice nine-hole course, big pool, tennis courts. Hey, it could be worse."

"Okay, book me."

"You're kidding! What about Del Mar? I thought you never worked during Del Mar. You rotten degenerate!"

"I'm ready," I said. "I think Charlie will be back full-time in a couple of weeks and I'll be through. I've had enough of horses for a while."

"What? What did you just say? Are you running a temperature? Did I hear you wrong?"

I ignored the sarcasm. "I presume room and board are included," I said.

"Of course. What kind of an agent do you think I am?"

"You're a sweet and sensible soul, Hal, and I love you."

"I just threw up on my shoes. Good-bye."

Betty Ruth Baldwin was sitting behind a fifteenth-century French escritoire when I was ushered into her presence. Everything in her office, I soon realized, was an antique and precious. The walls were decorated with framed caricatures and cartoons that looked vaguely familiar, but which I couldn't place. Betty Ruth herself would have looked at home in them; she was a big, stocky woman, with a lantern jaw not unlike her brother's and a broad forehead. Her hair was gray and cropped short, she wore no makeup, and her clothes were what country people call sensible—flat-soled brown walking shoes, a brown skirt, a green silk blouse pinned together at the neck by a cameo brooch, and a square-cut brown jacket. She wore a single strand of pearls around her neck and no earrings. Not even a handsome woman, but she gave an impression of quiet strength. She stood up when I came in and shook my hand firmly. "Sit down, Mr. Anderson," she said. "Would you like some coffee?"

"No, thanks," I said, my eyes scanning her walls. "I feel as if I've stepped back in time."

"Ah, yes, he's one of my favorite artists," she said, "a fine painter as well as a caricaturist. Merciless about bourgeois society. We don't have anyone like him today."

"Maybe Conrad. Do you ever see the *L.A. Times?*"

"Rarely, but I know his work. It's very fine, but heavily political."

I gestured at her walls. "And this man . . ."

"Daumier," she said, coming to my rescue. "He portrayed the society of his time in a less direct manner. I love the genre artists, you know. Is that what you came to talk about?"

"In a very general way," I said. "I'm profiling a number of people in the smaller cities and towns who are active in museum work and the arts in general."

"Ah, and what magazine are you with?"

"Travel and Leisure," I lied.

"Good, we need a little publicity these days, with public funds for the arts drying up everywhere," she said. "What would you like to know? I'd be happy if we talked more about the museum and less about me."

I produced a pad and took notes, mostly about her early involvement in the arts and her years in Paris, then her return to Louisville and her indefatigable championing of the arts in her hometown. "Basketball and horse racing, you know, that's mainly what this town has always been interested in," she said. "I've tried to make a difference. It hasn't been easy, but we've made a little headway. Have you seen the collection?"

"Not yet," I admitted. "I'm planning to, as soon as we finish here."

"I'll arrange to have one of our able volunteer docents show you around. How long will you be here?"

"Till tomorrow."

"Fine." She started to reach for the phone.

"I wanted to ask you a little bit about your background," I said. "You mentioned horse racing. Wasn't your family deeply involved in it?"

"Oh, yes, my father founded Clarendon. But I've never been interested in that at all. My brother runs that now."

"Ah, I see. So you've never been involved with horses?"

"Well, the money comes from the success of the farm," she said, "so you could put it that I was able to accomplish what I have because of it. But otherwise, no."

"And is your brother involved in the arts as well?"

"Not at all," she said. "He has his hands full with the farm."

"I hear it's not going very well," I ventured. "I think there was a story in the *L.A. Times* a while back about some financing difficulties. That doesn't affect you?"

"No, thank God," she said. "I separated myself from it years ago. I decided to let Roger have it, knowing perfectly well that he would make a mess of it. When was this story you mention?"

"A few weeks ago, I think," I said. "I remember reading about it. Something about bank loans, overseas investments, and so on. Mostly speculation, I guess."

"Oh, there's probably some truth to it. Roger's never been a good businessman. And he and my father never got along. I think Roger's ruined his life by trying to prove himself to his father. First when he was alive and now to his ghost. It's sad. I don't want to talk about it."

"No, of course not." I stood up. "Thank you very much for your time." I started to leave.

"You don't want to see the collection?" she asked.

I turned back. "Of course. I'm sorry."

Again she started to pick up the phone, then thought better of it. "Who are you?" she asked instead.

"Who am I?"

"You're not a reporter," she said. "Who are you? What are you? Why did you come here?"

"You're a very smart woman," I said.

"You really came to ask me about my brother, didn't you?"

"Yes."

"He's in a lot of trouble, isn't he?"

"I don't know. I thought you might."

"What are you, a private detective? Whom do you work for?"

"May I sit down again?"

"No. Tell me who you are and what you want."

I told her in some detail who I was and what I was doing there. "Charlie's worried about it," I concluded. "I have no deep interest in this except that I'm a friend of Charlie's and I've been working for him while he's recovering from his surgery. I guess I owe you an apology, but I figured you wouldn't want to see me, if I told you why."

"You're right." She paused, as if weighing whether to tell me anything or throw me out. "I don't want to talk much about it," she said at last, looking away from me out the window toward the office building across the street. "My father was a very difficult, tyrannical man and I didn't get along with him either. The difference is, I got away from him and made a life for myself and Roger didn't. I'm sorry for him, but I can't help him. We were never close and I was away in Paris during his teenage years. Then we had a fight over the inheritance and that pretty much soured us permanently on each other." She laughed, but there was no humor or warmth in it. Then she turned back to look at me very directly. "I'm not going to talk about this anymore. It's ancient history now. My father was what he was and Roger's a big boy. All I will tell you is this: Roger's involved with an overseas bank of some sort. It has an Italian or Spanish name, Banco or Banca del something or other. It has an office in New York and, I think, Las Vegas, of all places. That's all I know, Mr. Anderson."

"There's a man named Gene Aramis. Ever heard of him?"

"Blond fellow, with an appalling Yugoslavian girlfriend. Yes, I met him at the Derby. Roger introduced him to me."

"Oh, so you do go to the races."

"The Kentucky Derby, once a year," she said. "Everyone goes to the Derby, Mr. Anderson. The museum has a box, it's a tradition. Roger and I don't see each other, but we're cordial. No reason not to be, especially in public. This man Aramis was with him. The girlfriend monopolized everyone's attention."

"I've met her. She's very pretty."

"She's a slut and she's very loud. It tends to attract attention, even at the Derby. Good-bye, Mr. Anderson. I hope things work out. I don't wish my brother any harm. I feel sorry for him."

"Yes, I understand. Thank you." At the door, I turned and looked at her. "By the way, how did you know I wasn't a reporter?"

"You're writing a piece about the arts, you walk into my office, and you obviously don't know who Honoré Daumier is," she said. "Really, Mr. Anderson. I hope you're better at fooling people as a magician."

13 / Heat

TWO DAYS AFTER MY RETURN from Kentucky, Old Roman ran again, this time against winners. He drew the four hole in a field of ten, three of them well-bred animals with credentials to become nice horses. Old Roman was listed as the favorite in the program and once again he was backed down to less than one to two, with money coming in on him in big chunks, as had become usual with the Clarendon horses. None of us bet on him, though he turned out to be a safer investment than most banks. With Wib Clayton up, the colt broke cleanly this time, dueled briefly for the early lead with the other contenders, then spurted away from the field on the turn and came romping home by six lengths, running so willingly and easily that Clayton never had to even tap him with his whip. "I think what we're looking at here is a potential eight-hundred-pound gorilla," Jay Fox informed us after the race. "Pickard must be happy."

"He is," I said. "I think it's making him well."

Charlie was indeed doing much better. He'd put on a couple of pounds, his face had some color in it and he was showing up in the mornings, except on the days he had therapy. He was becoming impatient with that regime, however, and had told Eddie and May he'd be back full-time in another week or so. This suited my plans, because I had to leave for Las Vegas in eight days. "You can go, Shifty," Charlie had told me when I asked him about it. "I'm going to be okay. I sure appreciate your helping out here."

"It was fun," I said, "but I also learned something about myself."

"Yeah, what?"

"I'm not a horseman," I said, "and I'll never be one. I love this game, but it's not where I live."

"Hell, I could have told you that," the trainer said, grinning. "You're a horseplayer."

"It's not a bad thing to be."

"Didn't say it was, Shifty. Without you guys, how would any of us make a living?"

I had given Charlie a full account of my adventures in Kentucky and he had listened intently, smiling a couple of times when I'd talked about J. B. Tender and the other hardboots. "I guess what it all means, Charlie," I concluded, "is that Clarendon is in financial trouble and that some foreign bank this guy Gene Aramis is connected with may be holding liens on the property."

"I guess I can't worry too much about that, can I?" he said. "About all I can do is keep training these horses."

"Somebody's still plunging on them."

"Yeah, that worries me some," Charlie said. "Nobody's asked me nothin' about it, so I'm just going to keep on doing what I'm doing. One thing I don't like is I still got to ride this boy Spencer. He's driving me nuts."

"Is he pulling stuff?"

"No, that ain't it," Charlie said. "He's riding okay, except that one time on Bellringer. It's just that I can't take much more of the Jesus talk."

"You aren't religious, Charlie?"

"If I was, I wouldn't want to go to any heaven filled with Jesus freaks," he said. "I always figured if there was a God, He'd at least have a sense of humor. Although, if you look at the world today, there sure ain't much to laugh about."

"What about Bellringer?" I asked.

"He'll run next week, next to last day of the meet," the trainer said. "I'm going to send him long again and this time the jock better not screw up or I'll kill him."

When I walked out of the track that morning, Abel Green was standing outside Delmonico's stall with Ginger, Angles's ex-girlfriend, hanging on his arm. He was dressed normally for him, in baggy gray slacks and a green-and-white striped sports jacket, and she was in high heels and a miniskirt practically up to her hips. He'd apparently been giving her a tour of his horses and she was hanging on to his arm in what I took to be adoration. "Ah, Shifty, you know my friend Ginger?" he said, slightly ill-at-ease.

"Never had the pleasure," I said.

Ginger and I shook hands. She had a grip like moist flannel. "Nice to meet you," she said. "I've heard a lot about you."

"Really? From whom?"

"Abe told me you're a wonderful magician," she said. "I'd love to see you work."

"Come to Las Vegas next week. I'll be at the Nirvana."

"Is that so?" Abel Green said. "You know, we might do that, Shifty. We've been planning a trip."

Ginger squeezed his arm and snuggled up to him. "Oh, could we, Abe? I've never been to Las Vegas. Could we?"

The two of them together reminded me of one of the Daumiers I'd seen in Betty Ruth Baldwin's office in Louisville, a picture of an aging bourgeois out on the town with dancing girls. I wondered if I should ask him about his wife, but smothered the impulse. It wasn't any of my business and I had to admit that Ginger was a delicious little morsel, especially for a middle-aged capitalist with a roving eye. "Congratulations," I said instead. "I heard Delmonico won last week."

"Too bad you were away," he said. "He paid nine-eighty."

"I know. I called up and got down on him."

"Charlie tell you?"

"No, but I knew about it." I started to move past them toward the end of the shedrow, where May and Clara Wilson were working with the Clarendon two-year-olds. "Nice to see you, Abe. Nice to meet you, Ginger."

"Likewise, I'm sure," she said. "Can we go now, Abe?"

"Sure, honey," he said. "I wanted to show you Stilton. He's around the other side."

"Oh, do we have to, honey?" she said. "There's so much horseshit."

"You shouldn't have worn high heels, sweetheart."

"You didn't tell me, Abe," she said. "How was I supposed to

know? I mean, look at my feet. I'll get an infection." She reached up and kissed him on the cheek. "Please, Abey, can we go now?"

When I last saw them, they were heading back toward the parking lot. They had their arms around each other and his right hand rested on her buttock. "That's the goddamndest thing I've ever seen," Charlie said, watching them go from his tack room doorway. "Millie's going to kill the both of them."

"His wife?"

"Yeah, and she's a tough lady."

"Hasn't he ever fooled around before?"

"Sure, with hookers, mostly. This time the old jerk has fallen for her. Who the hell is she?"

"She's a waitress at Denny's," I said.

"Not anymore, she isn't," Charlie said. "He's set her up in an apartment. He's spending money like water on her."

"Abe? He's a terrible tightwad."

"Was," Charlie said. "It's amazing what women can do to a guy. Haven't you ever noticed, Shifty?"

"I've noticed. I've even participated."

"Yeah. I don't think May missed you much while you were gone."

"No? What makes you think so?"

"You taken her out yet?"

"We're having dinner tonight. What did you mean by that, Charlie?"

"Forget it, Shifty. I was just shooting my mouth off. You know me and women."

I did, but still the remark bothered me. I'd been back three days and though May and I had seen each other around the stable and spent some time in the cafeteria together, she'd put me off every evening until tonight. Would Heloise have put off Abelard after he'd had to make a little journey into the provinces? Would Isolde have asked Tristan to come back another night? I doubted it. My romance was clearly not too hot to cool down, as the song goes.

"What we are having is very good sex," I said, as we lay in bed together that night. "What we are not having is a love affair."

She sat up in bed. "I gotta go pee," she said, bouncing to her feet and scurrying into the bathroom. When she came back, she sat down on the end of the bed and peered at me through the soft light reflecting into the room from the kitchen. It was our love-making light, blurring outlines, softening blemishes, but allowing us to see what we were doing. Her eyes gleamed as she stared at me. "What's the matter, honey?" she asked. "Ain't we makin' good love?"

I sat up too, propping myself against the pillows. "Come on, May," I said. "I thought we had something going, the two of us. I really like you, don't you know that? You're not just some casual lay. What's the matter with you?"

"What am I doin' wrong?" she asked.

"Nothing," I said. "You're not doing anything wrong. Wrong is not what I'm talking about."

"I don't know what you want from me. Ain't we havin' a good time?"

"A good time is not what I'm talking about."

She didn't answer me right away, but sat there very quietly on the end of my bed, looking at me as if she had never quite seen me before. The soft light was kind to her, imparted an almost angelical air to her stillness, making her seem to be a figure in a dream. Her body was lean and muscular, but it was also appealing in a very feminine way, with those long legs and hard little breasts and strong hips. In this light her scar was invisible, as were the small, hard lines at the corners of her eyes and the cynical smirk her mouth sometimes assumed as a defensive shield against life. But she carried other invisible scars of her past around with her and even in her lovemaking there was a note of abandoned desperation, as if she were offering herself up to pleasure as a last resort. It was this quality in her that troubled me and that I blamed for our inability to proceed together beyond mere friendship.

"All right, Shifty," she said at last, "I ain't gonna marry you. I ain't gonna marry nobody."

"Marriage is not what I'm talking about," I said. "Whoever said anything about marriage?"

"Well, honey, you're talkin' about somethin' permanent, ain't you? I mean, what is it with you? You know I can't be here every night. I can't travel with you. I got a life, Shifty."

"What do you want from it, May?" I asked. "Tell me what you want from it."

"I'm gonna do somethin' with it, that's what," she said.

"Clara and I been talkin' a lot since she got here. We're gonna get our trainer's licenses, that's what. And then we're gonna get us some horses of our own."

"I think that's a terrific idea," I said. "It's going to take time."

"I know it. I know it better than you."

"You're going to have to persuade owners to give you their animals," I said. "That isn't going to be easy. Macho is the name of the game in this sport, but you know that."

"I know it and so does Clara. That's why we're in this together. We can help each other."

"Fine. Wonderful. I'll help you all I can."

"You will?"

"Of course. Why wouldn't I? Have you talked to Charlie about it?"

"No, not yet. He don't like women, you know that."

"I think he may surprise you, May. Charlie's the best horseman I know. He respects talent."

"Man talent."

"I'd talk to him, I really would," I said. "What do you have to do to get your license?"

"There's a test," she said. "You go up before a board and answer a lot of questions."

"You can do that."

"I ain't got schoolin', honey, and these good old boys don't like girls, not competin' with 'em."

"So you keep trying," I said. "Where it gets real tough is getting clients."

"Yeah, we know that. But we're goin' for it."

"Good. So what's this got to do with us?"

"Shifty, I ain't got time for more than we got," she said. "You got to live with that."

"Okay," I said, "I'll try. Just don't shut me out."

She moved up the bed toward me. "Shut you out?" she whispered. "I want you in me, honey." She rose above me and descended into my arms and we made love for the second time that night, more elaborately than ever before, with long, absorbing variations. And it was during them that I noticed that she had partially shaved herself, leaving only a tuft of hair above her sex. I was so engrossed in what I was doing with and to her at the time that I didn't mention it until after we had finished and were lying spent in each other's arms. "I did it for you, honey," she said. "You like it?"

"Yes. Want me to shave mine?"

"You serious?"

"No. The itch would drive me crazy."

She laughed and this time it was my turn to get out of bed to pee. When I came back, she was sitting up, her folded arms resting on her knees. "I got one guy might buy us a horse," she said.

"Who's that?"

"Some rich guy, friend of Mr. Baldwin's," she said. "He come around the other day with his girlfriend and spent a lot of time talkin' to me."

"About horses?"

"Yeah. He's got a funny name . . . Armor or somethin'."

"Aramis?"

"Yeah, that's the one."

"He came around to talk to you?"

"No, just to look at the horses, I guess. He asked me a lot about them and she did too, but she's kind of crazy. She's got an accent. She German?"

"Yugoslavian. Croatian, actually."

"Where's that at?"

"Europe."

"Oh. I never heard of it. I'm just ignorant."

"But smart. What exactly did they ask you about?"

"All kinds of stuff about the horses, and then she asked me a lot of questions about me. She like girls?"

"I haven't the faintest idea. I've only met her once. Did she come on to you?"

"Not talkin', but she looked me over pretty good, like a guy would. I never thought about it, but Clara caught it and she ought to know."

"Be careful, May."

"Honey, I ain't gonna have sex with anybody just to get me some horses. No, I think they was serious about maybe gettin' into it. Not him, her. I think he just goes along for the ride, if you know what I mean."

"Did she ask you about training horses for her?"

"Sort of. I got the message over that that's what I'm gonna do and she seemed interested. There was one guy there I didn't cotton to."

"Dark, hairy guy who drives for them? Was he there?"

"Yeah, name of Ted. He kind of stayed separate from 'em, but he sure looked me over good, like I was a piece of meat. He didn't say nothin', but he's not good folks."

"No, he isn't. He's some kind of gunsel."

"A what?"

"Like a bodyguard. Watch yourself, May."

"Honey, I can take care of myself. I been doin' it a long time."

"Are we going to see each other again before I go to Vegas?" I asked her a little later, just before we went to sleep.

"Yeah, maybe," she answered, "but definitely in Vegas. I'll get a couple of days off. We never did have our weekend, did we?"

"No."

"You gonna do good magic, Shifty? For me, huh?"

"That's what the world needs more of."

She went to sleep in my arms. I lay there awake for quite a long time, mainly because I couldn't get the image of Ted Mendoza looking her over out of my head. He scared me too.

The night before I left for Las Vegas, Jay invited the regulars in the box to dinner at Barzini's, an old L.A. restaurant in Westwood that was largely patronized by Hollywood and racetrack people. I'd been there before, but it wasn't one of my regular hangouts, mainly because I thought it was overpriced. The food was decent, featuring mainly pastas and steaks, the drinks were generous and the furnishings comfortable, with lots of big padded booths that could seat up to eight. The main asset was the owner, Russ Barzini, an aging track degenerate who supported his losing betting habits by overcharging his customers. But he was basically a decent guy, loyal to his friends and in love with life. Jay liked the place, because he had often put Barzini onto a winner and he rarely had to pay for a meal there. This time he had included Russ in a Pick Six ticket that had hit for a net profit of nearly eight thousand dollars, of which Jay had retained twenty percent, and the evening had been scheduled as a celebration.

It was crowded, as usual, when we arrived and we had to

stand at the bar for half an hour while waiting for our booth. Barzini, a chunky little man of about sixty with the face of a Calabrian peasant, set off by a single black bushy eyebrow that stretched from temple to temple, plied us with free drinks. Then, when the booth he had reserved for us showed no sign of emptying, he took direct action. It was occupied by a party of four middle-aged, conservatively-dressed couples, almost certainly from out of town, who had been lingering for forty minutes over coffee while paying their check and were showing no inclination to depart. Barzini walked over and informed them that he had a party waiting for their table. Apparently one of the men objected to being rushed and Russ promptly tugged the tablecloth out from under them, sending plates, cups, glasses, and silverware flying. "What the fuck do you think this is," he shouted, "a goddamn bus station?"

A bartender and two of the waiters hurried over to calm the outraged group and move them toward the exit, while Barzini stormed away toward the kitchen, muttering imprecations. Five minutes later, we were ushered grandly toward our seats and a new round of free drinks appeared as soon as we had settled in. "I like that," Arnie commented, raising his glass to toast the occasion. "I wish Russ would run for President. He knows how to clean house."

"Yeah, who needs tourists?" Angles agreed. "I wish he'd clean out the betting lines, where they got people who don't know how to bet. There should be a special window for them, with a trapdoor that opens under them when they take more than two minutes."

Jay was in his element, receiving accolades from nearly everyone in the place, since Barzini had evidently spread the word and had also cut in some of his staff and friends on the action. Everyone had cashed tickets on Jay's selections and the mood was festive. "My only regret," Jay said, "was the horrible ride on Bellringer. If he'd have come in at six to one instead of the favorite, we might have had the only ticket. That would have been worth fifty or sixty thousand."

"Would have, could have, should have," Arnie observed, "the horseplayer's lament."

"He's right, Arnie," Angles said. "That lousy jock stiffed the horse."

For once I had to agree with Angles. I'll probably never forget the look of pure consternation on Charlie Pickard's face after the start of the race that afternoon, when Daryl Spencer, up on Bellringer, had pulled him up out of the gate and cost him five or six lengths before allowing him to run, then rushed him up four wide on the first turn. He had finished sixth, beaten five lengths for all the money.

Charlie hadn't said anything. Together we had gone down to the track to meet the returning horses. When Spencer had come galloping up on Bellringer and dismounted, the jockey had looked ruefully at Charlie and said, "He had his head turned when they opened the gate and I had to steady him. I'm sorry, Mr. Pickard. The good Lord wasn't with us today."

I looked at Charlie. His face was red with anger, but he said nothing, simply turned on his heel and walked away. Spencer looked only mildly distressed. He smiled at me as he headed for the weigh-in scales, his tack in his arms. "It's a shame, Lou," he said. "But God must have a plan for this horse. There must be another day for him. I sure am sorry."

"I don't know about God," I said, "but somebody has a plan for him."

"I'll pray for him tonight," the jockey said.

"It's going to take more than prayer, Daryl," I said. "It's going to take an honest ride."

Spencer's expression hardened and he walked past me without another word. It was May who had reminded me of another curious factor. "Shifty, did you notice?" she said, before she and Eddie led Bellringer back toward the barn. "There wasn't much action on him today."

It was true. It was the first time in weeks that a Clarendon horse hadn't been bet down way below his morning-line odds. As Angles had put it later, when we had gathered back in Jay's box, "They're settin' him up. The angle is to get the price up and then he'll pop. You watch."

After that little exchange, we pretty much forgot about Spencer's horrendous ride, at least for the rest of the evening. We had a victory to celebrate, so we ordered expansively and picked out a couple of bottles of excellent California zinfandel to wash it all down. Barzini joined us periodically to exchange jokes and stories and we were all having a terrific time when, just as we were finishing our main course, Abel Green and Ginger Beaucaire appeared in the entrance.

Barzini hurried over to greet them, then led them past our booth to another one across the room. "The usual, Russ," I heard Green say, as he and Ginger sat down. She looked adorable and waved to us as she slid into her seat.

"Look at that," Angles muttered, "look at that bitch with that old man. It's sickening!"

"Calm yourself, Angles," Arnie admonished him. "It is all an aspect of the varied human condition. Be at peace with yourself, resign yourself to your loss."

"What the fuck are you talking about?" Angles said. "He's two and a half times her age, he's a sack of flab. What does she see in him?"

"He lavishes gifts, flattery, and attention upon her," Arnie pointed out. "All you ever did, Angles, was try to put her on a winner. Did you ever send her flowers?"

"Flowers? What for? She ain't dead."

"Ah, Angles, is there no end to your boorishness? You have no soul." Arnie raised his glass. "A toast," he said, "to life, liberty, and the pursuit of the ultimate exacta."

"I can't stand this," Angles said. "I'm going to go over and punch the old fart out."

"No, you're not, Angles," Jay said. "It's my party and you're going to behave. You can leave, if you want to."

Angles lapsed into a long, sullen silence, picking at his food with his head down. The rest of us ignored his distress and went on partying. Green had spotted us, of course, and waved. I waved back. When he heard from Barzini about Jay's big hit, he sent over a bottle of champagne and we all toasted each other across the room. Only Angles refused to participate. When Barzini brought the champagne and poured for us, he turned his glass upside down on the table.

"Angles, that is not merely a bit of the old bubbly," Arnie informed him. "That is Dom Pérignon. Don't be a cheap plater all your life."

"Yeah," Barzini said, "old Abe made me lay in thirty cases of the stuff, on account of that's all the broad will drink."

"Since when?" Angles asked. "She's a waitress at fuckin' Denny's. She don't drink that there, that's for sure."

"He got her hooked on it," Barzini explained. "It costs a fortune, but that's all she'll drink, he says. So I laid in the cases for him. Nobody else here drinks it. It's too expensive these days for most of my customers. Anyway, only frogs drink the stuff. Me, give me a good wine anytime."

"They come here a lot?" Jay asked.

"Three, four times a week."

"What does he tell his wife?"

"Who knows, who cares?" Barzini said. "You ever seen his wife? She used to be a looker, but she's got a face today that would stop a thousand clocks. He bought the chick an apartment and set her up, I hear."

"Is he going to divorce Millie?" I asked.

Barzini shrugged. "Ah, I don't know. Probably not. He'd have to give her half of everything."

"He won't divorce her," Jay said. "Why should he? And Millie wouldn't care anyway, would she? They probably haven't made it in years."

"You conjure up a vision from one of the seamier scenes of Hogarth," Arnie said. "Spare us the unseemly details of a coupling too loathsome to envision."

"Jesus, Arnie," Angles said, "I'm gonna puke." He got up, rushed out of the restaurant, and did not return.

"A sore loser," Arnie observed later, as Jay was paying the check. "In life, as in horse racing, the next best thing to winning is losing. Angles has never mastered the subtlety of that painful reality. He is doomed to suffer forever from the indignities and vicissitudes life inevitably showers on all the participants in the great game. For with loss comes wisdom."

"Arnie," Jay said, smiling, "if you weren't a diseased horseplayer, you could have been a philosopher."

"I'm still here, aren't I? Surviving, that's the highest achievement," Arnie said. "Philosophy is for the non-participants."

14 / **M**ucking

Las Vegas in August is a broiler. The heat rises off the desert floor in waves, blurring the outlines of buildings, casting a haze through which the surrounding barren mountains loom dimly, as if seen through half-closed eyelids. At night the twinkling neon lights along the Strip and downtown turn the sky pink, blotting out the stars, while groups of scantily-clad citizens shuffle along from one emporium to another, gawking at the garish sights, disappearing inside the casinos from time to time to try their luck at the tables and the machines. The city is an electronic meatgrinder, chewing up hopes and dreams to the beat and clank and burp of fifty thousand rigged games. The world's largest carnival erected in the middle of nowhere to separate the suckers from their cash.

I spent my first three days in town holed up inside the Nirvana and concentrating on my act. I used several of my more flamboyant moves, mostly with cards, and developed a patter of jokes and sly asides to keep my ruthlessly middle-class audiences awake. It wasn't easy. The sun and the gaming grind seemed to have baked the joy out of them and mostly they sat through my

153

routines with glazed eyes, as if stunned out of their senses. I concentrated on my performances, imagining that I was executing my best moves for a single other magician in the room, and counted the days till I could depart. At Del Mar, the horses were running, the golden girls were on the beach, the air was cool and clean with summer breezes; I must have been mad to have accepted this gig, I told myself.

At breakfast, on the morning of my third day in town, I idly picked up the telephone book and turned to the yellow pages. I scanned the names of local banks and came across the only one Aramis could possibly be associated with. It was called the Banca del Tirreno, located on Convention Way between the Strip and Paradise. I'm not sure why I decided to look him up, but probably it's because I'm always fatally attracted by skullduggery. Nothing he and Alma Glocken and Ted Mendoza were associated with could possibly be on the level and I thought that the least I could do for Charlie and May was find out, if I could, exactly what they might be up to.

The Banca del Tirreno occupied a single, dark suite on the second floor of an eight-story glass-and-steel office building surrounded by undeveloped lots. When I opened the door and walked in, a pale young woman looked up from behind her desk and blinked in surprise. "Yes?" she asked, as if I had somehow intruded into a sanctuary. "You are?"

"Perhaps a potential customer," I said. "You are a bank, aren't you?"

"Not for deposits and withdrawals," she said. "We are an international investment company."

"I guess I knew that," I said cheerfully. "Is Mr. Aramis in?"

The woman looked surprised, having already eliminated me from consideration as anything but a blundering outsider. "Who shall I say is calling?"

"Lou Anderson, Charlie Pickard's assistant."

"Ah, yes. You have an appointment?"

"No, obviously not, or you'd have known about it, wouldn't you? I'm in town and I thought I'd drop in."

The door to one of the inner offices suddenly popped open and Alma Glocken appeared. She was dressed in very tight short shorts and a halter, as if she had stepped out of a chorus line. She was amazed to see me, but quickly recovered her composure. "Anderson?" she asked. "What is wrong? It is Anderson, yes?"

"Yes," I said, smiling. "I'm in town on a job. Thought I'd pop in and say hello."

"Hello," she said. "What do you want?"

"Nothing. I thought we might talk horses."

"How boring."

"You spoke to a friend of mine about buying some horses of your own, you and Mr. Aramis. I thought maybe I could help."

"How?"

"I was Charlie Pickard's assistant. I know something about the game," I improvised. "May's a fine horsewoman, but she doesn't know much about the business end. Maybe I could help."

"You are the magician, no?"

"Yes. I also know about racing."

"Ah. One moment." She shut the door in my face and I could hear a conversation going on inside. I smiled at the receptionist, who stared blankly back at me, and sat down. A couple of minutes later, the door opened again and Alma stuck her head out. "Come in," she said.

Gene Aramis, impeccably attired in a dark business suit, was sitting behind his desk. He did not rise to greet me, but waved me into a chair across from him and smiled. "The ubiquitous necromancer," he said. "How is it that you are here?"

I explained, improvising as I went along, painting a picture of myself as a disillusioned performer anxious, now that I'd had a taste of the backstage world of horse racing, to improve my financial lot and become an administrator in the sport. "May told me about your interest and that you spoke to her about getting some horses of your own," I concluded, "so, as I'm in town for a couple of weeks, I thought I'd drop in and talk to you about it. You're going to need someone to handle your affairs on a day-to-day basis and I can do that for you."

Aramis did not answer right away. He sank back into his chair, placed the ends of his fingers together, and looked thoughtful. Alma had perched herself on a divan across the room to my left, her long legs crossed and her arms resting against the back of the sofa. She looked naked and lethal, a smirk on her face, as if what I had said confirmed whatever she and Aramis had been talking about before my arrival. "I told you, Gene," she said. "Ask this man what he wants for this."

Aramis glanced impatiently at her, then at me. "Well?"

"Nothing now, obviously," I said, "since you have no horses.

Two hundred and fifty a week when you want me to start, then, after six months, if I've done a good job for you, we can talk about a real salary."

Aramis took this in, his fingers still steepled, as if he were weighing a truly heavy proposition, then said, "We'll see. Where are you staying here?"

"I'm at the Nirvana for two weeks," I told him. "Then I go to Del Mar for the rest of the racing season."

"Oh, come on, Gene," Alma said. "It's a bargain."

He turned his head grimly toward her. "Alma, we have quite enough investments in this area."

"It's only for me, you know," she said. "We are talking toys, my darling, and toy money." She stretched and her breasts pressed against the cloth so that I could see her nipples through it. "You promised, you know."

"I promised nothing," he said, suddenly bouncing to his feet. "Good-bye, Anderson. I will contact you perhaps, yes."

"Are you and May lovers?" Alma asked, as I turned to leave.

"We're good friends," I said. "Does it matter?"

"Not at all," Alma said. "I only wish to know everything that is going on in the game."

"What game?"

"This one we are playing now, of course," she said. "I love games. I imagine that she must be very good in bed, eh?"

"You'll forgive me, I'm sure, but I don't think I'll discuss it with you."

"Ah, no, of course not," she said. "What a pity. I have my own ideas on everything. I always am very out front, is that how you say it in California?"

"Up front."

"Ah, yes, *up* front, thank you. Tell me, is it possible to be up front and also laid back simultaneously?"

"Sure, why not?"

"I adore California," she said. "I think it is a place that was created just for me, you know."

"Alma, that's enough, really," Gene Aramis said. "Good-bye, Anderson. If we do decide to invest personally in some horses, perhaps you will hear from us."

"Thanks. I hope so."

When I walked out, Alma had stretched herself out on the

sofa. She was smiling broadly at Aramis and raised one long, naked leg in the air, as if beginning a set of exercises. I decided that she was probably the single most dangerous person on the scene and I told myself as I left that it had become important to find out exactly what she was up to. Aramis may have been the head of the Banca del Tirreno, but in life he was Alma Glocken's creature.

Vince Michaels showed up for the early show my third night in town. For his benefit, I executed a couple of my better moves, including that great classic, Cups and Balls. After the show, we had a drink together in the main lobby bar. Vince was very complimentary, which pleased me, because praise from a master magician is what closeup artists live for. It certainly isn't the money. "So where do you go from here?" Vince asked, as we sipped beers. "Back to L.A.?"

"Del Mar, Vince," I said. "Surely you remember that every summer I'm committed to Del Mar. Jay and I rent a condo down there for the season."

"Oh, God, how could I have forgotten? Actually, I'm surprised to find you here at this time of year."

"Me too," I said. "Vince, do you have a stockbroker or an investment counselor?"

"Yes, I do," he said. "Why? Are you becoming a serious citizen?"

"Me? No chance. I'm trying to find out something about an outfit called the Banca del Tirreno. They have offices here in town. I'd like to know what this bank does, who they are, that kind of thing. I figured you probably have a contact."

"Sure." Vince reached into his pocket and produced a business card on which he scribbled a name and phone number. "Tim Galway at Island Investments. He handles my very modest portfolio and he's a good guy. Maybe he can tell you. If not, he'll put you on to someone who can. Why are you interested?"

"It's run by a guy named Gene Aramis and—"

"Aramis?" Vince said, astonished. "Hey, I know about him. I worked a private party for him. He's becoming a legend in this town. You should have been at this party. He's got this girl-friend—"

"I know her."

"Yeah? You should have seen her," Vince continued. "I did my act, mostly standard stuff to entertain their guests, then she came on and did the most terrific striptease you've ever seen. I mean, Shifty, she peeled right down to her skin and she's got a body on her. She had these musicians who played for her and a couple of hired chorus girls to help her and at the end she also undressed the chorus girls or hookers or whatever they were and they did all kinds of wild routines, winding up with the three of them singing happy birthday from the floor at his feet, as if she and the girls were presents for him."

"They probably were. So then what happened?"

"I don't know. I picked up my check and left a few minutes later, but I heard the party went on and got pretty wild. I asked about them and my friend Lorenzo Black, who's one of the pit bosses at the Xanadu, told me she's a huge player, bets tens of thousands at a pop."

"At what?"

"Anything, everything, you name it. A lot of the time she uses a beard to front for her."

"Ted Mendoza."

"I don't know, some guy. She apparently loves baccarat and she's at the tables in the Xanadu nearly every night. Then there's the horses. She bets tons of money. The books here won't touch her, so she bets mainly at the Hilton and the other sports books that are linked to the betting pools at the tracks."

"That accounts for it."

"For what?"

"They have an interest in Clarendon Farm," I explained. "Every time a Clarendon horse runs in California, it gets bet way down. Somebody hammers the tote, up to fifty, a hundred thousand dollars a pop."

"Wow, that's heavy money."

"You'd better believe it. That's why I want to know about the Banca del Tirreno. I'd like to know where all this money comes from."

Vince leaned back in his chair and gazed at me thoughtfully. "Oh, oh," he said at last, "you're involved in some sort of mess again, aren't you? These people could be dangerous, Shifty. Why are you doing this? Why don't you just be a great magician? You have the skills."

"Well, it's personal, Vince," I said. "They're fooling around in ways that could hurt my friends. I'd just like to know what they're up to."

Vince sighed. "You have a gift for this sort of thing."

"A gift? I don't know. Maybe it's a curse. I seem to wind up in the middle of a lot of nonsense everywhere I go. A lot of it pisses me off. I can't help myself, Vince. Maybe I should have been a cop. I really enjoy nailing the bad guys."

"You're right, it is a curse. Watch yourself, Shifty. Where money moves, people will do anything."

"That's why I love horses, Vince. I never knew a horse I didn't like more than most people."

Tim Galway turned out to be an accommodating sort who called me back within a couple of hours of my first conversation with him and told me what he had been able to find out. "The feeling seems to be that the Banca del Tirreno is pretty much of a front," he explained. "It seems to be a conduit for funneling money in and out of the country. It also acquires interests in businesses and real estate. It's currently being investigated by the Justice Department for currency violations. This guy Aramis has been in and out of Washington recently, testifying. He's represented in D.C. by one of the biggest law firms in town. It may be hard to pin anything on him."

"Where does the money come from?"

"Mostly out of Italy. The bank has a branch in Trieste and there's some speculation about capital coming into play from parts of what used to be Yugoslavia."

"That's interesting."

"Yes, I thought so," Galway said. "The most serious charge against the bank seems to be that it's also acquiring arms and shipping them to some of the warring factions there. This man Aramis acts as an agent for several arms manufacturers here and abroad."

"It makes me wonder why they'd bother to mess about in the horse business," I said.

"Well, you might consider this," Galway suggested. "Running large sums of money through casinos and racetracks is an excellent way to launder funds. Also, investing in breeding and racing operations is a good screen for moving money around. Banca del Tirreno reportedly owns a controlling interest not only in Clarendon, but in several smaller farms and one big one in upper New York State."

"Do you know who actually owns the bank?"

"The home offices are in Trieste," Galway said. "It's been in trouble with the Italian authorities as well. That's about all I know, Mr. Anderson."

"Well, thanks. You've been a big help. I appreciate it."

That night I dropped by the Xanadu after my last show and strolled over to the baccarat tables, which were located in a secluded alcove off the main gaming area. I didn't see Alma or Aramis, but Ted Mendoza was sitting at one of the tables with a huge stack of hundred-dollar chips in front of him. I lingered for a couple of hands, long enough to watch him lose seven or eight thousand dollars, then I went back into the casino and asked for Lorenzo Black.

I had to wait for him at the bar for about twenty minutes, until he could take a break, but he soon showed up and turned out to be an affable sort who just happened to be crazy about magic. He was about forty, with rust-colored hair and a mischievous-looking face half-hidden behind tinted glasses. "The neon lights in these places give me migraines," he explained, as we shook hands. "How are you, Shifty? I know all about you from Michaels. He says you're a great card man who would be even greater if you weren't a horse junkie."

"I guess that's accurate," I said. "Please come see me work, if you get a night off. I'm at the Nirvana doing two shows a night."

"So Vincent said. I'll definitely get over. What's on your mind?"

I asked him about Aramis and his friends. Lorenzo Black grinned. "They're crazy," he said, "especially the woman. She's here every night, almost, when they're in town and she gambles like a maniac, hundreds of thousands of dollars a night. Sometimes she wins big, but most of the time she loses. She seems to have unlimited funds."

"Anything else?"

"She came on to one of our dealers one night, really harassed her, threatened to get her fired if she didn't play along."

"Her?"

"That's right. I guess she swings both ways."

"You know her boyfriend, Gene Aramis?"

"No. He's hardly ever in here. Usually, there's this guy Mendoza with her. We know about him."

"What do you know?"

"He's an ex-cop out of Boston turned thug," Black said. "Not a nice man, Shifty. Stay away from him."

"He gambles with her?"

"No, only when she's not around. Like tonight, he's sitting in for her. When she shows up, he'll leave the table. They also both like to play the horses and heavy."

"Yeah, I know. They've been betting horses heavily that are trained by a friend of mine. He's worried about it, so I'm trying to find out what's going on here."

"I'd stay away from Mendoza, if I were you," Lorenzo Black said. "He's not a nice guy."

"I think I already know that, Lorenzo," I said, "but thanks for telling me."

After Lorenzo Black went back to work, I stopped by the baccarat tables again and found Alma. She had taken Mendoza's chair and was evidently on a winning streak. She presided over a small mountain of chips and was playing with the verve and abandonment of a winner on a hot streak. She looked up at me once, flashed me a smile and winked, as if she and I were engaged in a small conspiracy.

I lingered for a few minutes, then left and wandered through the casino until I spotted Mendoza. He was seated at one of the poker tables, playing five-card stud. It didn't take me very long to figure out that he was not a good player, but I also noticed something else. I left and went to look up Lorenzo Black, whom I found in the main gaming area talking to a colleague behind a busy craps table. He came over to me and I tugged him aside, so we wouldn't be overheard. "Lorenzo," I said, "you've got a situation going on at one of your poker tables." I told him about Mendoza.

"What about him?" Black asked. "He plays here a lot and loses most of the time. Not much, not like her, but we think it's his own money. He's just waiting for her to finish, then he'll drive her home. He's a hired hand, that's all."

"I guess he must be playing his own money and he got tired

of losing," I said, "because I just saw him palm an ace of spades into his hole card."

"Is that so? You sure?"

"I'm sure."

"We'll alert the spotters to him."

"I've got a suggestion."

"What?"

"I'll put him out of action for you. Give me one of your decks and let me into the game. Clear me first."

Lorenzo Black looked at me and smiled. "I like it," he said. "Give me a couple of minutes." He left me and walked over to a house phone.

Ten minutes later, with a new house deck of cards in my pocket and a new dealer in the game, I took the one open seat at Mendoza's table, directly across from him.

The gunsel was riding high. He had a solid stack of hundred-dollar chips in front of him and his habitual dour expression had softened into one of smug self-satisfaction. I decided to enjoy myself.

Three hands went by, with Mendoza dropping out early, then I saw him move the ace of spades into the game again. He did it so clumsily and obviously that I couldn't imagine him having gotten away with it before. I found myself wondering whether he had an accomplice up above. When it came my turn to look at my first two cards, I wired my top card, a seven of hearts, with the seven of spades. Mendoza was showing a ten.

Three of us remained in the hand, with the man to my right obviously going for a flush. He dropped out on the fourth card when he failed to fill it. Mendoza drew the ace of clubs and pressed. I saw him and now it was up to the two of us, with a nice pot of seven hundred dollars to contend for. Mendoza glowered at me across the table, but I smiled back. "Got your ace wired, eh, Ted?" I said. "Nice going."

"It'll cost you to find out," he said, shoving another stack of chips into the pot. I shrugged and followed his lead. I needed a bit of luck at this point and I got it, when I was dealt a five of hearts. I was now showing a possible straight, if only my hole card could be a six. Mendoza and everybody else at the table had to have me figured for a pair of sevens and he was almost smiling in anticipation of his coup. I glanced around the table and saw only one other six showing, then I carefully leaned over to check my hole card, substituting the six of diamonds for the seven I no longer wanted.

"Well?" Mendoza said.

I pretended distress. I frowned. I chewed my lip. I sighed. "Well, I've come this far," I said. "I've got to look at you." I pushed my money into the pot.

Mendoza uncovered his ace. "You don't know shit about poker, do you?" he said, reaching for the pot.

"No, but I guess I'm just lucky," I said, displaying my straight.

Mendoza looked amazed. "You stayed in on nothing?" he said. "You got to be kidding!"

"No, I'm not," I said. "Excuse me." I gathered in the chips.

Mendoza stood up. "You sonofabitch," he said.

"Ted, I'm sorry," I said. "I thought you were bluffing. I was hoping for a small pair, but I got lucky."

Without another word, Mendoza picked up his greatly diminished stack of chips and left. I headed for the cashier's window, then I went to see Lorenzo Black again.

"He has to have an accomplice upstairs, one of your spotters," I told him. "His move is so clumsy almost anybody could spot it. What time does he play?"

"Every night, after ten," Lorenzo said. "When the woman shows up, he heads for the poker tables."

"Do you have a shift change?"

"At ten."

"Better check it out, Lorenzo," I warned him. "This guy's your real basic hand mucker, but very crude. He works only with the ace of spades, which means he's got the card bent so he can palm it. Real crude stuff. He can't keep running in the same card on the same players either. If he were working alone, he'd have been caught first or second time."

"Thanks, Shifty, we'll look into it."

I got a phone call in my room, sometime after two A.M. "Shifty? Lorenzo here. Sorry to wake you up," he said. "You were right. We hired a new guy three weeks ago and he's the one who's in charge of the poker tables on that shift. He's already admitted it. He's been fired and told to get out of town."

"What about Mendoza?"

"We're not going to risk losing him," Lorenzo Black said. "The woman's the biggest high roller we've got. We'll just watch him real close from now on. Thanks. What did you win?"

"Eighteen hundred," I said. "It was a nice hit."

"Keep it," he said. "On the house."

It wasn't until the next morning that I found out about Algonquin. I had bought the *Racing Form* and I was having breakfast in the Nirvana coffee shop. The front-page headline jumped off the copy at me: "Algonquin Found Dead in Stall." The story described how the stallion had been found by one of the Clarendon employees and that the cause of death had not yet been ascertained. An autopsy would be performed by a team of veterinarians, including one from the insurance company. The stallion had not been ill and had no history of illness. His death was considered a heavy blow at Clarendon at a time when there were rumors that the farm was in financial difficulty. Algonquin had been insured for eighteen and a half million dollars.

I called the stable at Del Mar and found Charlie at his desk in the tack room. "I don't know anything about it," the trainer said. "I figure at this point the less I know, the better off I'll be. It can't be good, Shifty. Algonquin was the biggest asset Clarendon had. You want to talk to your girl? She's right here."

"Ain't it terrible, Shifty?" May said, as soon as she came on the connection. "I'm sick about it. What do you suppose killed him?"

"I don't know," I said. "It could have been a heart attack. Or it could have been money. I miss you, May."

"I miss you, baby. I'll be out next Monday for two days. You don't have to meet me."

"Why not?"

"Mr. Aramis is sending his car for me," she said. "They want to talk to me about buyin' some horses. And, honey?"

"Yeah?"

"I got my license." She sounded very excited.

"That's great. What does Charlie say?"

"He's gonna help Clara and me get started," she said. "He's gonna give us two stalls. And we can go on workin' for him, too."

"I told you. Clara coming with you?"

"No, they only need to talk to me. Oh, baby, I'm so excited. I'll come to you right after our meeting, okay?"

"I'll be waiting."

"You better be," she said. "I'm real horny now."

15 / Firing

"WE'RE GOIN' TO A PARTY tonight," May said on the phone.

"Honey, I'm not through at the Nirvana until midnight," I said. "Where are you?"

"In Mr. Aramis's office," she answered. "I can't leave just yet. In fact, they want me to stay with 'em tonight. Is that okay?"

"What for?"

"They want to spend a lot of time with me, I guess, get to know me better," she said. "Shifty, they're gonna buy horses for me and Clara to train. Ain't that great?"

"Sure, but why do you have to stay with them?"

"I told you. It's just for tonight, honey. Tomorrow I'll be with you. Anyway, there's this big party. It's Alma's birthday. And you're invited. You can come right after you're through, right?"

"I suppose so. May, be careful."

"Careful? About what, honey?"

"Something's going on here I don't like," I said. "Watch yourself."

"Oh, Shifty, you're just bein' silly. Look, we still got work to do here. There's a sale in Del Mar next week and we're goin' over the catalogue. Then we're talkin' about maybe claimin' somethin' or buyin' a horse private. Shifty, they're givin' me two hundred thousand dollars to get some horses."

She sounded so excited and upbeat that I couldn't bring myself to cast any more cold water on her joy, so I let her babble on, wrote down the address of the house where the party would be held, and let her hang up on me.

It was nearly one A.M. by the time I found the place. It was a big ranch house on the outskirts of town, well beyond several large new developments southwest of the Strip. I had to get through a security check at the front gate, then I was allowed to drive into the grounds up a long, curving road between rows of towering palms. The valet service consisted of two girls dressed in short skirts, boots, and bras, one of whom whisked my rented Geo away. I stood by the front door; then, on an impulse, I turned and walked around the side of the house toward the rear, where most of the noise, in the form of a salsa beat and loud talk, was coming from.

As I turned the corner of the house, I passed a bedroom window with drawn venetian blinds. The slats had not been closed, however, and I could look into the room. Three naked young men were rolling about on the bed, obviously performing, and I'd have awarded them a ten for their sexual gymnastics. In the far corner of the room, Gene Aramis sat, quietly observing the goings-on. He was fully dressed in a dark business suit, complete with necktie, and appeared to be only mildly interested in the proceedings. They seemed, in fact, to have been choreographed and I guessed the show was part of the general festivities. I didn't linger very long, but continued on my way toward the rear of the house.

Most of the party was taking place around the pool. A small band of three musicians was playing on a platform behind the diving board and there were bars at each end, as well as a long table to one side heaped with food, though at this hour few people were eating. Mostly, there were couples dancing, groups of guests talking and laughing, and couples obviously heavily involved with each other. At first glance it appeared to be just another big, splashy Hollywood-style party, but I soon became aware that it had a distinct professional flavor and a conspicuous dearth in one category. There were no older women. The male guests were of all ages, but the women were all in their twenties or early thirties. I suddenly had the odd feeling that I had blundered onto the set of a pornographic movie and I even looked around for a camera crew.

I didn't recognize anyone. I picked up a beer at one of the bars and walked around the pool, then strolled into the house through the sliding glass doors giving onto the patio. Inside it was quiet and dark; the living room was empty. Not sure what to do, I sat down in a corner armchair to sip my beer.

I was still sitting there quietly in the darkness when May suddenly appeared. She was dressed in a black miniskirt, pumps, and a sequined white silk blouse, with long pearl earrings and a single strand of pearls around her neck. She didn't see me, but hesitated, apparently unsure whether to go outside, presumably to look for me, or wait. Alma Glocken stepped out of the hallway behind her. She was dressed only in a long scarlet kimono down to her ankles and her long blond hair hung loosely to her shoulders. "Where are you going?" she asked.

"Shifty said he'd be here," May said.

"He's not coming," Alma said. "Come here."

May didn't answer her, but took another step into the room. Alma came up behind her, put a hand on her left breast and kissed her neck. "Don't do that, please," May said, pushing her arm down.

"You liked it a few minutes ago," Alma said. "I know you like it. Turn around."

May turned to face Alma and a smile of pure anticipatory lust spread over the woman's face. "Show me your breasts," she said.

"No."

Alma reached out with both hands and suddenly tore the blouse away, then seized May's nipples between thumb and forefinger and squeezed. "Like that," she said. "I like them pointed, no? You don't like?"

May didn't answer. Alma went down to her knees and tugged May's skirt and panties down to her ankles. "Step out, please," she said.

"Not here," May said.

"Yes, here. Now," Alma ordered. "I decide this."

"But what if—"

"It does not matter," Alma said. "If he sees you, he will know and he will know sooner than later. Others, what do they matter? Let them look. I might even let them have you."

"No."

"I decide. Over there." She pushed May toward a large ottoman, then made her lie down on it. She knelt in front of her and pushed her legs apart. "Up in the air, open, like that," she said, then moved in, her head descending between May's thighs.

May moaned with pleasure, as Alma's lips and tongue fastened on her sex and her hands went up to her breasts, seizing her nipples and pinching them.

I couldn't move. I sat in place, hardly daring to breathe. I felt as if someone had hit me very hard in the stomach and I wanted to cry out, but I couldn't catch my breath. As I sat there, immobile and sick, I saw May's body rise up to meet Alma's tongue and I heard her cry of animal pleasure. Then I watched Alma get up and tug May to her feet. "Come," she said, "I am not finished with you. Oh, no, we have a night ahead of us, my dear."

She pulled May out of the room after her and they disappeared into the interior of the house.

I stood up, not sure what to do. I heard a door shut behind me and then a rush of footsteps down a corridor. Two naked men came running into the room, laughing, and bounded out through the open doors to the pool area. People shrieked and laughed as they hurled themselves through the guests into the water. Three or four other people, fully clothed, jumped in after them. A woman climbed up to the diving board and began to do a striptease, tossing each discarded article into the water below.

I quickly let myself out through the front of the house and walked down past the palm trees to find my car. My dismay had given way by this time to a dull rage that engulfed me like a rising tide. I drove quickly back to my hotel and shut myself up in my room. I felt like a wounded animal, gone to ground to save himself but full of hate, lying in wait for the hunters.

It must have been well after three o'clock when my telephone rang. It was May. "Shifty, where are you? You didn't come."

"I started to," I lied, "but I changed my mind."

"I waited for you."

"Not too long, I hope. I was just tired."

"You want me to come over?"

"No, not now."

"I meant in the mornin'."

"Sure."

"What's your room number? I'll come on up."

"Never mind. I'll meet you in the coffee shop at ten o'clock."

"Shifty, I guess I'm gonna be stayin' here till I go back," she said. "They kind of want me to."

"That doesn't surprise me," I said.

"You ain't mad?"

"Just a little," I confessed. "I'll see you at ten."

"I'll make it up to you, Shifty, I promise," she said. "And I want to tell you about the horses. We're gonna bid on three two-year-olds at the Del Mar sale."

"That's good. I hope you don't pay too much for them."

"Shifty, it's my big chance," she said. "You understand, don't you, honey?"

"I guess. I'll see you at ten, May."

When I came down to the coffee shop the next morning, she was waiting for me at a corner table. She looked worn, with little makeup on, but happy. Her hair had been pulled back away from her face into a small ponytail, which made her look about fourteen years old. I sat down and she kissed me. I waited until my coffee arrived and then I told her. "I was there last night," I said.

She looked stunned. "You were? I didn't see you. I was lookin' for you."

"I was sitting in a corner of the living room having a beer," I said. "You didn't notice me."

Her face went white. "Shifty, it ain't what you think—"

"It's not? It looked pretty definitive to me. What else did Alma do to you?"

She looked away from me and didn't answer right away. "It don't mean nothin' to her," she said. "I ain't never met nobody like her. She just takes what she wants."

"And what she wants right now is you."

"It don't mean nothin', Shifty. It ain't gonna last. She wants me to do what she calls scenes with her for her boyfriend, but I ain't gonna do that."

"Why not?"

" 'Cause I don't want to, that's why. I already told her."

"And she's not going to make you?"

"No, I ain't gonna do that stuff, no way."

"From my point of view, it doesn't make a lot of difference what you do now, May," I said. "You want her to buy the horses for you, don't you?"

She didn't answer and looked away from me again. "Listen, May," I said, "I was pretty angry at you last night. Today it doesn't matter. Let's just go our own ways. Maybe we can remain friends."

I started to leave the table. "Wait," she said, "I got somethin' to say."

"Go ahead."

She hesitated, as if unsure of herself. "Shifty," she began, "you ain't never been where I've been."

"Where's that, May?"

"I mean, you ain't never had nothin', been no one. You don't know what that feels like. I have."

"I'm listening."

"When I was just a kid and Clara come on to me, if I hadn't been with her I'd have been throwed out of the Wilson place. Clara was in love with me and it didn't seem so bad to be with her. I needed a home, Shifty. I learned early on that just about the only thing I had to bargain with was my body. Every man I was ever with never did nothin' for me less I fucked him. You ain't no different."

"I'm not? I thought I was."

"Well, you don't care enough about me to try to understand, do you?"

"Understand what, May? That you sell yourself to get ahead? I understand that. But I don't like it. You expect me to like it?"

"You make it sound bad."

"Well, that's because I think it is bad."

May began to cry, but as much out of anger as grief. She looked at me fiercely, almost defiantly. "Well, maybe that's what I am," she said, "a damn hooker. I sell my body to get ahead. That's what I'm doin'."

"That's how I see it, yes. You hurt me last night, May. I sat there and watched that woman make love to you and it damn near killed me. But you don't give a shit about that. All you could think about was what Alma and Gene are going to do for you.

What's wrong with doing scenes for him? What difference would it make? You see, if you cared for this woman, it would hurt, all right, but I could understand it. It would be like losing you to another man, but I could understand it. But the idea that you're just giving yourself away to get ahead, that I can't accept. And if you don't see the difference, then I'm sorry for you. I can't explain Verdi to somebody who's tone deaf. You get the analogy?"

"Don't use them big words with me," she said. "You know I don't understand 'em."

I stood up. "So long, May," I said. "I'll sign for the coffee. Have a successful life. I hope they buy you some good horses."

"You ain't never been poor, Shifty," she said. "You don't know what it is to have nothin', be nobody. This is my one big chance and I got to take it. A person's got to be somebody, don't they?"

"No," I said, "I don't see the necessity."

I walked away from her without looking back. I couldn't hate her anymore and I hoped with all my heart that Alma and her rotten boyfriend wouldn't betray her. As for me and my future as a lover of women, I began to consider the cloister as a happy place to be. Perhaps I could go to Denmark and have my sex removed. Not changed, merely removed. The end of every love affair is like a hall of mirrors in an amusement park, a gallery of distorted images in which you see unrecognizable replicas of yourself in a dozen lugubrious poses and the music playing is a dirge in a minor key.

Two days before the end of my gig in Las Vegas, Bellringer ran again. I went to the Xanadu to see what would happen and quickly spotted Mendoza. He was standing in one of the aisles facing the screens. It was about fifteen minutes to post time at Del Mar and Bellringer was showing odds of seven to two. That was significant enough. He'd been listed in the morning line at twelve to one and he was being asked again to go a mile on the turf. Furthermore, he had drawn the eight hole, an outside post, at a distance that favored the inside. I figured he should have been fifteen or twenty to one.

Over the next ten minutes, Mendoza went back to the windows two more times and the odds on the horse dropped first to three to one, then five to two. I followed him and bet two hundred dollars to win on him.

It was no contest. Spencer broke the horse perfectly this time, tucked him in around the first turn so that he was only three wide, then allowed him to settle into stride in fifth, about four lengths behind the leader. Three-eighths of a mile from home, the jockey swung Bellringer out into the middle of the track and asked him for his speed. The gelding responded with a move that brought him up alongside the leaders at the head of the stretch. A tap of Spencer's whip was now all that was required. Bellringer shot to the lead and came home about two lengths in front of his nearest pursuer. He paid $7.20 to win and I was over five hundred dollars richer.

"Nice hit," I said to Mendoza, as I came back from the cashier's window. "It took you a couple of races to set him up, but you did a nice job. What's Spencer's cut?"

Mendoza had also been on his way to the cashier, but now he came after me and grabbed my arm. "Hey, you," he said, "I want to talk to you."

"What about, Ted?"

"I got lots to talk to you about," he said. "Let's take a walk."

"Where to?"

"Never mind. Just follow me."

"I don't think I'll do that, Ted."

He leaned in close to me and I could smell his breath, compounded of garlic, cheeses, and beer, not pleasant. "Listen, I could have fixed you good several times and I could fix you good now," he said. "The only reason I don't, see, is on account of Mr. Aramis wouldn't like it. He thinks it would be not so good for business. Me, I don't give a shit. You keep pushin' me and I'll do somethin' about it."

"Like you did with Benny Wilder?"

He stepped back and stared at me for a very long second or two. "You kiddin' me? You want to die, fella?"

"Not like Benny, Ted," I said. "I was hoping to make it to a ripe old age. Maybe you ought to be aware that the cops here know a lot about you and they also know enough about you and Benny Wilder to maybe ask you about it someday. Now, if something were to happen to me, Ted, I imagine the investigation would heat up some. What do you think?"

We were standing in a corner area of the main casino by this time, next to one of the three bars and at the end of a double row of slot machines. Without saying anything, Ted now reached over to a container full of swizzle sticks, grabbed a handful of them, and smiled at me. "You know, I figure maybe if you're a magician, it wouldn't be too good if you was to have a finger broken," he said, snapping one of the sticks in half. "Hear that? It don't sound so different when it's a bone." He broke another one in two. "I like the sound of it." A third one went. "And I like the sound that comes out of people when things get broken. I really enjoy it, you know? Or maybe you don't know. Do you or don't you?"

I looked at him and tried to remain calm. Once, as a kid of twelve, I had been walking in the woods at a summer camp I attended, had turned a corner and come face to face with a mountain lion. I had frozen in place and tried to make myself remain absolutely calm. The big cat had snarled, then bounded away from me. I felt that way now, as if my very life depended upon remaining absolutely cool and seemingly in control. One sign of panic and I knew Mendoza would have me. I forced myself to smile and I hoped it looked genuine. "Very nice, Ted," I said. "I do know. But you don't know me, do you?"

"I don't give a shit about you," he said. "You're just some dumb fuck gettin' in the way, messin' around in stuff you don't know nothin' about. It's like I'm givin' you an education, you know what I'm sayin'?"

"I doubt very much you have anything to teach me," I said. "Look, if you break my fingers, Ted, you're going to have to kill me, see. The reason is you'd take away most of the reasons I have to live. And as soon as I healed, I'd come after you."

"Hey, you're makin' me piss in my pants."

"The smell would go well with your breath," I said.

He hit me, very quickly and suddenly, a short, hard jab into my stomach. I doubled over and fought for air. He leaned in on me. "See what I mean, fella? You ain't got a chance," he said softly, almost caressingly. "Do yourself a favor, bug off. Forget you know me. Forget you know Mr. Aramis. Disappear."

I got my first breath of air and brought my right foot down hard on his instep. He gave a sort of bark and lurched to one side. I kicked him in the other leg, just below the knee, and he went down along a row of slot machines. Two middle-aged women who had been playing the machines screamed and ran out into the main lobby. I knew security was on its way, but I had time for one more shot and I gave it to him. My second kick caught him in the jaw and slammed him back against one of the machines, which now gurgled and lit up, then sent a shower of quarters tumbling over his head. "Another nice hit," I said, as the first security guard reached us. "Officer, this man threatened my life."

"Ernie, we know about this guy," Lorenzo Black said in my defense. "He's a hood out of Boston, works for this guy Aramis and his girlfriend. Shifty here put us on to a scam he was working at the poker tables. I think we ought to drop charges."

Ernie Loquasto looked at me. He was a heavyset, gray-haired man with a lined face and a small mustache nestling under his thick, flat nose. He looked like an ex-fighter, which he had been in his youth. He'd fought Ali and gone ten rounds with him, then lost a couple and hung up his gloves to go into private business with the casinos as a guard. He was now the head of security at the Xanadu. "Where'd you learn that kicking stuff?" he asked.

"A women's defense class," I told him, "taught by a friend of mine, Mary Conroy."

"She must be some dame."

"She is," I said. "She taught me everything I know. Ernie, this guy first threatened to break my fingers, then he hit me in the stomach. I'm pleading self-defense."

Ernie glanced at Lorenzo Black. "Lorenzo here says they're big customers, high rollers. We can't have you beating on them in the main lobby, for Christ's sake."

"I understand that, Ernie," I said. "I'll stay out of your way from now on. I'm only in town a couple of more days."

"You should see this guy do closeup, Ernie," Lorenzo Black said. "He's over at the Nirvana in the lounge, two shows a night."

"Yeah? A magician, huh?"

"Yes. My only problem is I can't make people disappear," I said.

"Don't try that in here," Ernie said. "Not the high rollers. You could make my kids disappear. They're a real pain in the ass."

I stood up and shook Ernie's hand. "Thanks." I turned to Lorenzo. "You too, Lorenzo. I appreciate it."

"Shifty, stick to magic, will you?"

"What are you going to do about Mendoza?"

"Nothing," Ernie said. "I'm going to suggest that Mr. Moncrief, he owns this place, go and talk to this guy Aramis."

"That might help," I said. "I don't think he needs a lot of publicity right now."

16 / Connections

TED MENDOZA CAUGHT UP TO ME the day before I was scheduled to leave for Del Mar. He was waiting for me in the Nirvana parking lot at about five in the afternoon and must have been there for some time, as he had no way of knowing when I might appear. I didn't see him, because he was sitting in his parked car and came up swiftly behind me just as I was inserting my key into the lock of my Geo. He rammed the muzzle of a gun against the small of my back and leaned into me. "This way, asshole," he whispered.

He forced me to walk over to his car, then made me put my hands behind my back and handcuffed me. He climbed in behind the wheel and started to ease the car out of the lot.

"This is not a good idea, Ted," I said. "They know all about you in this town. If something happens to me, they're coming after you."

He swung his right hand out and caught me in the mouth. "Shut up," he said. "I'll tell you when to talk."

I could feel my lips beginning to swell. Mendoza now turned out of the lot and away from the Strip, then drove toward the southwest. I guessed that he was headed for Aramis's place and I made no further effort either to speak or to escape. Perhaps I wasn't about to be eliminated after all.

Once inside the grounds, Mendoza drove around the back and parked in the garage, then made me get out and walked me toward the house. The sun was still up over the surrounding mountains and the heat rose in shimmering waves of light off the desert floor. We skirted the swimming pool and entered the house from the rear, through the same patio doors and into the living room where I had watched Alma make love to May. The house was dark and cool and silent. Mendoza again placed the gun against my back and urged me on into the interior, down a long corridor until we arrived at a closed door at the very end of the building. He knocked twice.

"Yes?" a voice answered.

"Mendoza," the hood said. "I have Anderson with me."

"Come in."

Mendoza opened the door and pushed me into the room. Gene Aramis was sitting behind a desk surrounded by a small bank of computer screens on which numbers were flashing. He was on the phone and speaking in French, but cut the conversation short as we entered. He was dressed in brown slacks and an open-necked green sports shirt. The blinds had been drawn and the light in the room was electric and cold, casting a hard, white glare over the corner where he worked. I guessed that this was where Aramis's real business was transacted and that the offices of the Banca del Tirreno were mostly a front. I blinked and tried to adjust my eyes to the light.

"Sit down," Aramis said, indicating a chair facing him. "What is the matter with your mouth?"

"Your hired hand here saw fit to hit me," I explained. "He's not a fan of mine."

Aramis did not smile. "Yes, I know that." He looked at Mendoza with distaste. "I told you not to harm him," he said. "Remove the handcuffs."

"He's got a big mouth," Mendoza said. "I had to shut it for him." He leaned down and unlocked the cuffs. I rubbed the circulation back into my wrists.

"I'm sorry," Aramis said to me. "I was afraid you would not come to see me of your own volition."

"Why would you think that?" I asked. "I came to you looking for a job."

"Ah, yes, that's it, you see," he said. "I'm afraid we didn't believe you."

"You want me to stay?" Mendoza asked.

"Sit down over there and be quiet," Aramis said. "I'm certain that Mr. Anderson will wish to talk to us now."

"Are we going to talk about my possible job?"

"Why should we waste time doing that?" Aramis asked. "No, Mr. Anderson, what I need to know from you is whom you are working for?"

"I don't work for anybody," I said. "I'm a closeup magician by profession."

Aramis looked pained. "Oh, Mr. Anderson, come on now," he said. "You ask a lot of questions of a great many people. You travel to Kentucky and you ask more questions. You come to Las Vegas and present yourself in my office as a would-be administrator, a profession that in horse racing, I am told, hardly exists. You must not take me for an idiot, Mr. Anderson. Of course you are working on behalf of someone. I wish to know who that someone is."

"Well, you're right," I said. "I did ask a lot of questions about you. The main reason is my friend Charlie Pickard. He had a heart attack and a bypass. I went to work for him, helping him run his stable while he was convalescing. I began to notice the amount of action on the Clarendon horses. I'm a horseplayer, Mr. Aramis. When I see a horse knocked down in the tote—"

"I beg your pardon?"

"Heavily bet, very heavily bet," I explained, "then I have to ask myself what's going on. Who's betting all that money and why? That's all there is to it. And then, of course, I had the pleasure of watching your action with Bellringer. That worked out pretty well. I mean, I cashed a nice ticket on the horse myself."

"And this is why you are running around the country asking all these questions?"

"Yes, and it's a good enough reason, believe me," I said. "Charlie spoke to me about it. He's a straight arrow, Mr. Aramis—"

"A what?"

"An honest man," I continued. "He was worried that all this betting action on his horses would focus a lot of attention on him. He doesn't need to be called in and investigated by the stewards. The only thing Charlie cares about is his horses, Mr. Aramis. Especially one horse."

"Which horse is that?"

"Old Roman, the Clarendon two-year-old colt," I said. "He may be the best two-year-old in the country. Charlie wants to run him in the Juvenile at the Breeders' Cup in November. That's all Charlie cares about and I'm Charlie's friend. That's all there is to it. You can't imagine that what you're doing is going unnoticed, can you?"

"What are we doing?"

"You and Alma and Ted here are pouring tens of thousands, hundreds of thousands of dollars through the betting windows," I said. "That kind of activity does not pass in private. You're becoming legends in this town, and not just because of your action on the horses. Alma's the highest roller in the casinos here, or at least at the Xanadu. Surely you don't believe you aren't attracting a lot of attention? And then you give great parties."

"Who told you that?"

"I was at one. And a friend of mine worked at one, I think it was your birthday. He told me about it."

Aramis thought my answer over. He seemed undecided, not quite convinced. For a minute or two, he gazed impassively at me, then swung about in his chair and stared at one of his computer screens. "Who else are you working for?" he now asked, not turning back to me.

"Who else should there be?" I answered. "What you should worry about, Mr. Aramis, is not who I might be working for, but the kind of attention you and your associates are focusing on themselves. Mr. Mendoza here likes to go around breaking people's fingers and maybe worse. Your girlfriend gambles as if there's no tomorrow. People will talk. And I know why you're nervous about me, I can understand that."

"You can?"

"Oh, yes. I know about the Justice Department investigation."

The door opened and Alma Glocken walked in. She was dressed in black exercise pants that hugged her long legs and a tight black jersey and her hair had been pulled back into a small knot at the back of her skull. She looked slick and as lethal as a black panther. She also looked mildly surprised to see me sitting there, but not astonished. She walked past me and sat down behind Aramis on the window ledge. "Well," she said, "what have we here?"

"Mr. Anderson has been kind enough to drop in for a talk," Aramis explained. "It seems that he has been going around asking a great many questions about us, here and in other places."

"I'm a naturally curious person," I said, "and you have to admit that your activities might tend to arouse some curiosity."

"He says he has no interest beyond a quite natural concern for the welfare of his benefactor, Pickard."

"Who?" Alma asked.

"The horse trainer in California," Aramis said.

"Oh, that boring little old man," she said and stretched. Her unfettered breasts rose up against the thin cotton of her jersey. She had a spectacular body, no doubt about it, and no inhibitions about showing it off. "Send him away, Gene," she added. "We have matters to discuss."

Aramis regarded me thoughtfully, as if unsure about whether to release me or simply turn me over to the gentle ministrations of Ted Mendoza.

"Look," I said, "I have no interest in your business operations, except as they concern the horses. I don't care what the Justice Department investigation is all about. I imagine it has to do with far more important business. You're attracting a lot of attention in town here with your gambling, but Las Vegas doesn't care either what your motives are. Maybe you're laundering drug money, who knows? Who cares? But if you're worried about taking some of the heat off your activities, you might consider dumping your cheap gunsel here."

"What the fuck—" Mendoza began, rising to his feet.

"Sit down," Aramis snapped. Mendoza sank back into his seat. Aramis looked at me. "What are you talking about, Anderson?"

"Your man is under investigation for the murder of a small-time grifter named Benny Wilder, who was unlucky enough to work a hustle on him," I said. "I saw it happen and I'm sorry to say it was I who tipped Mendoza off. I didn't know that Mendoza is such a sicko that he'd actually do away with poor Benny. Then, in L.A., he murders a hooker he picks up, just for the fun of it."

Alma gazed wide-eyed at the hood. "Ted, you didn't? How perverse you are!"

"The police haven't put that killing together with the one here or with the others I'm sure Ted has committed over the past few years," I continued. "He enjoys torturing and killing people, so it's unlikely he'd have limited himself to the two I know about. But it's only a matter of time, you see, because he keeps drawing attention to himself. I caught him cheating at poker the other night and the casino asked me to put a stop to it, which I did. The only reason they haven't taken any action is because Ted works for you and they don't want to lose your business. But they've got a surveillance in place on him and so on you, too."

"How tedious," Alma said. "Ted, how could you be so stupid?"

Mendoza rose again to his feet and moved toward me. Aramis stood up. "Sit down!" he snapped, but Mendoza ignored him. I got up and retreated, ready to kick out at him. "Sit down!" Aramis said again. This time he was holding a revolver in his hand, aimed at his hired goon.

Mendoza stopped and glared at Aramis. "Let me take care of him," he said. "I'll get rid of him for you and nobody will know what happened to him."

"Wrong," I said. "The first place they'll come to is here. They know all about you, Ted. I told them and they've got an eye on you around the clock. They know where I am right this minute."

"He's lying," Mendoza said. "Nobody saw me with him. Nobody knows we're here."

"You want to take that chance?" I said to Aramis. "Is it worth the gamble? Lose this guy. He's a dime a dozen on the gunsel market. I have no interest in making trouble for you, Mr. Aramis. I'm a magician and a horseplayer, that's all I am. Do yourself a favor. Get rid of the loony here and you and Alma can go about your perfectly legitimate business."

"You know, I think that is quite sensible, darling," Alma said, smiling at me. "We can't have people watching all the time."

"Get out, Anderson," Aramis said. "Now."

"I have no car."

"Walk," he said. "You can walk, can't you? You can catch a

bus on the street corner, half a mile away. Turn right as you exit the property."

"Nobody is walking in this country, it's quite extraordinary," Alma said. "Darling, don't shoot him in here. I just had the rugs to be shampooed and it would be quite messy. Take him outside. The garage would be good, no?"

Mendoza lunged for Aramis and the gun, which went off just as he grabbed his wrist. The two men fell to the floor, struggling. Alma bolted from the room. I ran around the desk to join them and got there just as Mendoza was getting the upper hand. He was on top of Aramis and had grabbed one of the fingers of his left hand. He snapped it like a celery stalk and Aramis screamed. I kicked Mendoza in the face, feeling the toe of my shoe crunch against the bridge of his nose. The hood toppled forward, blood gushing from his chin. I kicked him again as he fell, then reached into his jacket and tugged his gun out of its shoulder holster. Mendoza reached out and grabbed my left ankle, then tried to pull me down on top of him. I hit him with the gun on the side of his head and he slumped forward on his face. I backed away toward the door. Aramis was leaning against the far wall holding his smashed finger and staring wildly at me out of a pale, sweaty countenance. He looked sick and I thought he might faint.

Still holding Mendoza's gun, I backed out of the room and ran down the corridor toward the living room. Alma Glocken came out of the bedroom holding what looked in passing like a .22-caliber automatic. She saw me and retreated inside. Before I could do or say anything else, the door to Aramis's office burst open and Mendoza lurched into the hallway. He had gotten hold of Aramis's pistol, but he couldn't see very well and was bleeding profusely from his nose. He sensed rather than saw me, turned and came for me, firing. He got off at least two shots, but the bullets embedded themselves harmlessly in the walls. Before I could shoot back or Mendoza could fire again, Alma stepped out into the corridor behind him, placed the small weapon at the base of his skull and pulled the trigger. Mendoza's head jerked forward and he toppled to his hands and knees, then flat onto his face and lay still. Blood oozed out of the back of his skull and more of it fell on the floor, spreading into a pool beneath him. Alma and I stared at each other. I stuck Mendoza's gun into my pocket. Alma looked down at the hood, then at me again. "Gene?" she asked.

"He's all right," I told her. "He has a broken finger."

Alma smiled. "Perhaps you'd better remain here," she said. "We will need help with the body."

"I don't think so," I said, turning to go.

Her first shot grazed my left cheek. I ran, crouching, out through the living room. She followed me and fired again. This time the bullet missed me completely, but I decided to give her no more opportunities. I ran out into the sunlight of the pool area and around the house down the driveway toward the front gate. Alma made no further attempt to kill me, but remained inside. I kept on going for several blocks, then slowed to a walk and tried to get myself together. It isn't every day that two people try to kill you. Mendoza's gun, with my fingerprints all over it, weighed heavily in my pocket. I walked to the bus stop and sat down on a bench to wait for public transport. I had no idea what to do now, but I figured I'd think of something by the time I got back to my hotel.

It was twenty minutes before the bus came and whisked me back toward the Strip. I got out at a corner about five blocks from the Nirvana and looked around for a public telephone. No sooner had I spotted one than I realized I didn't know the street number of the house. I had written it down on the day of Alma's party but had long since forgotten it, and I had thrown the slip of paper away on which I'd noted it. I walked back to my hotel, went out to the parking lot and got into my car, then drove away from the Strip back toward the general area of Aramis's house.

It took me about forty minutes to find it. I parked across the street and removed Mendoza's gun from my pocket. I carefully wiped it down with my handkerchief, then, after first making sure no one could see me, I stepped out and put the gun under a bush next to the front entrance. I got back into my car and returned to the hotel, went upstairs to my room and called the police.

A bored male voice answered. "Yeah?"

"There's been a shooting," I said and gave the address. "There's been a murder."

The voice asked for my name and phone number.

I ignored the request. "There's a gun under a bush next to the front entrance," I said. "It belonged to the victim, a man named Ted Mendoza." I spelled the name out for him. "Hurry up," I added. "It happened about two hours ago and they'll be covering up the evidence and getting rid of the body."

"Your name and phone number, please, where you're calling from—"

I hung up and went into the bathroom. My left cheek, where Alma's bullet had grazed it, looked as if someone had rubbed it raw with a nail file. I put some lotion on it and lay down on the bed. It was nearly seven-thirty by this time and the sun was low in the sky, just over the rim of the mountains visible from my window. I wasn't sure what to do, but I did know that I was not about to involve myself in a murder investigation. Vince was right, of course. I should have stuck to magic, because obviously I was in way over my head with these people, who thought nothing of corrupting and butchering each other and were involved in some sort of huge crooked scheme involving money moving across borders and being laundered in casinos. I wanted to have nothing to do with them. I'd finish up tonight at the Nirvana and go to Del Mar the next day and play horses and lie in the sun for the rest of the summer.

I showered and changed into my working clothes, a pair of gray slacks and a navy blue blazer, then went down to the coffee shop and had a sandwich and a cup of coffee. By the time I had to go on, I was in pretty good shape, though I stuck to tried-and-true effects that night, ones I could do in my sleep, almost. I didn't want to risk making a mistake. My mind was still back at the house; I could still hear Aramis's scream, see Mendoza topple forward, and the look of cold fury in Alma's eyes when she aimed her gun at me. I was lucky to be alive and I knew it. The realization did not give me the peace of mind I needed to concentrate on my craft.

I was halfway through my last show when I saw Alma come in. She was alone and sat down toward the rear of the room, which was half-empty. It was a slow night. She was wearing one of her tight black outfits that hugged her body as if she had been sculpted into it. She sat quietly at her table, smoking and sipping a tall, pink drink through a straw. When I finished my act and went backstage, I found the stage manager waiting with a note for me. "Meet me in the main bar," it said. "Come by yourself. Do not be stupid."

She was waiting for me at a table in the far corner and smiled when she saw me. "Sit down, Anderson," she said. "I wish to talk to you."

"I thought you might try to shoot me again," I said, remaining on my feet.

"Sit down. That was the hot of the moment, you know. All I could think about was the violence. I am sorry. It was not intentful."

"That's comforting," I said. "What do you want?"

"Sit down, please."

I did so, but I couldn't exactly relax. I considered her probably the most dangerous person I'd ever met, someone who would be able to snuff me out with no more hesitation than a housewife stepping on a cockroach. "Where's your playmate?" I asked.

"I took him to hospital," Alma said. "His finger is broken in two, very painful. An accident. While we were there, some police came. They found a gun under a bush outside and they believed someone was shot in the house."

"Really? How extraordinary."

"Yes. Some foolish person must have called them, you see. But nothing has come of it."

"No?"

"No. They came in and asked many stupid questions, but they found nothing. What is there to find?"

"I can't imagine. Where's Ted?"

"Oh, he has left us, you see. Very sad."

I leaned toward her. "Come on, Alma, let's cut this cutesypie crap and talk turkey."

"Talk what? Turkish?"

"Turkey. It means straight. What do you want? They'll nail you eventually, you know."

"I don't know. I came to talk about your job."

"My job?"

"Yes, didn't you ask Gene for a job with our horses?"

"Oh, *that* job."

"Well, we have decided that you are indeed the right person," she said. "We will pay you one thousand dollars a week, with a guarantee of two years. That is over fifty thousand dollars a year. You are a very good magician, but this is good money, no?"

"Yes, very good. When do you want me to start?"

"Tonight, now," she said. She opened her handbag, produced a bulky, sealed brown envelope and dropped it on the table between us. "Best of all," she continued, "all payments will be cash, for reasons that do not interest you. What you decide about taxes is not business of ours, you understand?" She patted the envelope. "You will find two months of pay in there. Take it."

"You're a very beautiful person, Alma," I said. "You have a very beautiful soul."

"Take the envelope, please."

I put the envelope into my inside jacket pocket. "Now what?"

"When are you leaving?"

"Tomorrow morning."

"And you will go to Del Mar."

"Yes, that's the plan."

"Good. We will be in touch with you through your friend, Miss Potter."

"Ah, yes, Miss Potter. How is Miss Potter?"

"You have not been in touch?"

"No."

"She has bought for us three horses. She will tell you about them."

"And what about the Clarendon connection?"

"What connection?"

"Alma, we're talking straight to each other, right?"

She smiled and leaned contentedly back in her chair. Somewhere in the background, from one of the lounges, an orchestra was playing a rumba, with castanets, the whole works. It added a faintly surrealistic touch to our conversation, as if whatever we were saying to one another could not possibly be taken seriously. Alma, I decided, had stepped out of the pages of a comic book I had read as a child; she was someone I now considered so spectacularly amoral that I was having a hard time believing in her very existence. "Come on, Alma," I insisted. "If you want me to work for you, I have to know what the Clarendon business is all about."

"You must ask Gene," she said. "He's the only one who knows. I believe that Baldwin owes him a great deal of money. That is what I believe, but you must ask him."

"So that's why Algonquin was killed," I said, "to collect the insurance."

"Who?"

"The stallion."

"Oh, that. No, I don't believe so. Gene was most upset by that. Yes, I do remember, most upset. But you must ask him." She stood up. "Good-bye, Anderson. Your magic is most entertaining, you know."

"I'm glad you enjoyed it. I didn't do my best stuff tonight. I was a little shaky."

"Really? I must come and watch you when you are doing your best. By the way, you will be discreet, yes? No more phone calls, no more police. Discreet is part of this job. That is clear, yes?"

"It is."

"Good-bye, then." She paused for a moment, then smiled brilliantly at me. "I am so sorry about your girlfriend," she said. "I find her so attractive."

"Yes, she is."

"And what we do together, you know, is what she likes."

"Fine."

"Nothing personally," she said. "I enjoy her very much." And she walked swiftly away from me, gliding between the tables around us like a cat moving through a thicket. I made myself wait until she had disappeared, then went to a phone and called Vince at the Three Kings, where he was working.

"Shifty, you've got to be crazy, man," Vince said. "You took the money?"

"What else can I do, Vince?" I said. "These people are playing for very large stakes. I'm safe for a while, as long as they think they've bought me. But I'm not going to spend the money. I'm taking it just to stay alive."

"What are you going to do with it?"

"You're going to open a special account for me, Vince," I said. "If anything happens to me, the money is yours." I indicated the envelope full of hundred-dollar bills resting on the table before us. "There's eight thousand in there. If any more comes in, I'll get it to you. I'm sorry to involve you, but I don't want this loot to go to waste, Vince. And I want you to know about everything in case I'm not around after a while."

Vince sank back into his chair and crossed his arms. We were sitting in his condo and it was dark in the room, with only one light on in a corner behind his desk. "Shifty, Shifty, how many times have I told you to stick to magic? You always get into these scrapes. Why don't you go to the police?"

"I tried that," I said. "It didn't work. Vince, these are pretty smart people. They're connected. I don't know how high the connections go, but high enough. They've got expensive attorneys in Washington and elsewhere. The horse business is just a lark to keep Alma happy, that's all, and I'm like a little mouse scurrying around in the dark trying to stay alive in a roomful of cats. Will you help me out, Vince?"

"It's the damn horses," Vince said. "If you weren't such a horse degenerate, you wouldn't be in this mess."

"Right, Vince. But then I wouldn't be having so much fun either. Isn't that what we're supposed to be getting out of life, Vince? A few laughs, a few thrills, and a little fun?"

17 / Messages

THE SCANDAL REGARDING THE Banca del Tirreno broke
over the Labor Day weekend. I was sitting early in the morning in
the track kitchen at Del Mar, sipping a very bad cup of coffee,
when my eye fell on the headline on the front page of the *L.A.
Times*. "Italian Bank Investigated," it read. The subhead named
the bank and the story went on to describe how the institution
had been under surveillance for months as a suspected money-
laundering operation for drug cartels. What the investigators
found instead, however, was a scheme connected to the transfer
of arms into what had been Yugoslavia. The bank, it continued,
had been used extensively as a front for the purchase of weapons
and ammunition for Serbian forces fighting their war of ethnic
cleansing in Bosnia-Herzegovina and Croatia. Payments for these
shipments, funneled out of the country largely through Mexico
and Panama, had been made into the bank and apparently sizable
sums had been laundered in Las Vegas and Atlantic City casinos
and also through the purchase of real estate and racehorses. Fed-
eral marshals had occupied the bank's two main offices and all
activities had been temporarily suspended. It was rumored that

the bank had interests in Kentucky and held liens on property controlled by Clarendon Farm, one of the most respected operations in the world of Thoroughbred horse racing.

I stuck the paper into my side pocket and walked over to Charlie Pickard's barn, which was located close to the guinea stand. "Hello, Shifty, where you been?" he said, when I showed up outside his tack room. "You don't come around much anymore."

"Maybe you didn't hear," I said. "May and I split up."

"I heard. You're better off. She's not here anyway. She's over at the track with her two-year-olds. One of them looks okay."

"I'm happy for her." I took the paper out of my pocket and dropped it on his desk. "Did you read this?"

Charlie glanced at the headline. "I know about it," he said. "It don't affect me, at least for now."

"No? Why not?"

"I talked to Baldwin yesterday. They're having some money problems, but he said not to worry, to go on doing what I'm doing. So what can I tell you?"

"You've heard the rumors about Algonquin."

"That the insurance company won't pay? No insurance company ever wants to pay, Shifty. That's not how they make their money. But they'll have to pay eventually. They didn't find anything in the autopsy."

"So what did he die of, boredom?"

"Who knows? Too much sex, maybe."

"Charlie, there's no evident cause of death. Wouldn't you be suspicious?"

"Sure, but they got to prove something. They ain't found anything, Shifty."

"What do you think killed him?"

"How should I know? I guess there are as many ways to kill horses as people, ways that don't leave a trace. A big shot of potassium chlorate or a vitamin. Somebody needs the money."

"Algonquin was the stable's main asset, Charlie. Whoever killed him could have wanted to ruin Clarendon and take it over. Aramis and his pals."

"Or they needed a sudden big influx of cash," Charlie said. "Like big lump-sum payments coming due. A desperation move to buy time, see."

"You think so? Yeah, I can see that."

Charlie shrugged. "I'm just guessing, like you," he said. "Buy off the creditors for a few months and maybe you can pull it out. Old Roman wins the Del Mar Futurity, then he goes on to win the Juvenile at the Breeders' Cup and suddenly Clarendon's got the best colt in the country and guess who his sire is? Algonquin, no less, so now he'll have immediate stud potential, even if he busts out as a three-year-old. You see the scenario, Shifty? Buy time now, hope for another big horse to bail you out later."

"Sounds desperately chancy to me, Charlie."

"That's what this game is, a day-to-day crapshoot, believe me." He stood up and walked out into his shedrow to give instructions to Eddie Graham, who was supervising the work of a couple of other grooms down the way. "I want the vet to see the filly," the trainer informed him. "Keep her out here for a few minutes. He ought to be along. He's next door right now."

Eddie nodded and went back to work. Charlie leaned against the wall of his barn and grinned. "I think she popped a splint," he said. "It's always one damn thing after another."

"How's Old Roman?"

"That little colt is a miracle," Charlie said. "Does everything right, no problems." He knocked hard on the wooden wall. "If he stays sound, this could be one of the ones."

"What my friend Jay calls the eight-hundred-pound gorilla," I said.

"I don't know about gorillas," Charlie said. "Can they run at all?"

"A metaphor, Charlie. Has that guy Aramis been around?" I asked. "Or his girlfriend?"

"They ain't been around here," Charlie said, "but May told me they rented a house on the beach here for the last two weeks of the meet. He has to go back East a lot on account of the investigation, but she's around. She's around too much, if you ask me. Shifty, I'd stay away from that scene, if I was you."

The vet came around the corner of the barn carrying a satchel full of instruments and medications and Charlie led him over to the ailing filly. I headed back to my car.

I heard the woman scream just as I opened the door to our condo. I shut the door behind me and stood in the hallway, waiting. She screamed again. I went into the kitchen, found a clean cup, and poured myself a cup of coffee from the electric pot I had plugged in earlier, before leaving for the backside. As I stood there, sipping it, Jay came out of the bedroom and headed for the bathroom. He grinned conspiratorially at me, then disappeared inside. I heard the shower go on. A couple of minutes later, the bedroom door opened and the woman came out. She had a sheet around her and giggled when she saw me standing there, with the cup of hot coffee in my hand. "Hi, Shifty," she said, "how are you?"

"Fine, fine. I hope I'm not interrupting you."

"Oh, no. I have to wash up and get out of here. Excuse me."

She quickly opened the bathroom door and joined Jay inside. They liked to shower together, and I had a feeling they might do a bit more than that to each other in there.

I freshened my coffee and went out on the terrace to finish it. Then I snapped open the *Form* and began to handicap the day's card, which looked chancy to me, with three maiden races on it. I was anxious to hear what Jay might have to say about it, but I knew he wouldn't be ready to offer an opinion until just before post time, if then. The woman was proving to be a distraction. I put the *Form* down and gazed across at the new, still-uncompleted grandstand. It looked like a giant breadbox to me, but it had its conveniences, I suppose, though I missed the old plant, torn down after half a century of loyal service to the betting public. The management of the track thought the new facility was one of the seven architectural wonders of the age, but to me it represented another splendid example of money wasted on the grandiose. Still, nobody could change Del Mar itself, with its beaches, clean surf, soft climate, and the horses running, as they always had every year since 1937, under the placid Pacific blue of the southern California sky. I loved Del Mar; I built my racing year around the place. What did buildings matter, so long as the sun kept shining and the horses ran true to form?

Jay and I had rented the same condo now for several years, a two-bedroom affair on the hillside looking out over the infield. It was comfortable enough for our summer purposes and had a terrace overlooking the stable area. Best of all, from Jay's point of view, it had an enormous dining room table on which the handicapper could spread out his charts and notebooks as he set about isolating winners out of the great snarl of statistics he accumulated daily. Over these stats he wielded multicolored pens like tiny knives, slicing and chopping away at irrelevancies until, on his best days, he had managed to carve out the solid betting propositions on which he based his whole existence. Watching him at work was not unlike witnessing the laborious toil of a medieval monk over an illuminated manuscript, a study in care and meticulous detail. No fact was too insignificant, no consideration too arcane to escape his scrupulous regard, so that by the end of every morning he'd be ready to confront the daily challenge. I sometimes thought of him as Siegfried, armed with the sword of hard knowledge confronting the dragon of uncertainty that is the racetrack. I admired his diligence, but that kind of patience I reserved for my own work in closeup. To each his own discipline.

This year Jay was having a harder time of it than usual, not only because the horses were not running true to his stats, but mainly because he was involved in this love affair that was interfering with his concentration. The lady's name was Babs Wistern. She owned a small dress shop in the Flower Hill Mall, a shopping center just down the road from us, and she was married. Her husband Tom operated a fitness center in nearby Solana Beach and he had more muscles than a mastodon. He was also jealous and highly suspicious. This excited Babs, who liked to make love dangerously. She and Jay had coupled savagely and briefly all over the area—in the back of her shop, in his car, in a hallway of the Auto Club, on the terrace of a friend's apartment, late at night on the beach, several times in our place. She screamed every time she climaxed, which increased their chances of being caught. I advised Jay to drop her, but he was as excited by the affair as she was. He could barely concentrate on the horses, but I knew that if his luck remained poor, he'd soon begin to identify the cause as Babs and she'd be relegated to history. "The only woman who could hold Jay," Arnie had once observed, "is one with a saddle on her back who can breeze in a minute and a nine out of the gate."

Babs Wistern now screamed again and I realized that they had resumed their lovemaking in the shower. This was an improvement, as far as I was concerned. The previous day I had come home to find them in the laundry room downstairs, where, Jay later informed me, Babs had insisted on being ravished while straddling our washer-dryer.

I went back to my *Form* and circled a few horses I thought might be competitive, then I went back to the kitchen for a refill. Jay and Babs, fully dressed, now appeared together hand in hand, looking as pleased with themselves as if they had dined expensively somewhere at somebody else's expense. "Hey, Shifty," Babs exclaimed, "do me some magic!" And she came up and gave me a quick, friendly hug.

I couldn't imagine what Jay saw in her. She was twenty pounds overweight and at least thirty-five, about ten years older than Jay's cutoff age. "Over twenty-five they're no longer hard bodies," he had once explained to me. "They lose that taut freshness that makes the heart sing."

"What heart?" Arnie had asked. "You don't have a heart, Jay. You're merely a sexist horseplayer for whom a female body is nothing but a vessel for pure gratification. Give the woman a break. Lose her."

Jay was clearly smitten. Something about her excited him and, as the summer had progressed, they had become more and more involved. I had no idea where or how it would end, but I hoped not with the arrival of the irate husband. Jay was an ex-athlete and still in good shape, but not on a par with Tom Wistern, who looked as if he could bend iron bars in his teeth.

"Want to run on the beach?" I asked, after she had gone. "Tide's out."

"Not today," Jay said, heading for his table of stats. "I'm three hours behind and it's a tough card."

I left him, went down to the carport, and drove to the beach. I parked just north of the bridge over the river, now almost dry after a long, hot summer, and began my run heading south toward the smokestack of the old abandoned power station behind the main lifeguard tower, about half a mile away. A train came hooting up from the south along the bluffs and a sea of bodies lay before me on the sand as I headed toward the hard, flat surface at the water's edge. A pelican skimmed the surf, looking for prey, and swimmers gamboled in the long, even swells. The tide was now coming in and sandpipers scurried along ahead of the waves, probing for goodies in the sand with their long beaks. I felt an enormous sense of peace and well-being. I began to run harder as I loosened up.

By the time I reached the lifeguard tower, I had worked up a good sweat. I ran another quarter mile beyond it, then slowed to a walk, turned around, and started back. About three hundred yards up the beach, I spotted Alma Glocken. She was sitting on the wall of her terrace overlooking the scene and she had already noticed me. She waved and beckoned me over. I turned right and came up through the soft sand toward her.

"Well, Anderson, how are you?" she said. "We haven't seen you at the races."

"I rarely go to the Turf Club," I said. "I presume that's where you hang out."

"Of course, darling," she said. "We have a table there. You must have lunch with us sometime."

"I don't think so," I said. "How's the money-laundering business?"

"Not good," she said. "Don't discuss this with Gene. It is a depression to him."

Despite the fact that I despised and feared this woman, I couldn't keep my eyes off her. She had the most perfectly-proportioned female body I had ever seen, with long legs and arms, broad shoulders, large breasts, a flat stomach, and a tiny waist, and she liked to show all of it off. She was wearing what amounted to a strip of cloth between her legs and another one over her nipples and that was it. Her skin gleamed with suntan oil and I found myself lusting for her. She read my eyes and smiled. "You like me," she said, "yes?"

"No, I don't like you," I answered. "You scare the shit out of me. But you have a beautiful body."

"Yes, and I know what to do with it. We're giving a party tonight, just a few friends. Come, if you feel like it. After the races."

"What's the occasion? A human sacrifice?"

"No occasion," she said, with a laugh. "Nothing formal."

"I can imagine. Where's your playmate?"

"Gene? He comes back today. The usual boring things with lawyers in Washington."

"I imagine the investigation is slowing your action somewhat?"

"Not really. We still like to make some gambles. You will see. You know that we bought some horses."

"Yes, I heard."

"May is training them with her friend Clara."

"Yes, I know that."

She smiled. "I'm sorry about your May," she said. "I did not know she was your girlfriend."

"It doesn't matter now and it wouldn't have stopped you, would it?"

"Oh, no. No, indeed," she said. "She has the most interesting body, you know, almost like a boy, so very strong, and with so many muscles. She likes what we do to each other very much and, of course, Gene enjoys it too."

"That's very interesting, Alma. I really appreciate your telling me all this. I'll see you around." I started to leave.

"You can watch too, if you like," she called after me. "See you later, darling."

I began to run again to get away from her. I plunged through the hot, soft sand till I reached the water's edge again, then turned north and started back toward my car.

Despite Jay's misgivings about the card, we had a profitable afternoon, with a couple of winners at good-enough prices to come out ahead for the day. Arnie went on a tear, bringing in every one of his five big show bets and picking up over a grand. We decided to have the wine ceremony, which consisted of bringing blankets, towels, chairs, and chilled white wine down to the beach. We hurled ourselves into the surf, all except for Arnie, whose contact with water was limited to whatever went on in his bathroom, then dried off, sipped the wine, and waited for the sun to set.

"This is the best," Angles said, "the very best."

"There's only two kinds of good days," Arnie observed. "This is the best kind."

"You mean winning?" Jay said.

"Sure. The best thing in the world is to win at the track," Arnie said. "The second-best thing is to lose at the track."

"That's an old one, Arnie," I said.

"Sure, but it's still true."

We sat there for nearly two hours, sipping and chatting or just quietly watching the leisurely beach action around us. A handful of surfers bobbed on their boards, occasionally rising to their feet to soar in toward us in the curl of a wave. Pelicans and gulls carried out closing forays over water and sand. Couples strolled hand in hand by the water's edge as the sun set in a red glow against the horizon, after which the stars and a pale sliver of a moon took its place, providing barely enough light for us to see each other. Up the beach from us, a murmur of voices and music could be heard from the terrace of Aramis's house. I tried to ignore it.

"Somebody's giving a party," Jay said. "Sounds like a good one."

"Maybe we could join it," Angles said. "I figure it's big enough nobody would notice us."

"Forget it," Arnie said. "They'd notice you anywhere, Angles. You are not socially acceptable."

"Ah, screw you, Arnie," Angles said amiably. "I can't stand the fuckin' rich anyway. They give me a pain."

We lingered for another half hour, after which Arnie, Angles, and Jay started back toward the parking lot. "I'm going to hang around a while," I said. "I've got some thinking to do."

"We'll be in J.J.'s later," Jay said, "the sports bar in Del Mar, till about eleven."

"I may see you there."

I waited until they had gone, then I quickly changed clothes in the darkness, put on a pair of sandals I'd brought along, and walked up the beach toward the terrace where the party was in full swing.

The first person to greet me as I arrived over the low retaining wall facing the water was a large black man of about forty in a dark business suit and tie. "This is a private party," he said.

"I was invited," I told him. "My name's Anderson."

"It's all right, Gerald," Alma Glocken said. "I did invite him." She detached herself from an older couple she had been talking to and walked over to greet me. As usual she was dressed in black, in a tight cocktail dress that showed off her incredible body. "Hello," she said, "get yourself a drink. I imagine you know a few people, yes?"

"Don't worry about me," I said. "I can take care of myself."

"I don't worry about you at all," she said. "And I know you can take care of yourself."

"Is Gerald your new hired hand?"

"We are trying him out."

"He looks the part."

"So far we've found him to be most efficient. Your girlfriend is here."

"She's not my girlfriend anymore."

"Sad, very sad. Anyway, mingle, enjoy." She patted my cheek with cool fingers and moved on to other guests.

I pushed my way through the crowd to the bar, picked up a glass of champagne, and looked around. Roger and Maddie Baldwin were standing in a group of horse owners that included Aramis, whose right hand was bandaged and in a splint. I joined them, much to Aramis's surprise. Evidently, Alma had not told him I might be showing up. I decided to milk the situation for whatever it might be worth. I wanted something to happen. I wanted to blow the lid of this cesspool. "Hello, Roger," I said, "nice to see you and Maddie again. I was sorry to hear about Algonquin."

"Yes, it was terrible," Roger said. "We still don't know what happened."

"Oh, I imagine you had him put down for the insurance money," I said, smiling.

"What?" Baldwin's face had gone white, as if I had spat in it. "What did you say?"

"Oh, I don't mean you personally, Roger," I said. "Maybe Phil did it. He'd know how, wouldn't he?"

"Are you crazy?" Maddie Baldwin said. "You get out of here! Get away from us!"

"Everybody's been talking about it," I said. "At first I figured it might be Aramis and his gang, a way for them to get control of Clarendon by doing away with your biggest asset, but then I decided they probably wouldn't do that. Aramis here could afford to wait and eventually Clarendon would drop into his lap. How much do you owe the Banca del Tirreno?"

"How dare you!" Maddie Baldwin said, her voice rising in pitch. "Roger, do something!"

"I'm only saying out loud what everyone else is saying in private," I continued. "No, I figure you had it done. The insurance company drags its heels for a few weeks or months, but eventually they pay you the eighteen and a half million and you stay in business maybe another year. You buy a little time, then there's always Chapter Eleven. That would buy you more time. Time is what you need most, isn't it, Roger?"

Aramis hurried away and I knew I would soon be leaving

myself, but I stayed in place, a smile frozen on my face, and finished up. "I guess you got in over your head, Roger, with these people," I said. "You expanded at a time the boom market of the eighties went bust. Bad timing, old man, but I do admire your dedication and spunk. It isn't everybody who has the guts to kill for money. I wonder what old Stormy Joe would have had to say about this."

Baldwin gave a sort of bark that reminded me of a dog in distress and lunged for me. I backed off, but then a huge black arm encircled my neck and a large hand grabbed the seat of my pants. I felt myself being suddenly rushed through the crowd and into the house. I glimpsed May's horrified face in the corridor, then Clara's as well; they must have been in the bathroom. At the front door, my attacker spun me around to face him and pulled me in close. He had very small black eyes and his breath smelled strongly of onions. "You ever come back here," Gerald said softly, "I'll break your arms, you understand me, fella?" He opened the door and quite literally flung me into the street.

"You went to that party, didn't you?" Jay said to me at J.J.'s, when I showed up at the bar a few minutes later. "And they threw you out. Man, you got bruises on your neck that look like plums."

"I was not a success," I admitted. "I couldn't get into the spirit of the occasion."

"What did you do?"

"I told the truth," I said. "Haven't you noticed, Jay, how unpopular that makes you?"

18 / Losses

OLD ROMAN WON THE Del Mar Futurity on getaway day by four lengths. He drew the outside post position in the ten-horse field, broke poorly, and was eight lengths off the pace around the clubhouse turn. Wib Clayton, however, did not panic; he knew he had a ton of horse under him. He tucked the gray colt in on the rail so as not to lose ground, then allowed him to move up on his own accord along the backstretch until he was about five lengths off the two speed horses dueling for the lead. At the three-eighths pole, he asked Old Roman for his run and the colt responded with an electrifying move that swept him past the leaders. He was clear by two an eighth of a mile from home and breezed in a winner on his own courage, with Clayton not having to do more than just wave his stick at him to keep his mind on business. It was an overwhelming performance that seemed sure to establish Old Roman as the favorite for the Breeders' Cup Juvenile at Churchill Downs in early November.

On that same day, one of May Potter's new two-year-olds, a filly she had bid forty-eight thousand dollars for at the Del Mar sale, ran a strong second in her first race, with the Jesus freak,

Daryl Spencer, on her back. Not a bad beginning for a fledgling trainer, but I didn't look her up to congratulate her. I stayed in the stands and watched her and Clara handle the returning filly down in front of the winner's circle. I was glad that at least May now had something to show for the price she was paying with her life. Or perhaps I was making too much of it, I thought; maybe her relationship with Alma would turn out to be what she really wanted, what she needed, no matter how sick I might think it was.

I packed up my stuff and drove home to L.A. that night and I was happy to be back in my own place at last. I immediately set up a practice schedule for myself and contacted the Magic Castle to work a few sessions in the closeup room, as I needed to polish some old moves as well as perfect some new ones I'd been working on. Between my stint in Las Vegas and my month in Del Mar, I hadn't been working very hard on my magic and it was time to get back to my professional world. I also found a call waiting for me from my indefatigable agent, Happy Hal Mancuso, saying that he had booked me for three days on an episode of a new TV series that required a magician to perform in a nightclub. I was happy to be working again and temporarily away from the racetrack, where it had been an agitated, drama-filled month.

I stayed away from the track completely during the L.A. County Fair meet at Pomona, where for three weeks the horses race at Fairplex Park, a five-eighths of a mile facility known as a bullring, with sharp turns and mostly mediocre horses competing. I usually used that time of the racing year as a freshener, three weeks away from the horses for rest and rejuvenation. By the time of the fall meet at Santa Anita, I was ready to return to racing.

I hadn't talked to any of my racetrack cronies for a while and hadn't even bought a *Form*, so I hadn't heard about Old Roman. Then I came across a story on the third page of the *Form* the night before Santa Anita opened that simply said that Old Roman had breezed three furlongs at Churchill Downs "under the watchful eye of trainer Phil Hardin, while prepping for the Breeders' Cup Juvenile."

The next morning I drove out very early to Santa Anita and went to Charlie's shedrow. When I got there, Charlie was nowhere to be found, but May and Clara were hot-walking two of their horses and Eddie Graham was busy in Bellringer's stall. "Where's Charlie?" I asked.

"He's at the track," May answered. "They're just comin' off the break. He's workin' two horses."

"What's going on with Old Roman?" I asked. "I read something about him breezing in Kentucky for Phil Hardin. Did he ship out early or something?"

"Ask Charlie," May said. "He'll tell you."

Eddie Graham came out of Bellringer's stall and came up behind me. "They took the colt away from him," he said. "Gave him to Hardin."

"What? After Charlie made the colt? Whose idea was that, Baldwin's?"

Eddie shrugged, his pale face looking even more mournful than usual. "I don't know," he said. "Charlie got the news a week ago."

I looked at May and Clara. "You know something about it?"

May shook her head. "Charlie was pretty upset about it," Clara said. "I figure he had a right."

I walked over to Clockers' Corner, where a small crowd of horse people and the betting public was watching the workouts. I found Charlie at his usual post, leaning against the fence as he watched one of his horses gallop past with Polo Rodriguez in the saddle. "Just breeze him, Polo," he called out. "He should go in about forty-eight, got that?"

"Yes, sir, Mr. Charlie," Polo called back and moved away up the track toward the half-mile pole.

I came up beside the trainer. "I just heard about Old Roman," I said. "What's going on?"

"All I know is what Baldwin told me," Charlie said. "They want to run the horse in the East from now on, so they're turning him over to Hardin. After the Breeders' Cup, they'll take him to Florida, give him a rest, then point him for the Flamingo. After that, they're going for the Triple Crown races. Now you know as much as I do about it, Shifty."

"You made that colt," I said. "It's a shitty deal."

"You want me to cry about it? It happens all the time in racing, Shifty, you know that. Anyway, ain't nothing I can do about it. If the colt stays sound, he ought to win everything in sight. He's one of the ones, Shifty. They don't come along but once in a lifetime, if ever."

"That's why it's a shitty deal."

Charlie shrugged. "That's racing." He turned toward the track, stopwatch in hand. "Now shut up and let me clock this horse, will you?" Just as Polo put the horse in gear at the half, Charlie clicked the stopwatch and together in silence we watched the animal run, moving gracefully around the turn toward the finish line all by himself. I felt badly for Charlie, but I knew there was nothing else I could say to cheer him up, so I dropped the subject. Phil Hardin would reap the glory and the man who made it happen would remain in obscurity. That was how the world worked and not only in racing.

An interesting aspect of the fall meet was the abrupt cessation of heavy action on the Clarendon horses. I asked Charlie about it, but he didn't know anything. He still had horses for Clarendon and he was still being compelled to ride Spencer on most of them, but otherwise he had heard nothing about anything back in Kentucky. Bellringer was stiffed again by Spencer, which indicated that another coup was being set up, but Gene Aramis and Alma seemed to have dropped off the face of the globe. Then, one morning in the track kitchen, May came over to where I was sitting, reading the sports section and sipping a cup of coffee, and sat down. "You mind?" she asked.

"No," I said. "How are you?"

"I'm okay," she said. "I guess I'm okay. Shifty, I'm sorry about what happened. I know you don't understand and I don't expect you to. I just want to tell you I'm sorry about what I done to you."

"Forget it, May. It's over. I hope you're a big success and win a lot of races. How are things going?"

"Not too good."

"What's wrong?"

"They ain't payin' their bills. I ain't had a cent from 'em since we put the horses in training," she said. "One of 'em picked up a little purse money and I been gettin' along on that, but them two other horses ain't ready to run yet and I ain't got the money to pay the feed bills even. I don't know what to do, Shifty. I can't even get 'em on the phone and I don't know where they are."

"I'm sorry, May. I don't know how to help you."

"I don't expect you to," she said. "I'm just talkin'. I guess I was a fool. Women ain't no better than men."

"Not some women."

"Well, I'll see you around."

"Sure. I hope things work out for you, May," I said. "You deserve better than this."

After she left me, I finished up my coffee and went to a public phone. First I called the Banca del Tirreno offices in Las Vegas, but the phone had been disconnected. Then I called Vince, who sounded breathless. "I've been running," he explained. "What's up, Shifty?"

I asked him if he'd heard anything about Aramis and Alma and he said that he hadn't, but that he'd make a few inquiries around town and get back to me. I thanked him and returned to my *Form*. I had a lukewarm feeling about the card that afternoon, but I was trying to isolate a winner or two to build my day around. So I forgot about May and Aramis and Alma, which is one of the great blessings the racetrack dispenses to its devotees; nothing matters at the track but the horse of the moment and the outcome of the race.

When I got home that night, after a tough losing day in which I managed to finish second five times, I found a message from Vince waiting for me on my answering machine. I called him back at the Three Kings and caught him on a break. "Shifty, the guy's in jail in New York," he said. "He was arrested two days ago and booked. They set a very high bail on him, because he's a foreigner and could easily skip the country, so they're holding him until he can raise the money. It's about half a million, I think."

"He'll raise it and that'll be the last of him," I said. "What about Alma?"

"Who?"

"His girlfriend. Is there any word on her?"

"No, I haven't heard anything. There's supposed to be a story about the bank in the *Wall Street Journal* a couple of days ago," Vince said, "but I haven't seen it. My broker told me about it. The Feds have seized the Banca del Tirreno and there's a big investigation into all its dealings, here and abroad. The government may have been involved in some of them, so it's a very big deal, but it's going to take a long time. There apparently was also some stuff about this guy and racehorses. They bought some or something."

"Yeah, I know about that."

"And they invested in Kentucky real estate, horse farms there."

"Anything about Clarendon?"

"My guy didn't mention it specifically."

After talking to Vince, I went to my local library and tried to look up the *Wall Street Journal* article, but it didn't have a microfilm service, so I was unable to read it. The next morning, however, the *L.A. Times* broke a story on the front page about the Banca del Tirreno and even mentioned Alma Glocken. "Aramis has a long and unsavory record in arms transactions and is reportedly connected to several French and German corporations that in the past have done extensive business in the Middle East, especially with Iraq in the years prior to the Gulf War," the article declared. "Operating mainly as a broker, the wily French-born financier has operated out of offices in Monaco, Liechtenstein, and Panama. Long suspected of involvement in money-laundering operations for drug cartels, Aramis has always denied this charge and represented himself as an independent investor with holdings mainly in real estate. In recent years, he has been seen often in the company of an ex-model named Alma Glocken, who once graced the covers of European fashion magazines and is known to be a heavy gambler. Since Aramis's indictment and arrest, Ms. Glocken has disappeared and is suspected of having fled the country."

The next morning, I went out early to Santa Anita again and talked to May and Clara. "You aren't going to see any money on these horses," I told them. "I suggest you inform the stewards about what's going on. My guess is the horses will be impounded, at least for the course of the investigation."

May didn't answer. She walked away from me down the shedrow to where the two-year-olds were stabled and took a look at them. "She's pretty upset," Clara said. "Hell, so am I. It was our one big chance. Who else is going to give us a horse?"

"I don't know, Clara," I said. "I'm sorry about all this. I know you and May are good horse people. Maybe something will break for you. Meanwhile, I guess you can go on working for Charlie."

"I don't know," Clara said. "He's down to eight now and with the big colt gone, ain't no way of knowing if he's going to get more horses."

I wanted to go down and comfort May, but I couldn't think

of any way to do it. What she had done to herself for the sake of moving up in the world no longer seemed so important to me. I didn't condone it, but I had managed to convince myself that I had no right to make a moral judgment about it and her. What she had said to me in Las Vegas was true; I had never been desperately poor or abused or had to use my body to survive on somebody else's terms. I had been lucky never to have had to pay a personal price for my freedom, and so I had always taken it for granted. I didn't love May anymore and I felt sorry for her, but I also wished her well.

Toward the end of the fall meet, Jay hit another Pick Six, a small one this time for only about three thousand dollars, but it led to another dinner celebration at Barzini's. Babs Wistern had somehow managed to get up to L.A. by convincing her husband that she had to see buyers or visit wholesalers or something, so she joined us at the restaurant. We sat in a corner booth, telling stories and celebrating, until Angles once again spotted Ginger. She was sitting by herself at the bar, looking lost and disconsolate.

"What's she doing here?" Angles asked Barzini, during one of the owner's frequent visits to our table.

"You didn't hear?" the owner said. "Abe had a heart attack last week. He's at Cedars Sinai in intensive care. It don't sound like he's gonna make it. Millie, his wife, grabbed the bank accounts and shut everything down. She had the chick thrown out of the apartment he rented for her and now she's in here every night, crying. She's asking me all the time, 'What am I gonna do, what am I gonna do?' And I'm telling her, 'What are you gonna do? Don't ask me. What am I gonna do with all them cases of that French champagne I laid in for you?' I mean, we all got problems, right?"

"That's very sympathetic of you, Russ," Arnie said. "You have an expansive view of the human comedy."

"Ah, fuck her," Barzini said. "Broads are a dime a dozen. You get a little money and they swarm all over you like flies."

"Gee, that's not nice," Babs said. "You don't like women."

"If you didn't have all that equipment on you and looked so good, who would pay any attention to you?" Barzini said. "I mean, it's a practical consideration. Guys got to get laid and broads make 'em pay the pussy tax."

"The man is a philosopher," Arnie commented, after Barzini had disappeared temporarily back into his kitchen.

"What about?"

"What do you mean, what about? She's a nice-looking girl. You treated her like shit and so she left you for a guy who was willing to spend some bucks on her. That isn't a capital crime, last I heard. We're celebrating a win here. Ask her over for a drink."

To my astonishment, Angles got up and went to the bar to speak to her. A couple of minutes later, he brought her back to the table and introduced her to Babs. She looked pale and worn, but still very pretty, and she was grateful to have been invited to join us. She sat down, and she and Babs immediately hit it off well and were deep in a dialogue of their own as we went on telling horse stories, many of which we'd heard before, but which never failed to amuse us. "Gee, you guys," Ginger said, an hour or so later, after another rehashing of an old tale, "you'd think that horse racing was all there was to life."

"Close," Arnie said. "Not quite all, but close."

"You know what I like about it?" Jay said. "It's the same great high, but it's safer than sex."

No sooner had he made this statement than it was put to an immediate test. Tom Wistern, looking like The Hulk, suddenly came through the front door of the restaurant and headed straight for our table. Jay's face went white. He managed to evade Tom's initial grab for him across the table and bounded out through the back door into the parking lot. Babs flung her arms around her husband's neck, but he shrugged her off and lumbered in pursuit. "My God!" Ginger screamed. "What's going on here?"

"You have just witnessed the proof of a theory in action," Arnie said calmly, as Barzini came running up to our table.

"What the fuck happened?" the restaurateur asked. "Who is that guy?"

"Merely another wronged partner," Arnie said. "Nothing to worry about, Russ. Now, why don't we open a bottle of that great Dom Pérignon you have in stock? This *is* a celebration, isn't it?"

"I'm not sure, Arnie," I said. "What are we really celebrating?"

"You tell me, Shifty," he answered. "Let's just drink to faster women, older whiskey, and winning tickets."

"I think I want that on my tombstone," Angles said.

E*pitaph*

IT RAINED STEADILY for three days before that Breeders' Cup at Churchill Downs, turning the racing surface into a sea of mud. None of us knew whether Old Roman could handle an off-track, but I had no doubt he'd be able to. Algonquin had been a superb mudder and the great ones are supposed to be able to run on anything.

I didn't go to Kentucky, mainly because Charlie no longer had the colt and I had no rooting interest in watching Phil Hardin reap the glory and the rewards. Jay and I drove together to Santa Anita that morning to see the seven cup races, which were scheduled to be shown on TV before the live card. The Juvenile was the third race on the program, with Old Roman listed at even money in the morning line. He had been training sensationally and was supposed to win easily.

It had stopped raining early that morning and the track had begun to dry out under a pale late-fall sun, but it would still be way off. The Sprint was run in glacially slow time and nobody expected any records to be broken that day. Which was why we were all astounded by Old Roman's opening quarter in twenty-

two seconds flat. The colt seemed to be skimming over the surface, while his competition floundered in his wake.

Wib Clayton prudently took a firm hold on the reins and
managed to slow Old Roman down to forty-six and three for the
half, but even so it looked as if the race was over. The gray colt
had eight lengths on the field and looked as if he would win by
twenty. I had bet three hundred dollars on him at four to five, a
huge wager for me, and I was already counting my winnings. At
the head of the lane, Old Roman had the lead by ten and now all
he had to do was come coasting home all by himself, like a rein-
carnation of Secretariat.

I'm trying now to recall exactly when it was I knew something was wrong. I noticed first that the colt was lugging out a
little bit around the turn. Then, just before the eighth pole, I saw
the horse take what looked like a little shuffle to the side. He
quickly straightened himself out and ran a few more strides forward, then suddenly he lurched heavily to the right, spilling Clayton into the mud. I remember jumping to my feet and shouting.
Old Roman got up and began to run again, but couldn't. His
right foreleg dangled uselessly, held together only by skin and
flesh. He fell again and once more tried to rise, though by this
time the first of the men running toward him had managed to
reach him. He grabbed the colt's head and held him down, so
he'd be unable to injure himself any more seriously. Wib Clayton
had remained huddled in a ball on the track as the rest of the
field ran over and past him, then had staggered to his feet and
had also headed for his stricken mount.

Someone screamed, but whether on screen or somewhere
around me, I can't now recall. The camera closed in on the ap-
palled face of Roger Baldwin, watching the events unfold from his
box seat over the stretch. He looked ashen, like a man who has
just seen his whole world crumble before his eyes, which, of
course, he had. I felt a twinge of pity for him, though not for his
wife, who was weeping beside him. Phil Hardin's face seemed
made of stone. When a reporter thrust a microphone at him for a
comment, the trainer pushed it aside and headed for the track
and the group around his fallen champion. I felt no pity for him
either, but only a dull rage, which increased as the TV coverage,
with the tastelessness so characteristic of the medium, now proceeded to play over and over again that terrible moment when

Old Roman went down, his leg snapping under him like a dry stick, bringing himself and his owners to ruin.

One of the vets put him down on the spot, behind a screen hastily erected to prevent the crowd from witnessing the final, agonizing moments of the drama. I got up and looked around for Charlie. I didn't see him, but I gave up trying to find him, as I felt sure he would not want to discuss the event with me. Later, maybe, but not now. I went into the men's room, shut myself up in a stall, sat down and cried.

I remembered then another horrifying scene from a previous Breeders' Cup two years before, when the great filly Go For Wand, locked into a head-and-head duel with her rival Bayakoa, had also destroyed herself before our eyes. I recalled Bayakoa's trainer, a humane and thoughtful man, saying to an interviewer that we have to realize that these beautiful animals we love so well give their lives for our enjoyment. At the end of every road, high or low, the killer waits. Not all the colors of the rainbow can permanently blot him from our sight.